"Writte... with wit and a good s...
and the younger generations. The good guys who live
in the old hotel are clear and memorable."

—*St. Petersburg Times*

"Gets . . . off to a fast start."

—*Orlando Sentinel*

HAPPY NEVER AFTER

"Fast paced, entertaining."

—*The Atlanta Journal-Constitution*

"Callahan and her cohort of continuing characters (her
mom, Edna; the ancient cleaning ladies Baby and Sister)
are great company. If *Happy Never After* were a song,
we'd all be dancing in the streets."

—*San Jose Mercury News*

BOOKS BY KATHY HOGAN TROCHECK

Every Crooked Nanny

To Live & Die in Dixie

Homemade Sin

Happy Never After

Lickety-Split

Published by HarperPaperbacks

ATTENTION: ORGANIZATIONS AND CORPORATIONS

Most HarperPaperbacks are available at special quantity discounts
for bulk purchases for sales promotions, premiums, or fund-raising.
For information, please call or write:
**Special Markets Department, HarperCollins Publishers,
10 East 53rd Street, New York, N.Y. 10022.
Telephone: (212) 207-7528. Fax: (212) 207-7222.**

LICKETY-SPLIT

A TRUMAN KICKLIGHTER MYSTERY

Kathy Hogan Trocheck

HarperPaperbacks
A Division of HarperCollinsPublishers

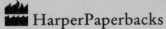 **HarperPaperbacks**
A Division of HarperCollins*Publishers*
10 East 53rd Street, New York, N.Y. 10022-5299

Copyright © 1996 by Kathy Hogan Trocheck
All rights reserved. No part of this book may be used or
reproduced in any manner whatsoever without written
permission of the publisher, except in the case of brief
quotations embodied in critical articles and reviews.
For information address HarperCollins*Publishers,*
10 East 53rd Street, New York, N.Y. 10022-5299.

HarperCollins®, 👑®, and HarperPaperbacks™
are trademarks of HarperCollins*Publishers* Inc.

A hardcover edition of this book was published in 1996
by HarperCollins*Publishers*

Cover illustration by Honi Werner

First HarperPaperbacks printing: January 1997

Printed in the United States of America

Visit HarperPaperbacks on the World Wide Web at
http://www.harpercollins.com/paperbacks

❖ 10 9 8 7 6 5 4 3 2 1

This book is dedicated with love to my dad, John Patrick Hogan, who let me dance on his shoe tops

ACKNOWLEDGMENTS

I wish to thank family, friends, and trusted advisers for the time, energy, advice, and support given me during the writing of this book. Any errors in fact or judgment are my own.

Special thanks go to Vey O. Weaver of the St. Petersburg Kennel Club. My parents, John and Sue Hogan, shared their betting system, knowledge of St. Pete, and too much more to mention. Jean Higham laid down the law for me. Doug Monroe told me about life at the wire, and Barbara and Steve Heckart gave me asylum in Yellow Springs, Ohio. Sallie Gouverneur made me keep writing, and Eamon Dolan made it better. And Tom and Katie and Andy reminded me of why I keep trying.

CHAPTER

ONE

TRUMAN KICKLIGHTER SPEARED A BIT OF HAM floating squarely in the middle of his split pea soup and smiled.

Friday was split pea soup day at the Ponce de León Room. Usually your chances of finding a piece of real meat in your bowl were about as good as the Tampa Bay Bucs' chances of winning a Super Bowl. Which meant not hardly.

He crumbled a corn muffin into the soup and flagged down Jackleen Canaday, who was speeding past with a bowl of cherry-banana Jell-O for Gladys Young, two tables over, who always ate dessert for lunch.

"Say, what about the fruit cup?" he asked.

Jackleen put on the brakes and backed up. "What about the fruit cup, Mr. K? You want dessert already?" She was watching Mr. Loring, at table three, counting out five pennies for her tip. And she'd made a special trip to the kitchen to get him toast instead of a roll, too.

"No. I don't want the fruit cup at all," Truman said. "That pineapple they put in it makes my tongue break out."

As Mr. Loring strolled past her in a cloud of mothballs, Jackleen sniffed and put him on her mental shit list. See if she gave him toast again. Not in this lifetime, buddy.

"Well, what do you want me to do about your dessert?" she asked, still distracted. The pennies were Canadian. It figured.

Mr. K was actually one of her favorite customers. New in the last six months, he was always careful to leave a straight 10 percent tip, and at Christmas he'd brought her a box of dusting powder and some chocolate-covered cherries.

Truman gave her a hopeful look. "Any of that apple pie left from dinner last night?"

She rolled her eyes. They were big and brown and expressive. And when she wore her hair straight, teased up on top, some people said she looked like Diana Ross, only with better boobs.

"Honey, you know that got gone. I got a dish of tapioca I could bring you instead. How 'bout that?"

"Never mind," Truman said quickly. "How about bringing me some more corn muffins and some more coffee?"

"I'll see," she said doubtfully.

But on her next sweep through the dining room she hotted up his coffee cup with a fresh pot and quickly slipped two steaming muffins into the roll basket on Truman's table.

"I saw that," a voice boomed out from the table directly to Truman's right.

Sonya Hoffmayer glared and waggled a finger at them. If there was one person at the Fountain of Youth Residential Hotel who got on Truman's nerves, it was Mrs. Hoffmayer. She was in her eighties, tall and thin, with iron-gray hair, beetling eyebrows, and a family connection to the owners of the hotel, which meant she thought she owned the place. Truman didn't know which was worse, Sonya or KoKo, the miniature schnauzer she carried with her everywhere in her pocketbook.

"Preferential treatment," she screeched. "I only got one corn muffin in my basket. And it was cold. My nephew will hear about this. See if he doesn't."

KoKo raised his head up out of the pocketbook she had placed on the seat opposite her and yapped angrily in agreement.

"Uh-oh," Jackleen said under her breath. "She already told on me last week 'cause my work shoes weren't polished. And the week before that she said I gave her coffee instead of decaf and she had a dizzy spell and nearly passed out. That biddy's gonna get me fired for sure."

"Better make nice," Truman said in a low voice.

Jackleen forced a stiff smile. "Oh, I'm sorry, Mrs. Hoffmayer, would you like another muffin? I was just coming to your table to check on you."

"You're sure they're fresh?" Mrs. Hoffmayer asked, her chins quivering.

"Right out of the oven," Jackie said from between clenched teeth.

"Well. Maybe two. The soup was thin today. And KoKo does love muffins."

"I'd like to poison the both of 'em," Jackie said under her breath. She sighed and then stormed off to the kitchen for more muffins.

Truman nodded sympathetically and shot Mrs. Hoffmayer a dirty look. But she was busy letting KoKo lick the remnants of the soup from her bowl and didn't see him.

In a moment, Jackie was back, depositing the muffins on Mrs. Hoffmayer's table and apologizing again for the oversight.

"Don't overdo it," Truman warned her as she approached his table again. "That kind, if she figures she can get under your skin, she'll only get worse."

"Easy for you to say," Jackie muttered. "She can't tell nothin' on you."

He didn't mention the hot plate and the tiny refrigerator he'd installed in his room, strictly against the rules. As was his habit of using two dryers at once in the basement laundry room and sneaking a cigar in the lobby after supper. Sonya Hoffmayer patrolled the hotel hallways and public areas like a rabbit-hungry beagle, snout down, always on the lookout for scofflaws like himself.

Instead he took a sip of coffee and looked down at the sports section of the *St. Petersburg Times*. He'd folded the page into a neat square and was scribbling notes on the page.

"You going to the dog track tonight?"

He looked up from his calculations. "It's Snowbird Special night. You know the Wisnewskis? Mel and Pearl? They're going too. They've got a free bus picking people up in front of all the downtown hotels. The Snowbird Special, they call it."

"Yeah, I know them," Jackleen said, setting her pot down on the table to get a better look at the sports page. "Don't they live in Pittsburgh?"

"They got in last night," Truman said, frowning slightly. "Mel was real tired. Pearl said he gets that way now. Has spells. But he'll be fine tonight."

"Hope so," she said. "Mr. Wisnewski, he's a real nice man. Likes hot tea instead of coffee, two eggs over easy. I didn't know you knew him."

"That's why I moved over here," Truman said. "After my wife died and I sold the house. Mel and Pearl talked me into it. That Mel could talk the birds out of the trees."

"Um-humm." She wasn't really listening, but was looking down at the listings. "I never been to the greyhound races."

"You want me to make a bet for you?" he offered. "Two dollars. Tell me your lucky numbers. That's how Nellie used to bet. Never did look at the dogs. Just bet our anniversary, or Cheryl's birthday."

She fumbled in the pocket of her apron, jingling the silver. She brought out a fistful of quarters and counted out eight, laying them in two piles of four on top of the newspaper. "My birthday's February 17. Two-one-seven. Will that work?"

He looked down at the listings. "The old perfesser likes a two-one-seven in the third. I'll play you a quinella. That suit you?"

She nodded and he raked the quarters into his hand and tucked them into a small black leather change purse.

"What's my cut if you win?"

She glanced down at the paper again. The two dog was named Attaboy, the one was Little Darlin', and the seven was called Mabel's Black Label. She said the names out loud, for luck, then glanced around to make sure she couldn't be overheard by you-know-who.

"Double desserts for a month."

Truman Kicklighter was built sort of like a greyhound himself, lean. If Nellie hadn't given his marines uniform to the Goodwill years ago, he bet he could still get into it. Five eight, 128 pounds, that's what he weighed, and he could eat as many bowls of peach cobbler and ice cream as he wanted without it ever changing.

"Deal," he said, slapping the table for emphasis.

"Gotta go," Jackleen said, jerking her head toward Mrs. Hoffmayer, who was clearing her throat loudly.

Truman deftly transferred the corn muffins to a paper napkin and transferred them again to the pocket of his navy-blue cardigan sweater. He liked a snack around four o'clock. When his Nellie was alive, she'd tucked something in his briefcase for his snack. Some vanilla wafers, maybe one of her homemade butterscotch brownies. No matter where he was or what he was doing, he'd stop work at four, have his snack, call home and see what she was up to.

"Trying to get some supper made, if you'll quit calling and pestering me," she'd say, acting like she was fussing, but secretly glad he called.

After he'd retired last year, she'd made it a new routine. He'd be out in the yard puttering around, or working on his scrapbook, finally clipping out all those stories he'd written over the years, and she'd make him stop for his snack. They'd have their four o'clock together, maybe sit outside and watch the birds at the birdfeeder he'd put up for her, or take a walk, if it wasn't too hot.

And then, like that, she was gone. It was after breakfast one day. She was going to go to the grocery store, but changed her mind at the last minute, said she had a headache. Truman went instead. And when he got home, there was an ambulance parked at the curb, lights whirling, and the paramedics were saying it must have been a stroke. He could still see the brown paper sacks of groceries sitting, untouched, in the front seat of the car. Ice cream melting, lettuce wilting in the relentless Florida sun.

Technically, she'd lived for another six months in what the doctors called a permanent vegetative state. She needed constant care, the kind that ate up your savings and made you go to bed praying that the next day would be her last. When the end finally did come, he'd sold the house six weeks later. No point staying there with Nellie gone.

The Fountain of Youth was home now. Saltines or sometimes a Baby Ruth served for his snack. He hadn't planned it this way.

He walked slowly out of the dining room into the sunlit lobby, the newspaper tucked carefully under his arm. He sat down in one of the green wicker armchairs in the lobby window, away from the mottled giant house plant whose leathery tendrils threatened to take over the whole room. His plan was to finish doping out his picks. After that, he'd be at loose ends again.

All the years he'd been with the AP, starting as a cub reporter, then chief correspondent, assistant bureau chief, and then bureau chief, he'd talked about his retirement. "When I retire," he'd say. And there were plans for trips, books he'd read, articles he'd write, hobbies he'd take up, maybe woodworking or boat-building. He was good with his hands.

"Next month," he kept telling himself. And then next month was here and he couldn't say what he'd done with the time.

No sooner had he settled himself with his newspaper than a crew of workmen arrived in the lobby.

There were two men. He watched while they brought large canvas dropcloths from the white van they'd parked out front and spread them over the terrazzo tile floor of the lobby. They brought in big plastic buckets of paint, long-handled brushes, rollers, and paint pans.

It took the two of them together to move the heavy concrete urn with the potted plant. That done, they opened the paint cans and started applying cream-colored latex to the wall nearest the front door.

Truman got up and wandered over to the reception desk. Cookie Jeffcote sat there motionless, her eyes glued to the page in front of her. It was funny, her being there. He wondered where Yvonne Sweatt, the receptionist, was. Cookie was the leasing agent and spent most of her time in her glass-walled office, talking on the telephone or fingers racing over her calculator.

He cleared his throat. Startled, she slid a magazine across the page.

"Yes?" She gave him that condescending smile. It was the same patronizing smirk he got from other people who assumed that everybody over the age of sixty was senile or incontinent, or both.

He tossed his head toward the painters. "Company coming?" he shot the smile right back at her.

Her cheeks flushed a little. She was pretty in a brassy way, long auburn hair, milky-colored skin, large breasts that jutted aggressively from everything she wore.

"Why do you ask?" she said, fluttering the eyelashes just a little.

Truman snorted. "I've lived here six months. Not that the place is a dump or anything, but it's the first time I've seen anybody as much as change a lightbulb. Old man Mandelbaum isn't known for spending money when he doesn't have to. What gives?"

She straightened the magazine so it covered the type-written page precisely.

"Regularly scheduled maintenance," she said, shrugging her shoulders so that her bosoms jiggled ever so slightly. "I hope the paint smell won't bother you."

What bothered him was the smell of old boiled cabbage that clung to the carpet in the dining room, the pine cleaner they used to mop the terrazzo, and that cheap flowery perfume Sonya Hoffmayer drenched herself in.

He knit his eyebrows a little. They were a surprising color, sort of a foxy gray-red. He took some pains with those eyebrows, touching them up with a toothbrush whenever he saw a white hair springing out. His hair really had been red once, long past his fiftieth birthday. Red, they'd called him during his days as a reporter for the Associated Press. Red Kicklighter. He'd started borrowing Nellie's Nice 'n Easy on the sly sometime after he turned sixty. She'd never mentioned the fact that now their hair had turned the same shade of auburn. Just like Nellie—she wasn't one to throw things in somebody's face. She just started buying an extra bottle every month when she went to Eckerd's for their toothpaste and shoe polish and such.

Now, of course, he bought the Nice 'n Easy himself, at the Rexall drugstore two blocks away. Had a senior citizen discount card to get it cheaper.

"While they're maintaining things, could somebody do something about the light fixtures in the rooms?" he groused. "I've seen better-lit caves in my day."

She picked up a pencil and scribbled something. "I'll make a note," she said brightly.

"You do that," he said, knowing what would happen to the note.

He rolled the newspaper up and tucked it under his arm. It was only half-past one; he had the whole afternoon ahead of him.

The painters had moved the furniture out of the lobby area now. He stood in the window and watched them outside, unloading ladders from their truck.

"Rroww-roww-roww." He looked down. KoKo, Mrs. Hoffmayer's dog, came tearing across the lobby floor, nails clicking on the terrazzo. The dog flung itself against the glass, barking furiously but ineffectively at the men outside.

"Aw, shut up," Truman told KoKo.

"Ahrrrrr." The dog turned and snarled, baring a set of

long ratlike teeth It darted toward Truman. "Rrowwroww." The dog was snapping at his ankles, nipping at his pant leg.

"Hey. Get away."

KoKo backed away a few inches and bared his teeth again.

Truman didn't have to think long about his course of action. The open bucket of white paint was right there on the floor, the paintbrush balanced on top of it.

"Arrrp-arrrp-arrrp." White paint dripped from KoKo's quivering, shocked-looking face. The stripe extended from his muzzle all the way to his stub of a tail.

KoKo tucked tail and ran, skidding around the corner toward the dining room.

Truman set the brush down with a sigh of satisfaction. He glanced at the dining room door. Maybe it was time for a walk. He could stroll over to the open-air post office. Check his mail, wander over to Chet's Newsstand. See who else was in town, pick up a race program for tonight. He patted his right front shirt pocket. Two cigars left. Maybe he'd pick up a pack of HavaTampas.

"KoKo!" he heard a woman shriek. "My precious! What's happened to you?"

He moved quickly out the front door and onto the sidewalk.

CHAPTER

TWO

IT WAS WARM EVEN FOR MARCH, HIGH EIGHTIES.
First Avenue was crowded. Big Lincolns, Buicks, and
Chryslers took up every available parking space as far as he
could see. The license plates told you what time of year it
was: Michigan, Illinois, Pennsylvania, Ohio. The snow-
birds had landed.

It was high season in the Sunshine State. Outside the
hotel the Fountain of Youth sign was lit up at night again
now, along with a No Vacancy sign. They'd cleaned out
the old stucco and tile fountain in the lobby and turned the
water back on again, and they'd planted bright red gerani-
ums in the window boxes outside.

He checked his post office box at the open-air. Nothing
but a bank statement and something from the hotel.
Probably another notice about not using electrical appli-
ances in the rooms. He had a hot plate and a toaster and he
used them any damn time he liked.

The newsstand was tiny; three people made it seem
crowded and there were two women inside already, studying the postcard rack.

Truman plucked a box of HavaTampas from the
counter display and looked around for the Derby Lane racing programs.

"Excuse me," he said, trying to wedge himself between the two muumuu-clad women. "You got any racing programs, Ollie?"

The dwarf behind the counter tried to peer around the woman who was pushing for the Silver Springs postcard. "Oh hi, Truman," he said. "Got 'em back here. Ain't even untied the bundle yet. The truck just dropped them off."

While Ollie rang up the women's purchases, Truman turned around to examine the magazine rack beside the glass-doored drink cooler.

"Going to the track tonight, Truman?" Ollie asked, sliding the race program across the worn wooden countertop.

"What?"

"The dog track," Ollie repeated. "You know, Derby Lane."

"Oh, yeah," Truman said, reluctantly turning from the rack. "Yeah." He put the cigars on the counter, then added a pack of Doublemint chewing gum. Pearl had made Mel quit smoking last winter, so he was a prodigious gum chewer these days A little present for his pal.

Truman fished a worn dollar bill and some silver from his change purse. "You wanna go with us? There's a free bus."

Ollie's face brightened momentarily and then fell. He was probably Truman's age, but his diminutive size made people treat him like a child. A sweat-stained St. Louis Cardinals baseball cap covered his thin brown hair, and the thick-lensed glasses made his eyes look outsized for his head. The Vandyke beard was a recent addition, to make people treat him with respect. He thought it made him look intellectual. Truman thought it made him look like the mayor of Munchkinland.

"Can't," Ollie said. "Promised my sister I'd come over for supper."

"Another time."

"Sure," Ollie said.

Truman tucked the cigars in his breast pocket and the gum in his trouser pocket.

"You get the notice about the church?" Truman was studying the latest issue of *True Caper*, one of those crime magazines he used to read in the barbershop. Twin red-heads dressed in white fur bikinis were posed on the hood of a red Ferrari, each with a pistol pointed right at the viewing public. Those girls had some lungs all right. He decided right then and there that now was the time to start catching up on his reading about current law enforcement matters. The magazine was three dollars, though. That would cut into his dog-track money.

"What?" he said, reluctantly putting the magazine back. "I'm not a churchgoer. Never have been."

"Yeah well, this is one church you better find out about," Ollie warned. "Seein' as how they're fixing to put you and me and everybody else over there at the Fountain of Youth out in the street."

"What are you talking about, taking over the Fountain of Youth?" he demanded. Ollie was bad to gossip. Every week he had some cockamamie new rumor about some pro sports team that was coming to town. Most of the time he was talking through his hat. "The Mandelbaums own the hotel. Always have," Truman pointed out. "I saw young Seymour just last week, in the business office. He didn't say anything about a church to me."

Ollie licked his upper lip excitedly. His tongue was huge for so small a guy. Truman wondered why he'd never noticed it before.

"Maybe old man Mandelbaum ain't told the kid yet," Ollie said. "All I know is, I got my notice in the mail this morning. Felt like I'd been kicked in the gut when I read it."

Ollie lived in what the hotel called a studio apartment just off the hotel lobby. It had actually once been a card room years ago. Now it had a toilet and a sink, and Ollie had his color television, a bowl of goldfish, and his adult tricycle in there.

Truman pulled the letter from the hotel out of his pocket and ripped it open. It was written on the hotel stationery.

"Tenant Notice" the top line said. Truman frowned. Notices never meant anything good.

OWNERSHIP HAS RECENTLY CONCLUDED NEGOTIA-
TIONS FOR THE SALE OF THIS PROPERTY TO THE
CHURCH OF COSMIC UNITY. THE CHURCH PLANS TO
CONVERT THE HOTEL INTO A RETIREMENT HOME
FOR ITS ELDERLY MEMBERS. REPRESENTATIVES WILL
CONTACT TENANTS SOON TO DISCUSS OWNERSHIP
OPTIONS. TENANTS WHO DO NOT PURCHASE THEIR
UNITS MUST TERMINATE RESIDENCY BY NO LATER
THAN JUNE 1.

The notice was signed by Arthur Mandelbaum, D.D.S.

"Regular maintenance, my ass," Truman said bitterly. "They're fixing the place up to sell it. Giving us three months to get out," Truman said in disbelief. "Three months."

He looked sharply at Ollie. "You got one of these?"

"Sure as I'm standing here," Ollie said. "I showed it to Howard Seabold when he come in today. Howie Jr., you know, is a lawyer. He promised to have the kid look into it for me."

"Says here tenants can purchase their units," Truman said. "Wonder how much? Not that I can afford it."

Ollie's tongue worked his upper lip. "What about me?" he said. "You got a pension, and a kid. All I got's this job here. Two-hundred-sixty-two dollars and fifty cents a week. I got two-hundred-fifty bucks I been savin' up in case of an emergency. My rathole money. I guess I'll be having a change of address pretty soon."

Truman felt for Ollie. He really did. His own pension from the wire service wasn't anything grand, but it was enough, if he was careful. And Truman was the careful kind. As for having a kid, well, Cheryl was having a rough enough time raising Chip by herself. He couldn't ask her for help.

He stood in the doorway of the newsstand and blinked

in the bright sunlight. He shoved the notice into his pants pocket. Church of Cosmic Unity. Christ. What next?

"Hey, Truman," Ollie called.

Truman turned around slowly.

Ollie held out the racing program. "You don't want to forget this. Maybe you'll win big tonight. Buy the Fountain of Youth yourself. Take the penthouse apartment. Maybe a trip to Hawaii."

"Yeah," Truman said, taking the program. "Maybe I'll marry Liz Taylor and move to Beverly Hills while I'm at it."

CHAPTER

THREE

COOKIE JEFFCOTE STOPPED AT THE DOOR TO
room 2711, fluffed her red hair out over the collar of the
mink coat, then smoothed the shocking-pink minidress
over her hips.

Michael liked her to look good. He didn't like anything that didn't look expensive or first class. The first
time they'd met, at the bar in the clubhouse, she'd had
on this mink, which was the only thing she'd gotten out
of her last boyfriend, a married lawyer who handled the
financial affairs of one of the residents at the Fountain
of Youth. (The scumbag, he should take poison and
die.)

She was standing there, waiting on her Rob Roy, when
Michael turned around, his elbows propped on the counter
like he owned the place. He gave her a good long look.
"Feelin' lucky?"

She'd giggled and shown him the fan of twenties she'd
already won that night.

"Not talking about greyhounds," he'd said coolly.

Cool. That was Michael all right.

She knocked the code. Shave-and-a-haircut. Two-bits.

He'd been in the shower. Drops of water glistened in
his wavy dark hair and clung to the thick, matted hair on

his bare chest. A towel was not so much wrapped as draped around his hips.

"Baby," she cooed. He didn't say a word, just grabbed her by the hand and pulled her into the room.

She'd just had time to rescue the mink from the floor before he was at her, tugging at the big zipper that ran down the front of the dress, pushing her toward the king-sized bed.

"Hello to you too." She laughed.

It had taken some doing to get out of the office this time of day. The Reverend Jewell Newby liked to keep a close watch on the sheep in his flock. Since she was handling the new condo sales, he was keeping an especially tight rein on her. Wanted telephone reports on everything. Screw that. She'd called in this afternoon to inform Newby that she'd be out all afternoon having dental work done.

"I'll pray for a healing," he'd said, in that preacher voice he used when he was talking about God.

Jewell Newby didn't give a rat's ass about any healing. If he was praying, it was to get her in bed. Cookie Jeffcote had been around men long enough to know when one wanted her. And that one wanted her in a bad way.

Right now, Cookie had something else on her mind. Michael Streck. She'd always had a thing for Italian guys, even though Michael swore he wasn't Italian at all.

Her first time had been with Frankie Lonardi, in the back of his mother's Buick Regal, at the Sky-Vue drive-in. And when she'd first met Butch Goolsby, his hair was dark, even though he still had that crew cut he'd gotten in the marines. By the time she'd figured out Butch was nothing but Baptist white trash from Pinellas Park, she was sixteen years old and three months pregnant, and her mama was screaming about sending her to the Florence Crittenden Home.

If she never saw a pair of greasy jeans or a pickup truck full of tools again in her lifetime, it would be just fine with Cookie.

She ran her long pink fingernails down Michael's back and let the big diamond solitaire dig into his nice firm buttocks. He was tan all over. She made a noise deep in her throat, like a tiger growling. She'd seen that in a movie once. "Ggrrrr," she purred.

"Ow," Michael said, looking up. "What the hell was that?"

"Three carats," Cookie said. "Feels good, huh?"

Later, he ordered drinks and hors d'oeuvres from room service and they did a couple lines of coke together. Cookie felt all warm and melty inside, like a Hershey bar that had been left in the sun.

Then the phone rang. He picked it up, listened, then turned to her. "You mind?"

She did mind, but she knew that tone of voice. She went into the bathroom and ran the water and stood at the door, trying to hear.

After she heard him hang up, she waited a moment, flushed the commode and came out. Michael was standing in front of the mirror, buttoning his shirt, getting dressed.

"Party's over, doll," he said. "I got business."

She plopped herself down on the bed. Michael never said what his business was, but she just assumed he was a member of the mob.

The first time she'd called it that, laughingly, he'd grabbed her wrist and twisted it angrily. "Don't call it that," he'd said. "It's family."

He tucked his shirt in, then came and sat down beside her on the bed, slipping his feet into soft leather loafers. He kissed her neck. "We'll do it again, later this week? Right?"

Cookie pulled on her stockings one at a time, leaning back on the bed, arching her back and cocking her leg in the air, like she'd seen Susan Sarandon do in that *Bull Durham* movie. Slowly and deliberately, she snapped them to the garter belt, then pulled her dress on over her head and zipped it up. Michael was frowning at an imaginary speck of dust on his slacks.

"What about tonight?" she asked.

"Tonight?"

"The track. I thought we could go. You've already gotten lucky once today, right?"

He turned and took the zipper in his teeth and moved it down an inch, kissing between her breasts. "I can't. I got a thing."

Cookie went to the mirror. She took a lipstick out of her purse and touched up her face and combed her hair. It was a mess.

"What about our thing?" she said, pouting. "We never go anywhere when we're together, Michael. Am I that awful, you can't be seen in public with me?"

"Something wrong with this setup?" Michael asked, gesturing at the room around them, with its heavy damask draperies, the patio that overlooked the Gulf of Mexico. "A two-hundred-fifty-buck room isn't good enough for you?"

"Nooo," she said, "but—"

"This is work tonight, doll," Michael said.

He wondered idly how old Cookie really was. She was older than the twenty-eight she had once claimed, that he was sure of.

"I guess," she said, shrugging, acting disinterested.

Michael went to the closet, got out a dark blue sport coat and slipped it on. "Next time. Okay?"

Cookie picked up her purse, looked inside, and frowned. "Next time. You guys don't seem to understand, a girl likes a little attention. I'm cooped up all day long in that dump downtown. And this new guy, the preacher who bought the place? He gives me the creeps."

"So get another job," he said, shrugging. "What's the big deal?"

She smiled, catlike. "Not just yet." Then she changed the subject. "So what's this thing you have working at the track tonight? If you don't mind my asking," she said quickly.

He shrugged, trying to act nonchalant. "It's just a thing I'm working on. This guy, he's got a system. A system of picking dogs. Says it's ninety percent accurate. So I'm gonna check it out."

"So you're going to the track after all?"

"I told you. It's business."

Cookie looked dubious. "He can pick winners ninety

percent of the time? What is he, a Gypsy? Why's he gonna sell it to you?"

Michael picked up the big diamond-studded gold watch from the dresser and slid it onto his wrist. He picked up the gold money clip, some change, and the room key and put it in his pocket. It was cute, the way Cookie was interested in business. She was a cute kid.

"He needs a backer, someone who can finance him," he said. "That's all. Hey, maybe if this thing pans out, we could work something out. I could set you up in your own place. How'd you like that?"

Cookie got out her car keys and glanced at her watch. She'd really have to go now, before all hell broke out down at the Fountain of Youth. "Maybe. That's all I ever get, Michael. A lot of maybes."

Curtis Goolsby ran the vacuum-cleaner nozzle over the front seat of the white Ford Escort for the third time. He'd already picked up one whole bag of trash from the front seat. Old newspapers, a half-full bottle of Sea & Ski, and a mildewed Holiday Inn bath mat.

But the sand. Jeez, that powder-fine white sand. It was everywhere. And it did not want to come up.

"These people must have slept on the beach, you know that, Dad?"

His old man, Butch, was not really listening. Butch sat in a wooden chair at his desk in the garage of Sun Bay Auto Rentals. He was reading. Butch was a great reader. He liked Harold Robbins and Louis L'Amour and Jacqueline Susann. Hell of a book, *Valley of the Dolls*. His specialty, though, was true-crime books. Had a shelf at the trailer with nothing but Ted Bundy books. Today he was reading the sports section.

The radio was on. Curtis could not work without music going. He was humming along to something, like always.

"What's that, son?" Butch asked, looking up from the sports page.

"Sand," Curtis hollered over the whine of the vacuum cleaner. All Butch could see of him was his butt sticking out of the front seat of the Escort. "The damn sand won't come out."

Butch glanced at the clock on the maintenance-bay wall.

"Just get the big chunks, son," he said. "Check the trunk for money or luggage, dump out the ashtrays and make sure there's no chewing gum on the seats." Chewing gum was a rental car's worst enemy.

Curtis switched off the vacuum reluctantly. He liked to do things right. He got out and flicked a rag on the hood of the car.

"You got anything doing tonight?" Butch asked, casual-like.

Curtis scrubbed at a spot on the hood that looked like seagull poop. "Me and Tammi were just gonna maybe go out to Sunshine Speedway. You wanna ride out there with us?"

"Might," Butch said. He let Curtis get the windshield of the Escort covered with window spray before he spoke again.

"Say, you remember that boy come in here and rented the green Cutlass a couple weeks ago? Blond college-look-ing guy?"

Curtis straightened up and thought back. "Guy said some colored dude stole his Porsche. That the guy you mean?"

"Yeah. That's him. He was supposed to come last Monday and bring the insurance money to pay for the Cutlass. When he didn't show, I took a ride over to his place. You know what he does for a living?"

"No, what?"

"He's kind of like a scientist. That's what. Works on some secret NASA space program. What he does is, he works on computers."

"Huh," Curtis said. "Did the boy give you the money?"

"No," Butch said slowly. "He said the insurance settle-ment ain't come in yet. We got to talking, though, and after I told him I was gonna have to hook up the Cutlass to the towbar and take it back, he told me about this deal he's got going. See, Wade—that's his name, Wade Hardeson III—old Wade has got this computer at his work rigged up to pick the Double Q out at the dog track."

"That's good?" Curtis asked.

"Yeah," Butch said, trying to be patient. "That's real good. They had a Double Q over in Tampa last season, woman won one hundred thousand dollars on a two-dollar ticket."

"Cool," Curtis said. He went over to the workbench, got a can of air freshener, and spritzed the spray around the interior of the Escort.

The fragrance of lilacs wafted through the garage.

Butch sniffed appreciatively. "You know, that stuff smells like the crap Cookie used to take a bath in. Not bad."

"Now, like I was saying," he continued, "Wade was telling me maybe he'd meet us at the track tonight, tell us which dogs to bet on in a couple of races."

"And then we'll be even," Curtis said.

"I was thinking though," Butch said, "maybe he should give us this computer thingy. So we could bet all the races. Win big."

Curtis looked doubtful. Frown lines crossed his grease-stained forehead.

"I don't know, Dad," he said. "That Cutlass has got about two hundred thousand miles on it and the transmission's shot. I don't think he's gonna think that's a fair trade."

"Maybe he won't," Butch agreed. "That's why I was thinking you could go with me tonight. You, me, and that .38 of yours."

"Ah-he-e-em."

It was an exaggerated throat-clearing. Both men looked in the direction it was coming from, from the doorway of the bay.

Tammi Stargell's body was outlined by the sunlight

streaming into the dim garage. She was tall and skinny, with long, stringy arms and legs. She'd cut her dishwater-colored hair short, bleached it blond, and she had these little strands hanging down over her eyes, like some kind of anorexic sheepdog. She wore dark brown eye shadow and pale pink lipstick. Butch thought she looked like something out of the late-night creature feature. Curtis thought she looked awesome.

"Somebody wants the Escort," she said. "You about done, Curtis?"

"Let me just gas it up and pull it around to the front and it'll be ready to roll," Curtis said, sliding in behind the wheel.

"About time," Tammi muttered.

After Curtis had backed the car out of the bay, she walked over to Butch, who was pretending to read the paper again.

"I heard that part about the gun," she said. "What kind of trouble are you getting him into now?"

"No kind of trouble at all," Butch said, not looking up.

"Then why the .38? He's still on probation from that last no-kinda-trouble-at-all you talked him into."

"We was set up," Butch protested. "How was I supposed to know there'd be a Doberman sleeping in that liquor store all night?"

"Why the gun?" she repeated.

Butch sighed. He might as well go on and tell her. If he didn't, Curtis would. He was so pussy-whipped by this skinny piece of tail it was pathetic.

As he filled her in, Tammi's close-set blue eyes narrowed to slits. "You're sure this guy really works at DataTrack?"

Butch held up a folded rental agreement. "Oh, yeah. When he was late coming back with the money, I called up the work number he gave. He works there all right."

She still wasn't convinced.

"There must be five, six hundred people working out there. How do you know he really works on computers like he says? How do you know he's not a janitor or something?"

Butch let his chair tilt back a little, propping his black lace-up workshoes on the metal desktop. He picked up the sports page again.

"He's no janitor," he said. "You ever hear of Wade Hardeson Jr.?"

"That the guy with the Cutlass?"

"His old man," Butch said. "That's Wade Hardeson Jr. as in chairman of the board of Orange State Savings and Loan. As in the big white house on the water on Snell Isle with the forty-foot Bertram tied up at the dock. As in rear friggin' commodore of the Yacht Club."

"If his old man's rich and such a big hotshot, why is the kid renting that piece of shit from us? And why's he owe us money?"

"Unfortunately," Butch said sadly, "in many cases the chip off the old block is in reality full of termites. Our friend Wade has got him a bad drinking problem and a spic girlfriend. His daddy's cut off Wade the Third's allowance. Now Wade's got this computer program. It could make him rich enough to tell his daddy to go jump in Tampa Bay. But Wade don't have hardly enough money to get in the pay toilet at the track, let alone into the clubhouse. He let on when I visited him last week that he was gonna try to sell the computer thingy to some high roller. What Wade told me was, soon as he gets the money from this guy, he'll pay us what he owes us, plus give us tips on a couple races."

Tammi's mind was racing along as Butch talked. "Why settle for a couple of races?" she asked. "Why not get him to tell us the races for the whole season?"

"That's just what I was thinking," Butch agreed.

Wade Hardeson III popped the top of a can of Pabst Blue Ribbon beer, took a long sip, and frowned. Five more cans littered the burnt-orange shag carpet around him. He poked one with the toe of his sneaker, just to make sure he hadn't overlooked anything. He hadn't.

He belched. Made it into a long drawn-out anthem. Shiiiit.

"What the hell," he muttered, and emptied the last can, drinking the lukewarm beer down in an effortless series of gulps.

A skinny orange kitten, only a little lighter in color than the carpet, crept into the living room where Wade was sprawled on the sofa. The cat sniffed daintily at the cans. "Get outta here, Asshole," he said, tossing the last can at the cat's head and missing.

Wade called the cat Asshole. Rosie, whose cat it was— hell, whose apartment this was—called it Punkin.

"Bummer." He said it aloud. Looked at the three hundred-dollar bills he'd laid out on the milk-crate coffee table. Some high roller. Some fuckin' stake. He said that aloud too. "Some fuckin' stake."

And tonight was the night. Big night. Wade's program was ready. He just needed the rest of the data Rosie was supposed to bring back from Sarasota.

"Hurry up," he'd told her. "This is important, babe."

She'd given him that look, in that way she had, those big black eyes unblinking. Telling him he'd gone too far.

"Listen, Wade," she said quickly. "This was my idea— right? You don't know anything about dog racing. You got that computer at work, and you know how to punch the right buttons. Make it tell you stuff. But you ain't nothing without me. I'm the one paying rent around here. And I'm the one knows the dogs. It's all up here." She pointed a red-painted fingernail at her head, the long black hair neatly parted down the middle, flowing down her back nearly to her waist.

Then she'd pointed to the stack of racing forms from Tampa Downs, the ones she'd meticulously marked up after every race during the six-month greyhound season in Tampa.

Six months. Her feet ached at the thought of it. Standing

around outside the front gate, dressed in her halter top and
cut-off jeans, and those ridiculous red spike heels. "Racetrack
Rosie Picks the Winners," she'd chant to the arriving crowd.
"You'll Smell Like a Rose with Rosie's Picks."

On a good night in Tampa or St. Pete she'd sell sixty or
seventy tout sheets at a buck a pop. Sarasota, where the
rich people lived, she could make a couple hundred bucks a
night sometimes.

Sarasota was where she'd met Wade Hardeson III to
begin with. The first night of the Sarasota season last June,
she'd hitched a ride over from St. Pete with her little
brother James.

This surfer-lookin' guy, shaggy sun-bleached hair,
white low-slung jeans, big blue eyes, bought one of her
sheets, went inside, and bet a couple of her picks. After
he'd won a trifecta in the third race, he'd come outside,
bringing her a beer to celebrate.

She'd thought he was cute, and he was definitely interested in her. He'd hung around all night, asking a lot of
questions about how a nice girl like her, blah, blah.

"I worked in one of the kennels while I was in high
school," she'd told him. "You pick it up."

The stuff about the kennel was true, as far as it went.
She'd actually gone to her first dog race at the age of five,
with her uncle Ernesto. Ernesto didn't seem to have a real
job, but he went to the dog races and the jai alai at home in
Tampa, and the horse track in Oldsmar, and a lot of other
places in Florida too.

She and James lived with Uncle Ernesto and Aunt Silvia
in a bright blue concrete-block house in a run-down part
of Tampa. Aunt Silvia worked at a dry cleaners. And Uncle
Ernesto hung out.

"Jobs are for fools, Rosita mía," he'd often told her.

That night in Sarasota. Well, James had come out after
the eighth race, flat busted. He never would try her picks.
James had seen her laughing and flirting with the blond
surfer guy, shrugged, and walked away. Rosie Figueroa
could take care of herself.

She could, too. Although why she fell for someone like Wade Hardeson III, she'd never know.

Yes, she did too. He'd been to college. He had a job where he wore a sport coat and necktie. He drove a Porsche. That night, after they left the track, he'd taken her to a swanky restaurant. She ate two orders of steamed stone crabs, the butter dripping down her chin.

"If his job's so great, how come he's living with you and you're paying all the bills?" James wanted to know. "What's he do over at DataTrack? They pay him to get blasted every night?"

"It's computers," she'd said quickly. "They do stuff for NASA, for the space program. We're going over to Cape Kennedy, next launch. Wade can get us right in. At least he don't walk around with Sheetrock dust in his hair and eyes and up his ass like some people."

What Wade actually did, she later found out, was sit at a computer all day and type in numbers—data, he called it.

Weather stuff, to be exact. He'd punch in temperatures, humidity, precipitation, barometric readings. And some-how, the computer could suck it in, then spit out the best time for a rocket launch.

"The computer decides what the weather's gonna be ahead of time?" Rosie had asked. "And it's right?"

"Ninety percent accuracy rate," Wade drawled, nib-bling on her ear with those nice straight white teeth of his. "Of course, a lot of that's because of the skill of the pro-grammer." He'd reached around to slip off her halter top, but she sat straight up in bed.

"If I could pick winners ninety percent of the time, hell, fifty percent of the time, I'd be rich," she said slowly. "Filthy, stinkin' rich."

"We'd be rich," Wade had said, drawing her back down toward him on the bed. "Now let me show you my money-maker."

After, when Wade was asleep, Rosie got up, pulled on a T-shirt and went out to the kitchen.

She got a Fresca out of the refrigerator and sat at the

dinette table with a pad of paper, a pencil, and some old racing programs.

She wrote down all the variables in handicapping that Ernesto had taught her. Stuff like the dog's dam and sire. Its weight, kennel, and trainer. Then there was the dog's previous finishes, its favorite running position, track length, weather conditions, health, and performance against other dogs.

Some of that stuff you got out of the programs, the rest of it you got by hanging around with trainers and lead-out boys and kennel hands. Rosie even knew a guy who worked for a veterinarian who took care of the dogs at some of the bigger kennels.

She wrote it all down. All the categories, in her neat block print, while Wade snored away in the bedroom. The next morning she'd told him her plan.

Tonight was definitely the night.

Wade had worked really hard programming in all the data Rosie had gathered from the Tampa season, but she'd had to go back to Sarasota to look up the old race programs at the track office, since she'd only started keeping records after their season was over. He deserved a beer or two. After tonight they'd be in high cotton.

He heard the chugging sound of her VW Beetle outside in the parking lot and hurriedly kicked the beer cans under the sofa. "Cheezit, Asshole," he told the kitten. "It's the cops."

Wade stood up, stretched, and scratched his belly, pausing to wonder at the paunch he'd developed since the summer.

"Wade?" Rosie called, letting the wooden screen door bang shut.

Her face was green.

"What happened?" he asked.

"I was at the top of the Skyway Bridge. Then some jerk ahead of me stops. He fuckin' stops. And my bug starts to roll backward. I pop it into first and it stalls. And rolls backward some more. And right behind me is the biggest mother tractor-trailer I ever saw. I thought I was gonna pass out."

"But you didn't," Wade said. Rosie hated bridges. Especially suspension bridges like the Sunshine Skyway. He opened one of the battered wooden cabinets and got out a ceramic mug and a jar of instant Folgers, spooned some into the cup, and ran some hot water over it.

"You want some coffee?" He put the cup in front of her. Then, casually, "You get the data?"

She heaved her fringed leather shoulder bag onto the kitchen table and took out a green steno pad.

"It's all right here," she said, patting the notebook. "What about the money? How much did your old man give you?"

Wade opened a brown-paper sack and took out a package of Ann Page sugar doughnuts. Rosie's favorite junk food. He set the doughnut box in front of her, got a plate, and put that there too. Then he bent down and kissed her neck.

She looked up, instantly suspicious. She smelled the beer on his breath. He'd screwed up again.

"How much?" she said sharply.

Wade sighed deeply. "Three hundred. The old bastard's still ticked off about the Porsche being repoed. But I can get—"

Rosie did not let him finish. She hurled the box of doughnuts, the saucer, and her purse at him.

"*You idiot!*" she screamed. Punkin fled the room in one elegant leap.

Next door, even across the weed-choked courtyard of the Bayside Tourist Court, the other residents could hear Rosie Figueroa screaming, first in English, then in Spanish. Moments later, Wade Hardeson III burst from the small, red-painted cabin, shirtless, covered in what looked like powdered sugar.

"Get the money," Rosie screamed, standing in the doorway of the cabin. "Get the rest of the money or don't come back."

CHAPTER

FOUR

BUTCH GOOLSEY SHOT CURTIS THE LOOK, BUT Curtis did not notice. The radio was playing and Curtis was humming along, nodding his head back and forth, using his fingers to drum the song's bass line on the top of his thighs. "Ooga-chukka, ooga-chukka," Curtis chanted.

When he'd had enough, Butch reached over and snapped the radio off with such force that the plastic knob came off in his hand.

Curtis looked hurt. "You broke the radio," he said.

"You gotta listen to that crap all day and all night? You look like one of them toy dogs setting in the back window of a car, head bobbing back and forth like some kinda moron. Can't you sit still?"

Curtis was humming now. Butch kept his hands tight on the steering wheel of the car, so he wouldn't reach over and slap Curtis.

Butch had been around. Done some time in the Pinellas County jail, and a short stint up at Starke for a misunderstanding concerning a concealed weapon and a clearly illegal traffic stop by a Florida Highway Patrol officer, so he knew it was not good policy to go around slapping somebody twenty years younger and sixty pounds heavier, even if that somebody is your only son.

"Look here," Butch said, "let's go over the routine for when we see our buddy Wade. I'm gonna remind him about the money he owes us for the Cutlass. And you're gonna sit in the truck. Don't say nuthin'. If this jerk-off Wade looks at you, give him your tough look."

"Tough?" Curtis was puzzled.

"Look mean," Butch explained. "Kind of narrow your eyes, like Clint Eastwood in them Dirty Harry movies. Think you can do that?"

Curtis squinched his eyes so that he looked like an idiot Chinaman. Butch sighed. "Here," he said, pulling the Smith & Wesson .38 pistol from under the seat of the truck. "If I give you the nod, you just hold this up real quick. Only don't shoot him. Not out in public."

"Okay," Curtis said. He squinched his eyes again for practice and stroked the pistol, humming again, but softly.

When they got to the Bayside Tourist Court, Butch pulled alongside the Cutlass, took a clean toothpick, and fitted it between his bottom teeth.

He knocked on the door of unit seven, scraping his knuckles on the peeling paint. After a moment, Wade Hardeson III stuck his head out the door. His face paled a little when he saw his guest.

"Who is it?" he heard a woman's voice call.

"Tell her somebody needs their battery jumped off," Butch said in a low voice. "We don't want nobody to get hurt."

"Be right back, Rosie," Wade called.

He closed the door quickly and stepped out onto the cracked concrete stoop. "What are you doing here? I told you I'd meet you at the track tonight. I'll give you a couple tips, and we'll be all square."

Butch shook his head. "Deal's off. The boss man's busting my chops about that Cutlass. You got the money?"

Wade's face fell. "No. I don't have the money. I got a cash flow problem. I thought we had an understanding."

"Uh-uh," Butch said. "No good."

He started walking away. Wade followed him out to the

parking lot. Butch leaned over and looked in the open window of the Cutlass.

"You got any personal shit in here, you better get it out.
Me and my boy gotta take it back to the shop right now."

He reached in his pocket and took out a round brass
ring loaded with keys, each with a small, round paper tag
attached.

"Curtis," he said, looking over at his son, who was sitting in the passenger seat of the truck, "let's go. I'll drive
the Cutlass, you follow."

When his father addressed him, Curtis stopped humming and quit tapping his feet. He squinched his eyes up.
"All right," he said, trying to sound tough. He jammed the
pistol in the waistband of his jeans, got out of the truck and
walked around to the driver's side and got in. At the same
time, Butch opened the door of the Cutlass and started
throwing Wade's belongings onto the pavement.

"Wait now," Wade said, panicking. "Man, I need my
wheels. I can't get to work or to the track without my wheels."

Butch let the toothpick droop in the corner of his
mouth. His eyes were half closed, and the reptilian expression on his face reminded Wade of the alligator who slum-
bered the afternoons away on the grassy bank of the pond
in back of the tourist court.

"Better get a bus schedule, dude," Butch drawled. "Your
credit's done run out with Sun Bay Auto Rental. My
records show you owe us six hundred eighty-three dollars
and seventy-two cents. Been owing it. You sure you ain't
got any of the money?"

"Not that much," Wade said. "Maybe a hundred, hundred twenty-five. Listen. If I can come up with a hundred,
right now, how about letting me keep the car? This thing
at the track, it's a sure thing. By the end of tonight, I'll
have every dime I owe you. How about it?"

Butch looked down at the clipboard with the rental
agreement in his hand. "My boss is back at the shop right
now. He's a mean sumbitch. Told us to get the car and the
money. Didn't he, Curtis?"

He shot his son an almost imperceptible nod, which meant that Curtis should not blurt out the fact that Butch was, in fact, the boss.

Curtis got the message. "That's right, Daddy."

"You remember what else the boss said?" Butch prompted.

This was the signal. Curtis took the pistol out of his waistband and stroked Wade's cheek with the gun barrel. Wade shrank away.

"The boss said to do whatever we had to do, but don't come back without the car and the money," Curtis said.

Without warning, Butch grabbed Wade, whirling him around and pinning his arms behind his back, twisting viciously.

"Shit, man," Wade cried, "you're hurting me."

"That's the plan," Butch said. He gave Wade a shove. "Come on. Let's go inside and see if your lady friend has any money. He's got a cute little old spic girlfriend in there, Curtis."

Now Butch was giving Curtis the high sign again, so he attempted something close to a leer. "Yeah, Dad. Let's get the chick."

Wade's face was contorted with fear and pain. The big kid had taken over holding him now, and he clamped his mitts around Wade's wrists like a vise. His hands and arms were throbbing.

He wasn't worried about Rosie's safety. Nah. If one of these two came near her, she'd knee them quick in the balls and run like hell. But if she found out how much money he owed these goons, she'd never let him hear the end of it. It wouldn't do to piss Rosie off. Not now. Not when they were so close.

"No, man," he gasped. "Leave her alone. Listen," he said, lowering his voice. "I'll give you the computer program. It's worth a lot more than what I owe you. Lots more."

"Program?" Butch said. "Would that be the thing you been mouthin' off about, the system to pick dogs?"

"Yeah," Wade said. He didn't remember telling this guy

about the program. He must have shot his mouth off while he was drunk.

"Lemme go, okay? And I'll tell you about it. Swear to God, this thing is guaranteed. Let me go and I'll go in and get the printout for you. Fourteen races. Fourteen guaranteed winners."

Curtis held on tightly, like a bloodhound with a treed coon.

Butch's toothpick rolled over to the other side of his mouth. "It's okay, boy," he said finally. "Let's go take a look at what Wade here has to offer."

Inside the cabin, Rosie watched through the dirt-caked window as the two thugs manhandled Wade.

"*Madre de Dios*," she muttered, locking the door and fastening the chain. She dragged a chair over to the door too, propping it under the doorknob. No telling what Wade was promising them.

Five more minutes. That's all she needed. She sat back down at the computer and tried to concentrate. Wade had designed a gridwork for predicting each race's outcome. There were fourteen grids to fill out, one for each race. Running vertically down the side of the grid she'd numbered the dogs, one through eight. Across the top, there were spaces for weight, age, speed, experience, post position, track length, breeding—all the factors she used for handicapping.

Then she'd filled in the blanks with numerical grades for each factor, all the material Wade had programmed into the computer.

She'd gotten picks for ten races, in different combinations, including a perfecta, an exacta, and a quinella. The first three races the computer ran, the results were nearly identical to what she'd predicted using her old hand-done method. But the results for the fifth, seventh, and tenth races were different. That's where they'd make their money, letting the computer figure in factors she couldn't.

She went into the bathroom and opened the Tampax box on the shelf in the bathroom, picking out the back row of tampons, the ones with the paper wrappers she'd carefully glued shut. She tore the wrappers off, took the rolled-up twenties out of the empty cardboard dispensers. Three hundred dollars.

She took the money and tucked it in her bra. She wanted the money against her skin, where she could feel it, for good luck.

Back to the program. She typed hurriedly, using the handwritten charts she'd worked on all week. She typed in the numbers for the twelfth race and tapped the enter button. The machine made a quiet noise, digesting, she thought of it. Rosie liked the computer. It was quiet. Competent. Like her, it ran on logic. Wade was a genius with numbers, but Rosie, she knew logic.

Wade. She ran back to the window. Wade's mouth was running a mile a minute. He was gesturing wildly, pointing toward the cabin, nodding confidently.

"Oh, shit," Rosie said, gritting her teeth. No fucking way. She hadn't worked this hard, come this far, to hand the program over to a couple of goons to settle one of Wade's bar bets.

She darted back to the computer. Pushed the print button. No time to run the last race. She'd rely on her own picks for that. She ripped the printout out of the computer, folded it in quarters, and stuffed it in the pocket of her jeans. She popped a diskette into the computer's hard drive and repeated the sequence of commands Wade had taught her.

Seconds later, after the computer screen flashed the words "file copied," she called up the file on the diskette. It was all there. Good. She took the diskette and put it in the zippered fanny pack she used as a pocketbook.

Now there were voices at the door, and the knob was turning. Wade's voice. "Rosie? Open up, babe. The door's locked."

"Be right there," she called. She called the program up

again on the hard drive, punched some keys, and typed out onto the command line: k-i-l-l. The computer made its quiet chewing sounds and then the screen went blank. Swallowed whole, Rosie thought.

She looked around the room regretfully. She didn't mind the clothes so much. But her books, a hundred paperbacks probably, picked up at the book exchange, she hated to lose. But there was no time. She grabbed her rose-covered hat and jammed it on her head.

"Rosie? Open up, dammit. This isn't funny."

"I'm in the bathroom," she called. "Be right there."

She went to the open window in the bedroom, and with one foot, kicked out the rotten screen. She had one leg out when the orange cat peeked out from under the bed.

"Punkin!" she called softly. In one swift move she was back in the room, grabbing the kitten and tucking it under her arm. Then she was out the window and running, darting in between the tiny tourist cabins, the cat tucked under the crook of her arm like a football.

Marguerite Streck was out in the front yard trying to get the Weedwacker to work when Michael pulled into the driveway.

"What are you doing home?" she asked him. Saturdays were the busiest times at the lot, where Michael worked for his uncle Earl. And this was a busy month too, with snow-birds shopping for double-wides to get away from those brutal winters in Detroit and Des Moines.

"You guys run out of mobile homes to sell?"

"Don't call it mobile homes," Michael snarled. "It's manufactured housing. Okay? Manufactured housing. And I'm home because I got somewhere to be tonight, if that's all right with you."

"Whatever," she said, turning her back on him and going back to the malfunctioning Weedwacker.

Michael loosened his tie as he walked into the house, going straight to the refrigerator for a beer. Then he went into the living room. From here he could watch while Marguerite slashed the hell out of his hibiscus and oleanders.

He took his cordless phone out of its stand and punched in a number. "Yeah," he told the person who answered. "This is Mikey. Lemme talk to Nunz."

Marguerite was kneeling on the grass now, pulling handfuls of tangled nylon line out of the Weedwacker. Her face was beet red from the sun, her hair damp and plastered to her head.

"Slob," he said aloud.

"Huh? Who the fuck is this?"

"Oh no, Nunz," Michael said hurriedly. "It's me, Mikey. No, I was talking about Marguerite, my old lady. She's out in the yard, sweating like a field hand. It's disgusting, you know?"

"You let your old lady do yardwork?" Nunz demanded. "What kind of man are you?"

Nunzio Gianni was very formal and old-fashioned. Michael had never seen him in anything but a dark suit and a white dress shirt.

"She likes to garden," Michael said. "It's like a hobby. Hey, Nunz," he said, changing the subject. "You know that thing I was talking to you about? It's all set for tonight."

"The thing?" Nunz had obviously forgotten.

"The thing. With the puppies. Remember, I told you I got a line on a guy who can fix the puppies?"

Nunz was still puzzled. "Puppies?" he repeated. "I got a parakeet. What the fuck do I need with puppies?"

Michael shook his head and rolled his eyes.

"Nunz. Remember? I got a guy who can fix those dogs over in St. Pete. The gray ones. Remember?"

"Gray dogs? Oh yeah, yeah. The thing. I remember. Sure."

"Great," Michael said, relieved. "So tonight's the night. The guy is supposed to meet me there, you know, to give it to me."

"He's gonna give it to you?" Nunz asked.

Michael chuckled, thinking about that dipshit Wade. He'd run into him at the track in Tampa, impressed after watching Wade cash in a handful of winning tickets. He'd bought the kid a few drinks in the clubhouse, then they'd done a line of coke in the men's room. He'd let it slip casually that he, Michael Streck, was close to Nunzio Gianni.

"No shit. You work for the Giannis?" Wade said, eyes widening.

Everybody in the state knew the Giannis ran the rackets in Florida. Almost everybody assumed Nunzio Gianni worked for his cousin the capo, Salvatore "Sallie Gee" Gianni. What few realized was that Nunzio Gianni had never really met his second cousin Sallie.

"With," Michael had corrected Wade, "I work with the Giannis."

Nunz and Michael were "like this," as Michael liked to put it, holding up two fingers pressed tightly together. Lately he'd been looking for something to solidify his relationship with the family and to get him the hell out of manufactured housing.

This computer thing, he knew, was it. He'd suggested to Wade that he might be interested in investing some capital, an advance, the way Wade the banker's son put it, against future earnings.

"The kid's got a system," Michael told Nunz. "Something that's a sure thing. What I need from you, Nunz, is some working capital for tonight, when I try the thing out."

There was silence at the other end of the line.

"How much?"

"I'm thinking ten."

Now there was button-punching, the sound of an adding machine on the other end of the phone.

"What kind of terms we talkin'?"

Michael was stunned. He'd been sure Nunz would give him the money just on a handshake. That was the way they'd done business before. Handshake. Man to man.

"Nunz," he said, "I thought we'd go partners. You

know. I get the system, you provide the up-front money, we split fifty-fifty."

"You thought," Nunz said. "We never discussed. Pick me up on the way to the track. I wanna meet this kid. See what the system is."

"Sure," Michael said. "We'll have dinner. Drinks. You'll see."

He hung up the phone and swore loudly.

"Shitfuckdamnhellpiss!" This was not how he'd planned the evening. The original plan went: Shake the kid down. Take the computer thing away from him. Lay down the bets. Then dinner, a nice rib-eye and caesar salad in the clubhouse. Maybe call Cookie from the track. He was sure he could find a way to get her to meet him. Winning made him horny as hell.

All that was off now. He'd have to get the program away from Wade but at the same time keep him away from Nunz.

"Shit," he said, this time with feeling.

CHAPTER

FIVE

SHE MADE HERSELF SMALL, NEARLY INVISIBLE, eyes cast down, arms held close to her body. It was a trick she'd learned in grade school so that the teachers wouldn't call on her and the bigger kids would leave her alone.

People got on and off the bus, laughed, talked, complained. If the driver noticed that she'd been riding for two hours, he said nothing. Finally, when the bus got to Williams Park, the central departure for every bus in the city system, she reluctantly got off. She had a plan now.

There was a pay phone on the corner, across the street from the old Maas Brothers department store. Rosie dialed James's number. It rang and rang.

She hung up, dialed her girlfriend's number. She had only a couple of real friends. But the answering machine picked up. Rosie looked at her watch. It was after four. Her friend Marion was probably on her way to work. Okay, she'd see her there.

The warm bundle around her middle shifted, and she heard a plaintive mewing. She looked down, saw the kitten's tiny pink nose poking out of the opening. She unzipped the zipper a little and stroked the kitten's head. "Poor Punkin." No way she could take the kitten to the track. Wade and those men would be looking for her, for sure. She sat down on one of the green benches. The fading afternoon sunlight still felt good and warm.

She got out the schedule she'd picked up and scanned it, looking for the bus that would take her to the track. There was a soft flapping noise and she looked up, startled.

Dozens and dozens of pigeons fluttered to the walkway in front of her. Parked in their midst was one of those adult tricycles, ridden by an old woman wearing a white sunbonnet, pedal-pusher slacks, and sunglasses with a white noseguard. The tricycle had a pair of wire baskets mounted behind the seat. In one basket sat a bored-looking dachshund, in the other there was a large bag of bread-crumbs, which the woman was dipping her hand into, throwing the crumbs to the flock of pigeons circling the bike.

Rosie sat up and watched. The old woman clucked and cooed to the birds. The kitten stirred again. She looked down at it, then got up and walked over to the woman.

The woman cringed and stopped throwing the crumbs as Rosie drew near. "I'm not hurtin' nobody," she said in a frail, high-pitched voice.

"I like the birds too," Rosie said. "And cats. You like cats?"

The woman nodded. "Buster and me love all God's animals."

Rosie dipped into the waistpack and brought out the kitten, who squirmed happily in her hands. "This is Punkin," she said. "I've got to leave town, but I don't have anybody to keep her."

"How much?" the woman asked.

"No, I want to give her to you," Rosie said. "Will you take her?"

The woman smiled softly, taking the kitten in her arms, turning to the dachshund. "Look, Buster, a kitty."

Rosie saw that the dog's eyes were filmed over with cataracts, the fur on its ears turning white at the tips. It turned its face toward the woman's voice and barked twice. "See, Buster's excited. She'll be fine," the old woman said.

She put Punkin in the basket. Then she got back on the bike and slowly pedaled away.

Rosie walked in the other direction, her fists clenched tightly. "Don't cry," she told herself. "Don't cry, dammit." She saw the number 8 bus, the bus to the racetrack, pull up to the curb and she quickened her step to meet it.

"Listen," Pearl said. "It's nothing. Really. Sometimes when I take the blood pressure medicine, I get dizzy and bump into things. I feel so stupid, running into my own bathroom door."

Truman lightly touched her cheek. A shiny, greenish-black welt was rising and her right eye was swollen almost shut. "We'll sit the track out tonight," he said.

Mel stood there silently, his hands jammed in his baggy pants pockets, jingling his change and car keys.

"Absolutely not." Pearl said. She gave Mel a little push. "You boys go on. I've got unpacking to do, and then Dotty Milas wants me to come down and play canasta. Go on now," she repeated. "I'm fine. I feel stupid, is all."

She handed Mel his hat, a beat-up straw fedora. Then she edged both men toward the door. She gave Mel a quick peck on the cheek, then turned to Truman. "Keep an eye on him, TK," she whispered. "He's not himself tonight."

"You sure this is all right?" Truman asked, alarmed. Mel had spoken only a couple of times since Truman had gone up to the Wisnewskis' room to see if they were ready to go. He wasn't even sure Mel recognized him.

"He's better if he gets out and doesn't sit around and stew," Pearl said. "He likes to be around people. But he forgets where he is sometimes, just sort of fades-like. You stay with him and he'll be fine."

So Truman stayed right at Mel's elbow when they got down to the street. They stood out in front of the Fountain of Youth, waiting with the good-sized throng for the Snowbird Special to pick them up.

It was twilight, and the sky was streaked pink, orange,

blue, and purple. There was a hint of a breeze coming off Tampa Bay a couple of blocks away, but it was nice and dry tonight, not like in the summer, when you wanted to pick a handful of that wet, suffocating air and wring it out like a washrag.

"So the trip down was good?" he asked Mel. "Traffic okay leaving Pittsburgh?"

Mel nodded enthusiastically. "Got twelve-point-four miles to the gallon. Put in a quart of oil when we got to Kentucky. The turnpike was murder, though. You never saw so many potholes."

Truman felt himself relax. If Mel was up to bitching about road conditions and bragging about the mileage on that Newport of his, he was feeling fine again.

"Whattabout it?" Truman said. "Think the Bucs can stay out of the cellar this year?"

"Don't start with me," Mel warned, his deep voice rumbling with pleasure. "We got the finest centerfielder in the NL. He's gonna hit .326, make the All-Stars. We're going all the way this year, my friend. It's the Pirates' year, all right, especially if—"

"Hey, Mr. K, Mr. Wisnewski," a young female voice interrupted. "How y'all doin'?"

Jackleen Canaday edged her way through the crowd to their side. She was wearing a big white tunic top with gold and silver sequins pasted on in a swirling design, tight white slacks, and gold high-heeled shoes. She had on a gold cowboy hat too, with her hair tucked under it.

Mel smiled uncertainly. "Hello."

Truman squeezed his elbow. "This is Jackleen. From the dining room. Remember?"

"Sure," Mel said. "Good to see you again, Jackleen."

"So, Jackleen," Truman said, "did you get the night off?"

A smile lit up her face. "LaWanda wanted to work double shifts today. All the girls put our money together." She held up a little white purse on a gold chain. "Thirty dollars. Enough to play every race. Talkin' 'bout big money."

"Well now," Mel said. He straightened his shoulders. "You don't mind being seen in the company of two old coots like us?"

"You can help me carry my winnings home," Jackleen said, grinning.

The bus pulled up to the curb then and made a loud snorting sound as the hydraulic doors were flung open. It was a standard green-and-white transit authority bus, but someone had pasted a big banner on one side. "Snowbird Special!" it proclaimed.

The pitch of voices raised, and the crowd began inching toward the curb. Truman caught hold of Mel's sport coat. "Stay by me now," he said, keeping his voice light. "I'm counting on you buying the first beer. It's your turn, remember?"

"Don't worry," Mel said, and then the crowd pushed them down the aisle of the bus, toward the back. They stayed standing, because all the seats were taken.

The bus bumped and lurched, but the crowd was packed so tightly that there was no chance they'd fall down. The air was hot and stale, it smelled like hair spray and Brylcreem and canned tomato soup. Truman wished someone would open a window.

When they all got off into the balmy night air, they were directly in front of the main entrance to the track.

Mel got off first, and the crowd seemed to swallow up the tall, straw-hatted man. Panicked, Truman tried to push his way through the throng, but it was too thick, too unmoving.

He reached into the pocket of his lightweight poplin jacket and pulled out his old press card.

"Excuse me," he said loudly, holding the white card aloft. "Working press. Coming through. Press here."

People looked at him curiously, but let him through. He managed to jostle his way toward the glass-fronted ticket booth. Mel Wisnewski stood there, anxiously looking for his friend.

"Truman," he said when he spied him. "What the hell

took you so long?" It wasn't until Truman reached the window and was reaching into his jacket pocket for his wallet that he felt the tugging at his coattail.

"Mr. K," Jackleen said breathlessly. "You run pretty good, you know that? I had to hang on for dear life."

"Never mind," Truman said. He hated to admit it, but his heart was racing with fear and excitement. God knows what might happen if he lost Mel in this crowd.

As long as he had the press card out, Truman thought, it wouldn't hurt to use it. After Mel and Jackie paid, he stepped up to the ticket booth.

"Working press," he said, flashing the card for a moment.

"What?" the girl said. "Can I see that card again?"

Truman's face flushed. His press card had expired last year. "I'm with the press," he said. "AP."

"What's that?" the girl said.

"Associated Press," Truman said, puffing his chest a little.

"Like a newspaper?" the girl asked. " 'Cause we got a separate press entrance. You gotta go around to the gate on the other side." She was already looking over his shoulder at the next person in line.

Truman shrugged and gave her a dollar. "Never mind."

Inside the gates the three walked quickly down a runway to the grandstand. Truman, in the lead, strode past the rows of green benches to the fence around the track. He stood and sniffed appreciatively. It smelled like old times. Cigar smoke mingled with perfume and the tangy salt of the bay. "Nice night," he said to his friends.

The three of them clung to the fence surrounding the track and drank it in, a postcard view of Florida. The white sand track had been raked smooth and it sparkled next to the lush green lawn of the infield. There was a rock fountain there in the middle, and it was outlined with some kind of frilly pink, white, and purple flowers. The tote board was lit up atop the bandstand, numbers winking on and off as the odds changed. On the bandstand itself a dozen red-jacketed men tootled away at "Sentimental Journey." Tall sabal palms swayed in the evening breeze.

Truman felt himself relax. As always, he wished fleetingly that Nellie were here.

"Twenty minutes to post time," the public address system announced. "Twenty minutes to place your bets."

"I gotta go find Rosie," Mel said abruptly.

"That your girlfriend?" Jackleen asked. "I'm gonna go call Miss Pearl and tell her on you, Mr. Wisnewski."

"Girlfriend?" Mel was puzzled for a moment. He blushed. "No, no, no. Rosie's a . . . uh, she tells people which dogs to bet."

"A tout," Truman said. "She's not too bad," he added grudgingly.

"I've got to go find her," Mel said.

"Later," Truman suggested. "Look, I got the *Times* and the program. They both got picks in them. See?"

He took the folded-up sports pages out of his jacket pocket, along with the rolled-up race program. "Let's box quinellas like we did last year. Double our money, right?"

"No," Mel said stubbornly. "Rosie's got a system. Something new. At the end of last year she told me a friend of hers was working on a new system, something with computers—"

"Yeah," Truman said, shaking his head in disapproval. "Everybody's got a system. Me, I like to watch the dogs when they lead 'em out. I watch to see which ones are frisking around, raring to go, which ones are rolling around in the grass. But the dog I bet, that's the dog that takes a dump. I figure he's gonna run that much faster. Right?"

"Hey," Jackie said. "You know Anne Marie, the blond girl who only works dinners? She's got a system too."

"Anne Marie," Mel said, interested. "Do I know her?"

"You know," Jackie said. "Kind of a hippy-lookin' chick. She wears those big black lace-up army boots and beads, got these little old round granny glasses."

"Big butt and good legs," Truman said.

"Oh yeah. Anne Marie," Mel said. "What's her system?"

Jackie took a sheet of paper from her purse. It was one of the coffee shop's paper placemats, the ones with the map of Florida attractions on it. The back had been written on with a green ink pen.

"She does the dog's signs," Jackie started to explain.

"Signs?" Truman said. "What kind of signs?"

"Their astrology signs. She's got all these books and charts and stuff."

"Wait now," Truman said. "How the hell does this girl know which dog is a Leo and which is a Taurus?"

He didn't advertise it, but Truman never missed his own horoscope in the *Times*. A Virgo, that's what he was. "Loyalty to a friend leads to new horizons," it said for today.

"No, Mr. K, see, they got it all right here in the program," Jackie said. She tapped the first race listing.

"See, this dog here, Andy's Candy? Look over here in the chart. He was born in February. That makes him a Pisces. So Anne Marie, she looks at how good a Pisces is gonna do today against, say, an Aries, or a Sagittarius, and she figures out who's gonna do best."

"You believe that crap?" Truman asked.

Jackie nodded quickly. "Anne Marie worked me up too. 'Financial windfall,' she said. That means money, right? I'm gonna win big tonight, for sure."

"Be right back," Mel said then, and before Truman could stop him, he was moving away rapidly, disappearing into the crowd.

Jackie saw the look of panic in Truman's face and started after the old man. "I'll go with him," she called over her shoulder.

"I'm right behind you," Truman said.

CHAPTER

SIX

WADE HARDESON'S RIGHT EYE WAS SWOLLEN nearly shut, his cheekbone and eye socket a swirl of purple and green. But he could see well enough to observe the woman with the flower-covered hat getting off the bus that was unloading in front of the main entrance to the track.

"That's her," he said, his words slurred through thickened, bloody lips. "In the hat with the roses. That's Rosie. Follow her and we'll get the program. You'll see."

Butch rolled the toothpick from one side of his mouth to the other and glanced over at Curtis, who was sitting on the other side of Wade, all three of them in the front seat of the Cutlass.

"She's cute," said Tammi, who was sitting in the backseat but leaning forward to get a better look. "How come she went with a loser like you?"

Wade scowled but said nothing.

"You been making promises about that program all day," Butch drawled. "And what have we got? Nothin'. That's what. We ain't got jack."

"You guys spooked her," Wade said bitterly. "She's smart. She probably saw you two banging me around out in that parking lot and figured out what was going on. If you'd just met me here, the way I told you, we'd have the program, tonight's picks, everything. But no—"

"Don't start," Butch warned. He nodded at Curtis. "You go inside with our buddy here, see if you can find the girl."

"You say she's got a favorite betting window?" he asked Wade.

Wade nodded. "Marion. Fat redheaded woman who works the number four window at the grandstand level. Rosie thinks Marion brings her luck. She won't buy tickets from anybody else. She's Cuban. You know how they are."

"Go with him," Butch told his son. "Get the chick. Show her your gun if you have to."

"He'll never get near her," Wade said quickly. His mind was racing. He had to get away from these two. Get hold of Rosie, sweet-talk her, get the picks, meet Mikey up in the restaurant. Twenty-five thousand. That's what he'd told Mikey he wanted for a copy of the program.

If only he could get these apes to back off.

"Wade's right," Tammi said, clutching Butch's arm.

Butch frowned. He'd been against bringing Tammi along. But Curtis had insisted.

"Let me go after her," Tammi said. "She's already seen you two clowns. And she sure as hell knows Wade. I'm the only one she hasn't seen. I'll go up, start talking to her, maybe bump up against her or something."

"Yeah, right," Butch said derisively. "What? You go pretty please and she'll just hand it over?"

Tammi's eyes narrowed. She opened the car door, got out, and patted the straw bag she wore on her shoulder. "You think you're the only guy in the world with a gun? I'll go on up to the ticket counter and try to make friends with Rosie. But maybe she'll be looking for us. Hey, genius, where else could she go?"

Wade shrugged. "Anywhere." Then he got an idea. "She's buddies with a cocktail waitress in the clubhouse restaurant. She might go in there, get her friend to lay down the bets for her."

He looked meaningfully at Butch and Curtis, who wore oil-stained blue jeans, flannel shirts, and thick-soled work boots. By contrast, Wade wore rumpled but clean khakis, his threadbare navy blazer, a dress shirt, and tie.

"You gotta be dressed up to get in that restaurant, huh?" Tammi asked.

"Yeah," Wade said. "They're pricks up there."

Butch sensed his control slipping away. "Okay," he said. "Here's the plan. Tammi, you hit the ticket window. Try 'em all, but concentrate on that redheaded woman. Wade, you can go up to the clubhouse. But Curtis is going to be right outside the door. You try any cute shit, Curtis goes to Plan B."

"Plan B?" Curtis said.

"The one where you drag Wade outta there and into the men's room, where you proceed to break his arms and legs," Butch said patiently. "Me, I'll roam around, see if I can spot her."

He glanced down at his watch. "Forty-five minutes to post time. Meet up at the bar at the grandstand level five minutes before the first race. We gotta get our bets down."

He grabbed Wade's arm and squeezed hard, watching with amusement as the blood drained out of the kid's face and his lips twisted with pain. "Don't screw up," he said. "I got big plans for tonight. Big plans."

Nunzio Gianni scanned the menu. He frowned, his heavy silver eyebrows sinking low over the deep-set black eyes. He took off his glasses, folded them, and placed them in his inside breast pocket.

"No pasta," he said. "What kinda restaurant you take me to, Mikey, a man can't get a plate of pasta?"

Michael smiled nervously. "I know, Nunz. What are you gonna do? They got only one game in town up here. Hey, you like steak? Try the New York strip. Honest to God, Nunz, it's great. Or the shrimp. Fried, steamed, any way you like. Right off the boat, honest to God."

"Shellfish?" Nunz recoiled. "Red meat? You trying to kill me? I got a condition, you know."

He thumped his chest for emphasis, then looked up at the waitress, who'd been standing, hands on hips, waiting.

"All right," Nunz said. He put the glasses back on, peered at the waitress's name badge, which was pinned over her left breast. "Shirley, that's your name, right?"

The waitress nodded.

"Shirley, you know how to make a nice tossed salad? Some nice romaine lettuce, some green peppers, maybe a cucumber or some peperoncini peppers, dressed with a little lemon juice, some olive oil. You think you could do that for me?"

"House salad," Shirley said, scribbling on her order pad. "You want the croutons or no?"

"Croutons?" Nunz said, horrified. "Just take the steak knife and put it in my heart, okay, it'll be quicker. No croutons. Bread. No butter. I got a condition."

She took Michael's steak order, promised to bring the red wine right away.

When she was gone, Michael scanned the room, trying not to look anxious in front of Nunz, who was babbling on about his left ventricle or something. Finally he saw what he was looking for.

"Nunz," he said. "I gotta go to the can. Be right back."

"I know how that is," Nunz said sadly. "Probably your prostate. My prostate, it's the size of an eggplant."

Michael walked quickly from the table. The kid was standing at the maître d's stand, gesturing frantically. Stupid jerk.

When he got closer, he knew something was wrong. The kid's face was beat to hell. And he kept glancing backward, toward the door.

"What's wrong?" he said when he got right up next to Wade.

The doorway was jammed with people trying to get seated before the first race.

"We got complications," Wade confessed. "Rosie shot

her mouth off about the program and then she skipped out on me with it."

Michael grabbed Wade's arm and squeezed. The kid gasped in pain and jerked away.

"You don't have it?" Michael said. "Are you dicking around with me here, Wade?"

"No sir," Wade said. "No. I mean, Rosie's got it. She's here. I just have to find her and get it from her."

"So do it," Michael said. "What's the problem?"

Wade glanced back at the door. "There's a guy out there. Rosie owes him money. Big money. He showed up at my door a little while ago. He's the one who did this to my face. He wants the program. Says he'll kill me if he doesn't get it."

Michael's fingers latched around Wade's forearm. He put his face very close to Wade's. "I'll kill you if you don't get it."

He spun Wade around and pointed toward his table. "You see that old guy sittin' there, talking to himself? That's the number-two man in the family there. He's got an envelope full of hundred-dollar bills in his pocket. We're ready to do business. And you're telling me you don't have the goods?"

"I can get it," Wade said. "But you gotta help. I can't get anywhere near Rosie with that goon on my back. You gotta help me get out of here, get him away from me so I can get to Rosie."

"Okay," Michael said. "Where is this guy? Is he carrying?"

"He's got a .38 in his jacket pocket," Wade said. "He's right outside, by the elevator. Big dude. Blue jeans, flannel shirt. His name's Curtis. He's big, but dumb as shit."

"Wait here," Michael said. "When you hear a commotion outside, duck out that door. Find the chick. My associate and I want that program. You understand?"

"Sure," Wade said. "No problem."

"What's she look like, this chick?" Michael asked.

"She's little. Maybe five two, good body, long brown

hair. Cuban. She's wearing a big straw hat with flowers all over it. Roses."

Michael opened the glass door to the hallway. The guy leaned against the wall by the elevator, hands jammed in his jacket pocket. He was singing softly and bobbing his head to some kind of secret beat.

Down the hallway was a ticket window. A track security guard stood watching people line up to place their bets.

Michael rushed over, a look of alarm on his face. "Officer?" he said, a little out of breath.

The guard eyed him cautiously. "Yeah?"

"There's a man," Michael said, "around the corner there. I think he could be some kind of criminal."

"Oh yeah?" the guard said. "What makes you think he's a bad guy?"

"I was at the ticket window downstairs, making some bets. I, uh, carry a lot of cash. I noticed this guy watching me. Then I came up the elevator to the restaurant, he came too. He's standing over there now. Just watching."

"Nothing illegal about that," the guard said.

"No," Michael agreed. "But I think I saw a gun in his pocket."

"That right?" the guard said, glancing around. "Let's check it out."

It hurt to laugh, but Wade did it anyway. The sight of the guard patting Curtis down, finding the gun, radioing for backup. Now there were two guards and they were handcuffing him, and he was hollering about his rights. Michael walked past the altercation, winked at Wade, and kept going, strolling back to his table.

Wade took off running and didn't look back.

At the table, Nunz was digging into his salad.

"Hey, Nunz," Michael said. "Sorry it took so long. You know how it is."

Nunzio rolled his eyes heavenward. A drop of olive oil

glistened on his chin. "Where's this guy with the thing?" he wanted to know.

Michael's face reddened. "That's what I need to tell you. There's a slight hitch. The kid says he hasn't got the thing."

Nunzio shrugged. He sipped his red wine. "This kid with the thing. What is he—stupid?"

"Nothing like that," Michael said quickly. "I'll be right back, all right? Ten minutes. Honest to God."

CHAPTER

SEVEN

MEL CLUTCHED THE FOUR QUARTERS TIGHTLY IN his right fist. People were pouring into the grandstand area now and he had to fight to keep moving in the right direction: an upstream salmon in a downstream-running river.

He was tall, though, and he stood straight and moved at a good clip. He could see over most of the crowd's heads, and they could see him, a scarecrowlike figure in the ragged straw hat, the baggy gray cotton slacks, and the loose flapping sport coat he wore over a worn cotton flannel shirt. Pearl tried to get him to dress up, wear the things she'd bought for him, but he liked his old clothes. Familiar things kept the confusion at bay. He felt confused a lot lately.

He was looking for another hat, that silly rose-covered hat.

"Racetrack Rosie. You'll smell like a Rose with Rosie's picks." He said it to himself and kept moving through the crowd, leading with his shoulders, not noticing the shouts when he stepped on a foot or bumped into someone in his way.

After what seemed like a long time he worked his way to one of the exit turnstiles. A uniformed security guard was just turning the corner and he looked at Mel in a funny way. "You going out, sir?" he asked politely. "Feeling sick or something?"

"No," Mel said, annoyed. "I'm fine. I'm just looking for somebody. Rosie—the young lady who sells the tip sheets?"

The guard thought about it. He was good-looking, maybe thirty, with sleek brown hair that brushed his shirt collar. Muscles bulged from his short-sleeved white uniform shirt. His badge said Roberts.

"You mean Rosie Figueroa?"

"That's the girl. Have you seen her tonight?"

"I seen her when I got here an hour ago," the guard said. "You might look for her by the grandstand betting windows, back the way you came."

Mel turned then and tried to go back. He could hear the band playing, something with a livelier tempo now. Was it "Alexander's Ragtime Band"?

"Five minutes to post time," the announcer called. "Five minutes to place your wager."

The runways were crowded. So many people. And now he needed a bathroom

He turned down a runway that should take him toward the elevators to the clubhouse level. There would be bathrooms there. But the lights in the hallway were dim. He was alone now. There was a doorway on the right side. He tugged on it. Locked. He could barely hear the crowd now. The hall was deserted and dark as a tomb.

Wait. Up ahead, light was coming from somewhere. And he saw something. A hat. A red-rose-covered hat.

"Hey, Rosie," he called out. He broke into a near trot. The bathroom was forgotten for the moment. Less than five minutes to post-time. He needed that tip sheet.

The tunnel lead back outside. Mel stood and looked around, trying to get his bearings. He could see those tall streetlights in the parking lots, and the cars parked a little way away from a tall chain-link fence that surrounded this place. Some kind of service area, maybe. Pickup trucks were parked here, and there were dogs in cages, greyhounds, yipping and pacing with excitement.

He couldn't see Rosie now. Didn't know where she was. The dogs kept barking and hurling themselves against those metal mesh cages.

What was he doing here? Where was Pearl? Was it time to go to work already? Who had put all these dogs in cages in his driveway?

He walked around a black truck and stumbled over something. He looked down to see what he'd tripped over.

It was a woman. A woman wearing a red-flowered hat. Pearl had a hat like that one Easter. And a blue sailor suit. Cute as the dickens. He squatted down to speak to Pearl, but she was holding her head funny, asleep maybe, but with her eyes wide open.

"Pearl?" He reached out and touched her shoulder. His hand touched something warm and sticky. He wiped his hands on his slacks. Pearl had a bunch of papers in her lap, they were being blown about by the breeze, white pieces of paper scattered all over. He sat down beside her. "Pearl," he said, shaking her gently. He had something all over his hand now. She didn't say anything. Mad at him. Giving him the silent treatment because he'd been late getting home, stopping for a beer with the boys. He reached in his pocket for his handkerchief, needing to clean his hands, but he didn't find one. Pearl always carried a hankie. She had a funny kind of pocketbook, a bright blue plastic pouch, strapped to her waist. Mel unzipped it, found a hankie, wiped his hands on it, then stuffed it back in his own pocket.

"Pearl?" He couldn't stand it when she gave him the silent treatment like this. It could go on for hours, days even.

"I'm sorry," he said loudly. "Real sorry. I didn't mean it, honey."

"Hey, man."

Mel heard footsteps and a voice. He looked up. A teenager dressed in gray work clothes came through a gate from the parking lot. He was dark-skinned, wearing a baseball cap. He walked quickly over to Mel. "You can't be back here, mister. This is a restricted area."

Then he was standing in front of Mel, looking down at him, the kid's eyes wide with terror. He was looking at Pearl.

"Holy shit," the kid said.

This old guy looked like a crazy person, all raggedy, with blood streaks on his pants and shirt, blood on his hands too. Holding some papers and shaking the woman, telling her he was sorry.

He wanted to run, but he made himself bend down, to get a better look, see how bad the lady was hurt.

"Oh man," he said softly. "Oh man. Why you wanna kill Rosie for?"

CHAPTER

EIGHT

"COMIN' THROUGH," JACKLEEN BELLOWED, trying to edge through the crowds. People were standing around, looking up at the closed circuit television monitors. She stopped, looking around helplessly. Truman was directly behind her.

"Working press," he bellowed. "Out of the way. Coming through."

The crowd parted, people giving them dirty looks as they went steaming by. But there was no sign of Mel.

"Maybe he wandered outside," Truman said, gesturing toward an exit sign.

The going was easier here, people moving briskly in both directions, probably because there were no television monitors. The hallway came to a T. Truman looked right and left. No sign of Mel. "Let's try down there," Truman said, pointing to the left. It was darker here, almost like a tunnel.

Up ahead, Truman saw a doorway, and through the doorway, what looked like the parking lot. He started walking faster and then they both heard it: sirens. Close by. He thought about the last sirens he'd heard this close, when Nellie had her stroke.

The sirens were coming closer. Truman could see the

area was enclosed by chain-link fencing. He heard the frenzied barking of dogs. Two police cars with flashing blue lights pulled up outside the fenced-in area and cops seemed to pour out of them.

"Mel!" Truman called. His friend was slumped against the fence, over to the right, his face buried in his hands. Mel was crying. "Don't be mad at me, Pearlie. Please don't be mad."

That's when Truman saw Rosie. She was leaning to one side, a flowery straw hat on her head, her eyes open but unseeing, and a gaping red wound across her neck.

"Sweet Jesus," Jackleen whispered behind him.

"Move away from the body, please."

Truman looked up. It was a cop, a St. Petersburg police officer, dressed in a white shirt and green uniform pants. "This is a crime scene, folks. You'll have to step away."

Mel was still crying. He didn't seem to have recognized Truman or Jackleen.

The kid was agitated. "I found this old dude here," he was telling the cop. "He was sitting down here beside the lady, talking to her, but she was dead. He kept saying he was sorry, you know? Callin' her Pearl."

One of the track security guards walked briskly up to the cop. He was muscular, with sleek brown hair and even white teeth. "What have you got here?"

"Looks like a homicide," the cop said. He looked at the guard's badge. "Do I know you?"

"Bobby Roberts," the guard said, nodding. "Yeah. I work a beat out of the downtown traffic precinct. You mighta seen me in traffic court. This is my off-duty job. You want me to secure the area or something?"

"That'd be good," the cop said. "We got detectives on the way."

Now the kid was pointing to Mel. "That old dude had a knife in his hand. I couldn't get him to put it down. Crazy old dude."

Roberts walked over to the body, crouched down, and looked. When he stood up, he was ashen-faced. "Anybody given you an ID of the body yet? 'Cause I know her. Name's Rosie Figueroa. She's a tout. Hangs around the track all the time."

The cop wrote it down in his notebook. "Spell that for me?"

"It's Cuban," Roberts said. "You got me how to spell it. And the old guy. He was looking for her. Comes up to me ten minutes ago, asks me have I seen her."

The cop wrote that down too. He looked up at Truman and Jackleen. "What about you two? Were you here when the body was found?"

"We just this minute walked up," Truman said. "My friend here has Alzheimer's. But he didn't do this. He must have found the body. He was lost."

The other police officer was kneeling down beside Rosie. He donned a pair of disposable rubber gloves and put his fingers on her wrist, trying for a pulse, then shook his head, snapped the gloves off, and threw them aside. "She's dead," he said, standing up now. "I'm gonna radio for homicide."

They used Jackleen's betting money to take a cab back to the hotel.

"Mel couldn't kill anybody," Truman said. He'd been saying that over and over.

"He had blood on his hands," Jackleen pointed out. "And he kept saying he was sorry. Only he was calling her Pearl."

"Poor Rosie," Truman said. "She seemed like a good kid. Always smiling. Couldn't have been more than twenty, twenty-one. Same age as my Cheryl when she got married."

When they got to the Fountain of Youth he went over to the lobby phone booth and dug a quarter out of his pocket.

The desk sergeant wouldn't tell him much, just that Mr. Wisnewski was being questioned by a Detective Rivers.

"You people have got the wrong guy," Truman said. He slammed the phone down.

Pearl's eyes got big and frightened when she saw who was knocking at Dottie Milas's door. "Truman?" She got up from the card table, knocking her chair over, she was in such a hurry. "What's wrong? Where's Mel? Is he okay?"

The plan was to tell her once they got back to the Wisnewskis' room on the fourth floor, but Pearl started crying, and Truman couldn't handle that. So he told her what little he knew. Then he called Howard Seabold's kid, the lawyer, Howie Jr., and set it up so Howie would meet them at the police department.

"He never even got a parking ticket," Pearl said when she could speak again. They were in Mel's car, the Chrysler. Truman drove, and Jackleen sat in the backseat, handing Kleenex to Pearl.

"I know," Truman said. His eyes were on the road, he wanted to make sure he didn't miss the turn into the police station. They'd built a new one in the years since he'd covered the cop shop for the wire service. Big and fancy. Justice Administration Building, it was called now. They could call it that. It was still the cop shop.

He wanted to ask Pearl about the knife they'd found on Mel, about that black eye she said she got from bumping into something, but every time he cleared his throat, he heard himself saying softly, "It'll be all right. It'll be okay."

The desk sergeant had a secretary take Pearl and Truman back to the homicide office, but he gave Jackleen the kind of look she was used to getting. A black girl, only nineteen, and St. Pete was still the South, no matter how many Yankees moved down. So she sat in the lobby, read a Rotary Club magazine, and fumed.

The detective was waiting for them outside the door to the homicide office. He was white, in his mid-thirties, wearing a white and red-striped shirt with his tie undone. His face was smooth and round, a baby-face, Truman thought, surprised. In his days cops were grizzled veterans of the field, chain-smokers and hard drinkers.

"Mrs. Wisnewski?" the detective said, putting his hand on Pearl's shoulder and giving Truman a quizzical look. "I'm Virlyn Rivers. Your husband is inside the office, talking to one of the other detectives. Has anybody told you what happened?"

"We know your people have the wrong man," Truman said, stepping forward.

"Sir?" the detective said.

"Truman Kicklighter," he said briskly, businesslike. "AP. Tampa. Assistant bureau chief. I was with Mr. Wisnewski at the track tonight. We're old friends. He was only gone a couple of minutes. The next thing we know, you people have hauled him down here like a criminal."

"You don't think he killed that woman?" Pearl said, her voice quavering, threatening to start crying again.

"Mrs. Wisnewski," Rivers began, apologetic, "your husband seems pretty incoherent. Has he been drinking tonight?"

Pearl gasped. "No! He has Alzheimer's. But I thought it would be good for him to get out tonight. He'd talked about the track for weeks."

"Has he ever been violent before?" Rivers asked.

"Mel's never been violent," Truman said, interrupting. "He'd cross the street to avoid an argument."

"My husband would never hurt someone," Pearl agreed.

Rivers shrugged. "The Figueroa girl's throat was slashed. Mr. Wisnewski was holding a knife when that kid found him. Blood all over him, kept apologizing, calling the girl Pearl."

Pearl gasped. "That's me. He thought it was me. He gets confused, that's all."

"Mel didn't do it," Truman insisted. "He's seventy-six years old, for Christ's sake, Detective. He's no killer."

The door to the homicide office opened then and an older black man stepped out. His eyes sagged at the corners, and he was thin to the point of emaciation. The man nodded at Pearl and Truman, handed a piece of paper to Rivers. "A fax from the Allegheny County Police Department."

The two men stepped away from Truman and Pearl and held a brief, whispered conversation.

"Thanks," Rivers said, scanning the paper. The man went back inside the homicide office.

Rivers looked up frowning. "Mrs. Wisnewski, at the end of the hallway down there, there's a break room. There's a fresh pot of coffee in there. It's not the worst coffee in the world. Why don't you go get yourself a cup, try to calm down a little? In a few minutes we may be able to let you talk to your husband."

Pearl nodded mutely and walked away.

Now it was just Truman and Rivers. Truman looked down at the younger man's shoes. Cowboy boots, hand-tooled, it looked like.

"Detective Rivers," he said. "What don't you want to talk about in front of Pearl?"

Rivers handed Truman the fax. "Your pal Mel has a record back up in Pittsburgh."

"What's that supposed to mean?" Truman snapped. "You must have the wrong Wisnewski, that's all."

"No mistake," Rivers said. "We used his Social Security number. He was charged with aggravated assault back in 1951."

"Does it say he was convicted? Huh?" Truman demanded.

"No," Rivers said slowly. "Captain Boykin there talked with somebody up in Pittsburgh. The old case report says Mr. Wisnewski was picketing outside a steel mill. Some nonunion laborers tried to cross the picket line. Your buddy and three other men beat him nearly to death. When the guy got out of the hospital, he was too scared to testify."

"So Mel was a hothead a long time ago," Truman said. "Lots of people were. It was a mill town. Things got out of hand. This is different. Besides, Mel isn't himself. He wouldn't kill anybody."

Rivers's gaze found Pearl, walking slowly toward them, sipping from a Styrofoam cup. "How'd Mrs. Wisnewski get that shiner? The old man give her a belt?"

Truman's lips tightened. "She walked into a door. That's all."

While Rivers took Pearl inside to talk to Mel, Truman went to get a cup of coffee. There was a little carton of cream sitting in a bowl of half-melted ice on the tray by the coffeepot and real sugar. "Look at this," Truman said to himself. It was a far cry from the inky sludge he'd guzzled back in the days when he'd covered the cop shop.

When he got back to the homicide office, Howie Seabold was sitting on a folding chair somebody had brought. He stood up when he saw Truman.

The two shook hands. "Pearl's inside with Mel," he told Howie Jr. Then he told him everything he knew about the night's events.

"Alzheimer's disease," Howie said, making notes on a yellow legal pad. "We should be able to get them to cut Mel loose tonight, if he's really as bad off as you say. I've never met this Detective Rivers. But I do know Jimmy Boykin, the captain. He's not a bad guy. And one of my former classmates is an assistant in the district attorney's office. Jean Rielly. I'll call her first thing in the morning."

The door to the homicide office swung open again and Rivers brought Pearl Wisnewski out. She was crying again, her lips pressed tight, tears streaming down her face. She shook her head when she saw Truman, unable to speak. He introduced Howie to Pearl and then to Rivers.

"I'd like to see my client now," Howie told Rivers.

Rivers nodded. "I'll take Mrs. Wisnewski out to the lobby. She says you have a friend there, waiting for you, someone who'll sit with her."

"Let me go in with you," Truman told Howie when they were gone. "Mel's only met you once or twice. Maybe he'll remember me."

Mel was sitting in front of a desk, his hands clasped in his lap, his hat on the floor beside him. His hair was white and mussed, and Truman noticed for the first time how bald his friend had gone in the past year. Mel's lips trembled when he saw Truman.

Truman knelt down beside Mel, shook his hand. "This is Howie Seabold Jr., Mel. Remember? We played golf with Howie and big Howie last winter, down in Bradenton."

But Mel was trembling, wringing his hands. "Pa, they made me stay after school, Pa. I got in a fight with Jacky Murphy. He started it, Pa. He called me a dirty Polack. I had to hit him, Pa. I'll do my chores when I get home, Pa. Okay?"

Truman grasped Mel's hand. It was cold and dry, covered with a network of tiny spots.

"It's me, Mel. It's me, sport. Your buddy Truman. Remember me? Truman?"

A single tear trickled down Mel's cheek. "I'll shovel the walk when I get home, Pa. I promise."

Truman sighed, stood up, and turned to Howie Seabold. "I've never seen him like this," he said. "This is a guy who could recite the box scores for every Pittsburgh Pirates game going back to 1939."

"It happens," Howie said.

Outside, in the hallway, Pearl and Jackleen were sitting, waiting. Jackleen gave Truman a questioning look. He shook his head. Not good. Pearl stood when the two men came out. "Did he tell you anything?"

"He thought I was his pa," Truman said helplessly. "He thought he was in trouble for fighting in school."

Pearl patted her purse. "I have his pills. They help sometimes."

Rivers took her back inside then.

"That's a hell of a black eye on Mrs. Wisnewski," Howie said, keeping his tone conversational. "Do you know anything about it?"

"She told us she walked into a door," Truman said.

"Could Mel have done it?"

"No way," Jackleen put in.

"Maybe," Truman admitted. "Not the old Mel, though. You know they've been married almost sixty years?"

"Any kids?"

Truman shook his head. "A son, Danny. He was the only child. He was in the navy. Got killed in Vietnam. They never got over it."

Detective Rivers came out of the office, and he and Howie strolled down to the end of the hall together, chatting quietly.

"They really gonna arrest him?" Jackleen asked.

"It doesn't look good," Truman had to admit. "That girl's throat was slashed. And Mel had a knife when they found him."

"What else?" she asked.

Truman frowned. "The cops dug up some old charge against Mel. From back in the fifties. He was arrested for beating up some scabs outside the steel mill where he worked. It was a long time ago, but it still makes Mel look like some kind of a thug or something."

"He didn't do it," Jackleen said stubbornly. "Not Mr. Mel."

Howie and Rivers returned then, nodded at Truman and Jackleen, and went back in the office.

A moment later, Pearl and Howie emerged, Pearl's face white and worn-looking. And she was crying again.

"Oh, Truman," she said, grasping his arm. "They're going to make him stay here. In a jail cell, Truman. Mel doesn't know where he is. He's all mixed up. And he's scared. So scared.

"Mr. Seabold," she said, turning to Howie, "why won't they let me stay with him? Or let me take him home? We'd bring him back in the morning."

Howie patted Pearl's arm awkwardly. "Mrs. Wisnewski, it's a murder investigation. First thing in the morning I'll call the district attorney. I'll talk to him. We'll get Mel's doctor back in Pittsburgh to call and tell the police about the Alzheimer's. I don't think they're really going to want to go to trial. I'm sure of that. Not with a senile seventy-six-year-old."

Pearl and Truman both winced at Howie's choice of words.

"I'm sorry," Howie said. "But his age and medical condition are the two strongest things he has working in his favor. You folks go home. Get some sleep. They'll keep him in an isolation cell here. Nobody else to bother him."

With Truman on one side and Jackleen on the other, Pearl walked out to the car. There was nothing left to say.

Truman drove home again. He switched on the radio. The eleven o'clock news came on and the announcer started talking about "death at the greyhound track." Truman reached out to switch it off, but Pearl caught his hand. "No. I want to hear. I need to know what they're saying my Mel did."

The dead woman's identity was being held pending notification of next of kin, the announcer said. And then he went on to announce that Derby Lane's Big Q would have paid a record-breaking $280,000 except that nobody had cashed a winning ticket.

CHAPTER
NINE

"**W**HERE'S THE JUDGE?" PEARL WANTED TO know. She glanced nervously around the courtroom at the rows of prisoners who lolled around on the benches, waiting their turn. Mel sat in the front row, slightly away from the others, who were all younger.

There was no judge's bench, no witness box, no tables for the state and the defense. Just rows of dark polished wood benches holding prisoners, with uniformed sheriff's deputies and bailiffs stationed around the room.

"There's a television camera," Howie Jr. explained, pointing to the front of the courtroom. Truman quit staring at the other prisoners and looked at a plain pine podium and a metal tripod holding a camera aimed at the podium.

"The judge is in his courtroom over at the county courthouse," Howie explained. "He's got a television too. He can see each defendant and hear what they say, and in that television monitor up there the defendant can see the judge and the state's attorney."

"It's on TV?" Pearl cried. "Does that mean everybody back at the Fountain of Youth will know what's going on? I'd die, I'd just die if everybody knew Mel had spent the night in jail."

"No, no," Howie reassured her. "It's closed-circuit. Just the judge and us."

It was the damnedest thing Truman had ever heard of, and he said so. "Looks like these judges could at least get off their keesters and come to court," he said. In his day, courtrooms were solemn, well-appointed places.

"It's supposed to save the taxpayers money," Howie said. He looked around and frowned. "Although I've got to admit, I don't like it worth a damn either."

"What happens next?" Pearl asked, clutching her purse like a life preserver in a monsoon.

"This is an advisory hearing," Howie said patiently. "They'll formally advise Mel and me of the charges against him. I'll ask that Mel be released on his own recognizance—ROR, they call it. Normally, with a homicide, the state's attorney would oppose it. But I've talked to my friend Jean Rielly and told her about the circumstances, and she's agreed that jail is not the place for Mel."

"Did you talk to Dr. Shrader back home?" Pearl asked. "Dr. Shrader knows all about Mel's problem. He's the one who gave us those pills, I forget what they're called."

"Cognex," Howie said. "He told me everything and faxed me the medical records, which I've faxed over to the state's attorney."

"All rise," the bailiff intoned. But no judge entered the courtroom. Instead they saw a light glowing red on the top of the television camera.

They all stood up. Howie gathered his papers. "They're going to hear Mel's case first," he said, "because of his medical condition."

Howie stood by Mel and took him gently by the elbow, steering him to the podium in front of the camera.

The judge on the television monitor was saying something, but Truman couldn't make it out. He was apparently asking Mel a question, but Mel, frail and confused, only looked around the room.

"Your Honor," Howie said loudly. "My client was diagnosed as having Alzheimer's disease six months ago. In light of his incompetence, we would ask that the district attorney drop all charges and that Mr. Wisnewski be released to his wife's custody."

The judge said something else then that Truman couldn't hear.

"Yes, sir," Howie said. "Mr. Wisnewski and his wife have wintered here for the past fourteen years. Mrs. Wisnewski has agreed that she'll make arrangements to stay in Florida for as long as the court stipulates. My client has ties to the community, and he has no record of forfeiting any bonds."

The picture on the television was so fuzzy, Truman couldn't make out whether the judge was a man or a woman. "Hell of a way to have a trial," he muttered to Pearl.

Now Howie was trying to object to something. "That incident was more than forty years ago and has no relevance to the charges against my client," he said, getting a little hot under the collar. "Mrs. Wisnewski has power of attorney and has stated that she is able to manage Mr. Wisnewski's care and supervision," he said.

Truman turned his head so that his good right ear was facing the television. He could make out the words "nursing home" and "condition of release," but that was all.

"What'd he say?" he asked Pearl. But Pearl shook her head. "I don't know."

A moment later Howie was ushering Mel away from the camera. He brought Mel to the back of the courtroom and motioned Pearl and Truman over.

"What happened?" Pearl asked. She grasped Mel's hand, but he tried to shake her off. She bit her lip.

"The judge threw us a curveball," Howie said. "I'd gotten the state's attorney to agree to dropping the charges with no stipulations, but the judge decided different. He'll drop the manslaughter charge, but only if we get Mel admitted to an approved nursing home."

"A nursing home," Pearl gasped. "I want him with me. I'll take care of Mel. He doesn't need to be in a nursing home. That would kill him."

"The judge doesn't see it that way," Howie said. "It's a take-it-or-leave-it situation. If we don't accept, Mel will go back to jail and he'll be tried for manslaughter. We don't really have a choice, Pearl."

"Mel?" Pearl put her face close to her husband's and cupped her hands on either side of his face. "Mel? Do you know me today?"

His pale blue eyes blinked furiously and he worked his mouth, but no sound came out.

"Oh God," Pearl groaned. "He's never been this bad. Never." She looked over at Howie. "When?"

The lawyer shrugged. "As soon as we can find an available bed. How's your insurance?"

"Insurance? Mel always took care of all that."

Truman put an arm around Pearl's shoulders. "Mel was always so organized. I'll bet he has all the papers right together. There's probably an insurance card in his bill-fold. It's funny. My Nellie was the one who took care of that stuff in our family. When she got sick, I had to take over. I can help, if you like."

"I'll have my secretary start calling around to look for a bed on Monday," Howie said. "Pearl, are you sure you can handle Mel by yourself for a while? Do we need to think about a private-duty nurse?"

"We'll be fine," Pearl said fiercely. "Just fine."

The dining room was almost empty by the time Truman sat down for lunch. It was nearly one now. The meat loaf special would be gone and so would the good desserts.

He'd picked up a discarded newspaper in the lobby on the way in. Now he unfolded it and began looking for the story of Mel's arrest.

He found it on the front of the local section. A twelve-inch story. More than was allotted to a domestic knifing in one of the city's public housing units, much less than the thirty-two inches allotted to a story about the arrest of Norman Giddens, the veteran weatherman on Channel 9, who'd been picked up for soliciting an underage prostitute in a strip joint over in Tampa.

Truman allowed himself a small chuckle over the police mug shot of Giddens, who had apparently tried to cruise incognito, disguising himself with a cheap toupee and ridiculous-looking glued-on sideburns and mustache.

Jackleen appeared from nowhere, sliding a steaming plate of meat loaf, mashed potatoes, and LeSueur peas in front of him.

"Here," she said. "I saved you a plate."

"Thanks," Truman said, meaning it. "I was afraid I'd have to settle for the salmon patties."

"You mean the sawdust patties? I wouldn't feed them to my worst enemy," Jackleen said. "How'd it go in court this morning?"

He handed Jackleen the newspaper. She set the coffeepot down so that she could read it.

"Says here the police confirm that someone was questioned for the murder, but there hasn't been an arrest," Jackleen said. "Sure looks like an arrest to me when they put handcuffs on somebody and put him in the back of the police car."

Truman finished chewing and took a sip of coffee. "These reporters today, they got computers, faxes, everything. The only thing they don't have is an instinct for news."

"What's your instinct telling you now?" Jackleen asked, glancing around to make sure Mrs. Hoffmayer wasn't watching.

"Mel didn't do it," Truman said. "Period."

"Okay," Jackleen said. "I believe you. But if Mr. Mel didn't do it, who did?"

He put the cup down. He'd dreamed about the girl last night. Rosie. So young. He could see the long dark hair in his dream, dark and damp with her own blood. But in the dream Rosie had had Cheryl's face.

"She hung out at racetracks every night," he said.

"Gamblers are a rough bunch. And she was young. Maybe she was mixed up with dope or something."

There was a small photograph of Rosie in the newspaper. It looked like the kind of picture they put on an ID.

"She had a nice face, huh?" Jackleen said. "Twenty years old. I wonder how she knew so much, to be able to pick winners like that. Mr. Mel, he said she was real smart about greyhounds."

"She was smart," Truman said thoughtfully. "Too smart, maybe."

He drank his coffee and brooded about it. "Maybe she got in with the wrong type of man," he said. "Girl that pretty is sure to have a boyfriend."

Jackleen nodded sagely. "Uh-huh. Now you talkin'. Probably some sorry-ass dude put her out there sellin' them sheets. Like a pimp, kinda."

"Doesn't sound like you have a very high opinion of men," Truman said, wiping a bit of gravy from his mustache.

"See, men my age, they're not like you, Mr. K," Jackleen said. "Don't want no commitment, don't wanna settle down, work a job, make a home. All they wanna do is be runnin' in the street."

"Surely not all of them," Truman said.

"All the ones I been mixed up with," Jackleen said. "Sorry, that's what they are. Now, take somebody like you. How long were you married?"

"Forty-five years," Truman said softly. "My sweetheart and I were married in 1949. Six weeks after we met."

"You're kidding," Jackie said. "You only knew her six weeks and y'all got married?"

"No point in waiting around," Truman said simply. "Never regretted it either. We had our fights. I won't tell you we didn't. But Nellie and I, we were a team. Best friends."

"You miss her, huh?" Jackleen said. Out of the corner of her eye she saw someone waving frantically to catch her attention.

"Gotta go," she said hurriedly. "I saved you back some apple crisp. You gonna want some more coffee with that?"

"Yeah," he said, meaning he missed Nellie.

He was polishing off the apple crisp when Ollie rushed up.

"I been looking all over for you," he said breathlessly. "We got a meeting, upstairs in the card room, four o'clock this afternoon."

"For what?"

"Christ! The church takeover, what else?"

"I'd forgotten," Truman admitted. Or maybe he'd deliberately put it out of his mind. How much was this Cosmic Unity outfit going to charge for an apartment? Truman had a room with a bed, a dresser, two easy chairs, and a nightstand. There was a tiny bathroom with a tub but no shower. For this he paid $325 a month. And after he paid his bills and helped Cheryl out a little, he had precious little left.

"Can't," he said quickly. He had no stomach for meetings today. "I promised Cheryl I'd go take a look at her bathroom sink. It drips."

"You gotta be here, Truman," Ollie insisted. "We need somebody nosy to keep these stiffs from pulling something over on us. We gotta stop 'em, Truman. You gotta help us."

Truman nodded his head toward a wizened gentleman sitting at a nearby table. The man looked away suddenly, as though he'd been gazing at something fascinating on the other side of the room.

"You want nosy, get Arch Barchie over there," Truman said. "The guy's a professional busybody."

"Yeah, yeah," Ollie said carelessly. "He's coming. Look, it's only one o'clock now. You go over to your kid's house, fix the plumbing, you can be back by four. Did I mention we're having cake and coffee?"

"Not interested," Truman said firmly.

Cheryl sat on the commode lid, watching while her dad turned the old red toolbox upside down. He glanced over and gave her a smile. She knew what he was thinking, that it was like the old days when she'd come into the bathroom on Saturday mornings and watch him shave, maybe even lather up her own face and shave with an imaginary razor.

Truman pawed through the tools laid out on the tile floor. "What happened to all the tools I gave you?"

Cheryl waved a hand. "Chip's been in them again. The lady across the street gave him an old busted-up radio and he took it apart out in the garage. He's convinced he can fix the thing."

"Chipper," Truman hollered. "Bring me a wrench. On the double."

He started to get up from the floor. "Ow," he said, wincing and rubbing his knees. "You know you're getting old when it hurts just to sit on the floor."

"You're not old, Dad," Cheryl said, "just experienced."

"My ass," Truman muttered, rubbing there too. It had been cold on that tile floor.

"Here you go, Grandpa." Chip stood in the doorway, his arms full of well-used tools. "Is one of these a wrench?"

"That's a pair of wire-cutters," Truman said, pointing. "That's a socket wrench. And this," he said, taking one in his own hands, "is an adjustable wrench. Now watch how I tighten this doohickey, so maybe you can fix it for your mom next time around."

Chip stood with his face inches away from his grandfather's, intent on watching the repair in progress.

"There," Truman said, wiping his hands on a towel. "Done."

"What would I do without you?" Cheryl asked, giving him a peck on the cheek. "You're staying for dinner, right?"

"Yeah, Grandpa, stay," Chip begged.

"I don't know," Truman said. "I had a late lunch."

The truth was, he was tired. He couldn't get Mel out of his head. Seeing him like that. Like a baby in a used-up body. He wanted a nap. Wanted to close his eyes and not think about hotel buyouts and Alzheimer's disease and a pretty girl named Rosie, dead at the age of twenty.

"Can't do it," Truman said. "I promised to be at a meeting at four o'clock."

The three of them walked out to the kitchen. The house was small, only two bedrooms, a bath, the abbreviated kitchen, and a living room. "Perfect for just the two of us," Cheryl had proclaimed the first time she'd driven by it with her parents.

Her marriage had lasted just six years. When Chip was two, Alex announced he was feeling suffocated in their relationship. Now he lived in Arizona with his new wife and their children, and he was always behind in his meager child-support payments.

Cheryl opened the refrigerator and handed her father a can of beer. He took it and opened it, but not without protesting. "You don't need to spend your grocery money on beer for me, honey. You've got tuition coming up, don't you?"

"Already paid for," Cheryl said proudly. "I've been doing some tutoring on the side. And the books I need next quarter I've already bought used. We're in clover, aren't we, Chipper?"

Her son nodded, biting into an apple.

"Besides," she added, "one six-pack every two weeks isn't going to break me, Dad. What kind of meeting are you going to?"

Truman put the beer on the table and sat down at the dinette. He looked around and liked what he saw. New peach paint on the walls, crisp gingham curtains fluttering at the windows. On the shelf above his head ran a row of pink-flowered cups and saucers, the china he'd brought back for Nellie after an assignment in Germany. Cheryl was like her mother, she liked things to be special.

He took a long sip of beer. She'd bought the premium stuff, not the generic kind he bought.

"Oh, everybody in the hotel is all stirred up," he said, trying to sound casual. "New management or something. Nothing for you to worry about, honey."

"You like that place, don't you, Dad?" Cheryl asked.

She worried about him sometimes, living in that tiny room of his.

"Like it fine," Truman assured her. "There aren't many places like the Fountain of Youth left around St. Pete. Downtown used to be full of 'em, the Pennsylvanian, the Princess Margaret, the Seabreeze. Now, I guess, people buy time shares or they go to one of those old folks' towns up there on U.S. 19. Sun City, those kind of places."

"I remember the Princess Margaret," Cheryl said. "When I was a junior I went to Boca Ciega High School's prom there."

"With a hippie kid whose hair was longer than yours," Truman said. "When your mother saw that tuxedo jacket he was wearing, with bell-bottom jeans, she nearly bust a gut laughing."

"I've got a picture of us that night around here somewhere," Cheryl said, "but what the heck was that guy's name?"

"I've forgotten," Truman said. "Maybe I'm getting Alzheimer's too." His expression was suddenly sad.

"You?" Cheryl scoffed. "The man who won three trillion dollars on *Jeopardy!* in one week? The man who remembers every card played in Hearts? Alzheimer's? Never happen."

"That's what Pearl thought about Mel," Truman said. "Last night, when we got to the jail, he thought I was his pa. And he doesn't know Pearl at all."

"How awful," Cheryl said, shaking her head. "But Alzheimer's wouldn't make somebody like Mel turn really violent, would it? He's always been such a sweet old guy. You don't think he did it—do you?"

"No," Truman said. "I've known Mel a lot of years. He couldn't do what the murderer did, slash that poor girl's throat. But who knows what Alzheimer's has been doing to his mind?"

"Another beer?" Cheryl asked, wanting to change the subject.

"Souchak," Truman said suddenly. "No thanks."

"What?" Cheryl was totally confused now.

"Steve Souchak," Truman said. "That was the kid's name. His old man ran for county commissioner that year. He was a real horse's ass."

"You're amazing," Cheryl said, giving him a hug. "I couldn't have come up with that guy's name in a million years. Not if you paid me."

"Souchak," her father repeated. "Maybe I'm not so senile after all."

CHAPTER

TEN

THE ROOM WAS STIFLING. IT SMELLED OF TALCUM powder and mothballs and medicine. Pearl gestured toward the bed. Mel lay on his side, legs curled to his chin, his eyes blinking rapidly. "He's been like that all day. I've tried to talk to him, tried to get him to eat, but he just blinks his eyes that way."

Truman tried not to look shocked at Mel's runaway decline.

"Has he eaten at all?"

Pearl bit her lip. "Jackleen, she's such a sweet girl, she brought up a tray. All his favorites. Mashed potatoes, macaroni and cheese, bread pudding. I managed to get him sitting up, and I put the tray on his lap. But, Truman, it was as though he'd never seen a fork before."

She wrapped her arms around herself and shivered, despite the heat in the room. "He's never been this way before." She paused "TK, I don't know what I'm going to do."

"How about I sit with him for a while? You've been cooped up in this room all day."

"No," she said quickly, "I couldn't leave him."

"Pearl," he said, trying to sound stern. "He'll be all right. If he wakes up, I'll talk to him. We'll talk baseball.

Go on now, get outta here. I'll bet you haven't eaten either."

"No," she said slowly. "I'd forgotten about food. I've been so worried . . . "

"Go on," Truman said, giving her a tiny push. "I don't want to see you for at least an hour."

When she was gone, Truman took off his cardigan and rolled up his shirtsleeves. He pulled a chair up beside Mel's bed. The patient had turned over and was facing the wall, not stirring.

Truman looked around for something to read. He found a neatly folded copy of the Sunday paper.

"Good," he said aloud. He'd only had time to read the local news earlier in the day. Now he took the front section and started reading, methodically, cover to cover, the way he'd read papers his whole life. When he'd been with the AP he'd read half a dozen papers a day, every day. The *St. Petersburg Times*, of course, plus the *Miami Herald*, and the *Orlando Sentinel*. Plus the *New York Times*, the *Washington Post*, and the *Wall Street Journal*. Most of the time, he'd see bylines by an old friend or former colleague. In those days newspaper journalism was a small world. Everybody knew everybody else or had worked with them at a smaller paper along the way. Now, though, he read only the one paper, and rarely saw a name he recognized. Newspapering was a young man's game now.

He heard the sheets rustling, looked over, and saw Mel sit up, surprised, as though he were Rip van Winkle waking up twenty years later.

"Hiya, Mel," Truman said quietly. "Pearl just stepped out to get a little supper. I got the sports section here. You wanna take a look?"

Mel blinked. In his thin cotton pajama top, with his bony sternum showing, he looked like an undersized plucked chicken. "How'd the Bucs do last night?"

Taken aback, Truman had to think about it for a moment. It was as if somebody had suddenly turned the light back on inside his friend's head. He wanted to run from the room, call Pearl, tell her, "Hey, look, Mel's okay. He's back. He's gonna be okay."

Instead, he opened the sports section to an inside page, took his reading glasses out of his breast pocket, put them on, and started scanning. "Lemme check the box scores," he said. "I didn't catch the news last night."

"That colored kid, Clemente," Mel said, "he's something else, ain't he? I think he's gonna be the greatest right fielder ever, best arm in baseball, hits the ball anywhere he wants. He makes Musial look like a sandlot chump. Where'd you say Pearl went?"

Mel was back all right, Truman realized. Back before his favorite ballplayer died in that 1972 plane crash. He'd heard somewhere that Alzheimer's affected short-term memory. How short term, he didn't know. Did Mel remember anything of last night or yesterday?

He chose his words carefully. "Pearl just went for a bite to eat. You've been sleeping most of the day. She's been real worried about you, pal, you not eating and all."

"The hell you say," Mel said, snorting. "She won't give me any food. I told her I was hungry, but she hid the food. I think she ate it all."

"No, Mel," Truman said, alarmed. "Pearl wouldn't do that."

He brought the tray over to the bed. "Look. Jackleen sent up some lunch. She's been real worried about you too."

Through a mouthful of pudding, "Jackleen?"

"The waitress in the dining room," Truman said. "The girl who always takes good care of us. She went to the track with us last night. Remember?"

Mel wrinkled his brow, then picked up a roll and started buttering it. "The track? I was at a ball game last night. Clemente hit a triple offa Gibson. I won twenty bucks in the office pool."

"Right," Truman said, depressed. "You want a cup of coffee?"

*   *   *

By the time Pearl came back, ten minutes later, Mel had drifted off to sleep again.

"Oh," she said, looking disappointed. "He never woke up?"

"Sure," Truman said, a little too heartily. "He woke up, talked a little bit about the Pirates, even ate some supper."

"Thank God," Pearl said. She looked at her wristwatch. "You better get going to that meeting or all the refreshments will be gone."

"I'm not going," Truman said. "If this outfit has already bought the hotel, there's nothing we can do."

"You've got to go," Pearl said, her voice rising. "We've got to do something. Nobody here can afford to pay the prices they'll be asking. Where'll we all go?"

Truman pulled the classified section out of the Sunday paper. "I was going to take this and start calling the apartment for rent ads. Face it, Pearl, it's too late. They had painters in here yesterday. That means the sale is final."

She snatched the classifieds away from Truman, trembling with anger and frustration. "There's got to be something we can do."

Her anger took Truman by surprise. "You've got a home in Pittsburgh, Pearl. It's not as though you lived here year-round, like me and Ollie."

"No," she said. "I've talked to my lawyer up home. I'm going to have to sell the house to pay for Mel's nursing-home fees and medical care."

"Sell it? Won't the insurance take care of everything? What about Medicare?"

"Medicare doesn't cover Alzheimer's," she said bitterly. "My lawyer thinks the house should bring enough money to cover the nursing-home bills, but just barely. I can't afford to live anyplace else, TK."

She stood there with her arms folded across her chest, glaring, waiting for him to say something.

"I'll go," he said reluctantly. "But don't get your hopes up."

CHAPTER

ELEVEN

THE MEETING WAS ALREADY IN PROGRESS. Arch Barchie stood at the front of the room, frowning down at a clipboard. At least twenty people were seated side by side in folding chairs. Cookie Jeffcote, the hotel's leasing agent, was seated in the corner, like a child being punished.

Truman slid into an empty chair in the back row.

An elbow dug into his side. "You're late."

It was Jackleen. She was still in her waitress uniform.

"What are you doing here?" Truman whispered.

"You ain't heard? Those church folks say they're gonna close up the dining room. Make it into an infirmary or something. It ain't much of a job, I know, but it's all I got, and if I can, I need to hang on to it."

Truman nodded. Up until now he'd thought of the Fountain of Youth buyout as an inconvenience. He'd have to move, rent an apartment somewhere else. The others in the room, like Ollie and Jackie and now Pearl, didn't have the options he had. Not that he had many.

"What's going on?" he whispered.

"I guess somebody appointed Mr. Barchie head man in charge. 'Cause he used to be an accountant probably. He was just saying how he called the Mandelbaums, even sent 'em a registered letter, asking 'em to come to the meeting."

"Obviously they declined," Truman said dryly.

"Cowards," Jackie said. "Instead, they sent her," she said, glaring at Cookie. "Mr. Barchie says she's from the new management."

"Now then," Barchie said, looking down at his notes. "The hotel has had an interesting history, which I'd like to share with you all before we begin. It was designed by the local architect Lowell Randolph in 1912, and constructed over the years 1912 to 1914, one of several hotels built downtown by the same firm. Early on the hotel was called the McLatchey, after the pioneer Florida family that used to own—"

"How much?" Sonya Hoffmayer's frizzy red head bobbed up from the crowd. She stalked up to Cookie Jeffcote, who looked alarmed at her advance.

"How much are we gonna have to pay?" Mrs. Hoffmayer repeated, pursing her Kewpie-doll-painted red lips.

"Thought she was part of the family," Jackie said, smirking. "Don't look like they're cutting her a discount, does it?"

"We'll get to that, Sonya," Barchie said, tugging nervously at his bow tie. "Now, as I was saying, the hotel was one of the earliest buildings in Florida to have steam heat and private tiled baths—"

"Ask that woman how much," Mrs. Hoffmayer insisted. "She's working for that preacher fella now. She ought to know."

"Yeah, Arch," came a high-pitched voice from the front. "Skip that other crap. We wanna know how much."

It was Ollie. He stood on his chair in order to be seen.

Arch Barchie shrugged. He could ignore Sonya Hoffmayer, but Ollie Zorn was a different matter. He turned to Cookie. "Miss Jeffcote?"

Cookie licked her lips and tugged at her short white skirt. She stood up and approached the microphone.

"Well," she said, looking around for an ally but seeing none. "Uh, Reverend Newby and the church elders have come up with a preliminary pricing schedule. Nothing is really set yet, so it's too early—"

"How much?"

Rosemary Pickett, the plumper of the Pickett girls, was standing now. "My sister and I have a small trust fund. We need to know how much our unit will cost so we can start planning."

Verbena Pickett stood up beside her twin. She was dressed in a blue flowered shift that was identical to her sister's pink one. "That's right," she said shrilly. "Papa was very conservative in his investments."

Cookie sensed that she was outnumbered. She ran her finger down the price chart Reverend Newby had drawn up and smiled brightly.

"It's actually a very affordable plan. For instance, units start at sixteen thousand five hundred dollars and cap at eighty thousand for a deluxe St. Peter's penthouse unit."

The room was quiet for a moment while the residents took it all in.

"What penthouse units?"

Truman found himself standing, addressing Cookie Jeffcote. "The only thing on the top of this building are six one-bedroom apartments. There aren't any three-bedroom penthouses here."

Cookie frowned, trying to remember the name of the wiry man with the strawberry-blond eyebrows. Kicklighter, she thought his name was. Recently widowed. Fourth-floor front. Troublemaker.

"Now that's the exciting part of the plan," she said. "The church will build two luxury units on that top floor. The St. Peter's units will have top-of-the-line amenities with European kitchens, garden baths, private entrance halls, and key-operated elevators—"

"Eighty thousand dollars!" Sonya Hoffmayer's face was an alarming shade of purple. "I live on the top floor. What happens to me?"

Cookie frowned. The Mandelbaums had cosseted the

old lady for years. Too bad for her that she came from the poor side of the family tree.

"All former Fountain of Youth residents will have an opportunity to purchase units," she said. "I'm sure one of the smaller units on the lower floors, say, one of our St. Luke efficiency units, which will be sixteen thousand five hundred dollars, would suit you perfectly, Mrs. Hoffmayer."

Ollie was jumping up and down on his metal folding chair. "Sixteen thousand five hundred for an eight-by-ten room with a toilet, a sink, and a view of the alley? You're nuts, lady. And you can tell that goddamn preacher he's nuts too. We ain't paying. And we ain't moving out, either. Are we?"

He looked around the room for agreement. The residents sat in their chairs, stunned, their hands folded in their laps.

"Are we?" Ollie repeated. "Come on, people, if we stick together, we can win this thing. We can have a sit-down strike. Refuse to be moved. Call the media. There's a guy buys the *New York Times* at my newsstand, he's something big over there at Channel 7 in Tampa. I say something to him, we'll be all over the news. What do you say?"

Myra Strickland, a tall, thin woman with hair wound into two white braids coiled on top of her head, stood up.

"A strike?" She pursed her pale lips in distaste. "No. Definitely not.

"As some of you may know," she continued, "I practiced law in Wisconsin for many years before my retirement. I've checked into Florida's condominium statutes, at Arch's request, and what I find, unfortunately, is that it appears that what the new owners of the hotel are doing is perfectly and unfortunately legal."

"Legal?" Ollie cried. His sweaty hair stuck to his scalp. His face was flushed. "It's legal to put retirees, folks who have worked hard all their lives, out in the street so some uppity-ass church can sell our homes to the highest bidder? How's that legal?"

A hum of voices rose around Ollie. People were nodding quietly. Cookie got up and made a beeline for the door. She'd had enough.

"Hey," Ollie called after her. "We're not through with you yet, missy. You tell that preacher we're not leaving. Hell, no, we won't go"

"You tell 'em, Ollie," somebody said. "Give 'em hell," another one prompted.

Arch Barchie had to pound his podium repeatedly with his wooden meat-mallet gavel to regain order in the room.

"Please!" he thundered. "Let's observe some parliamentary procedure, can't we?"

"What are we going to do?" Rosemary Pickett asked. "Verbena and I can barely afford our rent now. We don't have enough money for a down payment. And where else can we go? We've got to be downtown, close to the buses. Verbena sold our car three years ago."

"That's why we're here today," Barchie said, struggling to regain control of his meeting. "The first thing we need to do is appoint someone to get the church to give us full disclosure of pricing and financing for the conversion. Miss Rosemary, would you do that for us?"

Rosemary and Verbena Pickett nodded in tandem.

"Next," Barchie said, looking down at his clipboard, "we'll need a legal committee to explore our options pursuant to taking legal action to stop the conversion."

"Yeah!" Sonya Hoffmayer called out. "Let's sue the bastards!"

Barchie pretended not to hear her. "Myra Strickland has already agreed to head that committee. Sonya, perhaps you could assist her?"

"Hey!"

Barchie glared out over the rim of his bifocals at Ollie, but Ollie seemed not to notice.

"Has anybody here ever heard of this Cosmic Unity outfit?"

"Never heard of them before," Barchie admitted. "Anybody else?"

No one had.

"Somebody needs to find out who these people are," Myra Strickland agreed. "Are they even Christians?"

"That's what I'm getting at," Ollie said. "We need to dig up the lowdown on these scumbags."

Truman slid down in his chair and tried to cover his face with his hands. He sensed what was coming.

Ollie pointed to the back row. "There's Truman Kicklighter. He used to be a professional snooper. Big-shot newspaper reporter. He can find out who these characters are."

"Now look," Truman protested, "I'm retired. I don't have any press credentials. And I never covered religion. What we need—"

"Good idea," Arch Barchie said firmly, as though it were his own. "Truman Kicklighter will head up our fact-finding committee."

Jackie's hand shot up in the air. "I'll help out," she called.

"Me too," Ollie hollered.

"So moved," Barchie said. "Do we have a motion to adjourn?"

Ollie ran up to Truman. "When do we start work?"

Truman had been doing mental math. The numbers he came up with were impossible. By his calculations a "unit" like the room he'd rented for the past six months was going to sell for around $30,000. It might as well have been $300,000.

His gaze wandered to the door to the lobby, which Cookie Jeffcote had left open. He saw her at her desk in the lobby, talking furiously into the telephone.

He straightened his shoulders and took a deep breath. "Right away, Ollie," he said. "We start right away."

CHAPTER

TWELVE

THE CAMERA PANNED SLOWLY ACROSS THE tiny room, showing the goldfish bowl with its solitary tenant, the adult trike that took up one corner of the room, the stark rust-stained porcelain toilet and sink, the crumbling plaster, and the peeling linoleum. "Christ," the cameraman muttered to himself under his breath. "Criminals at Raiford got it better than this. This is killer stuff."

Carmen Quinones overheard his remark and smiled brightly, showing a set of gleaming, slightly oversized teeth. Joe was right. This was definitely lead-story material.

Now the camera panned to where the tiny man sat at the edge of a lilliputian cot. His hair gleamed with wet comb-marks and he was dressed in a faded cotton shirt, buttoned all the way to the too-large collar.

"Mr. Zorn," Carmen said, oozing concern, "we understand that this room we're standing in, which is no larger than the size of the average mop closet, would sell for sixteen thousand five hundred dollars. Can you afford that kind of money?"

Ollie shook his head sadly. "No way," he said. "I live on a fixed income. I don't have that kind of money."

Carmen turned to the camera so that it could capture

the empathy etched on her smooth olive face. "Then where will you go if the Church of Cosmic Unity succeeds in its plan to convert the Fountain of Youth Hotel to luxury condominiums?"

Ollie knew his cue. "I don't know," he said, near tears. "The streets, I guess. I got nowhere else to go."

Now the anchorwoman back in the studio was clucking her tongue sympathetically.

"A sad plight all too often shared by the hundreds of thousands of retirees living on the Suncoast on fixed incomes," Kristin Carpenter commented. "Carmen, does the Reverend Jewell Newby have any comment to make about this plan, which could put thirty or forty senior citizens out of their homes?"

A remote camera now showed tape from earlier in the day. Carmen Quinones standing outside an office door, gesturing toward the brass nameplate.

"We went to the new St. Petersburg headquarters of the Church of Cosmic Unity today and tried to speak to the Reverend Newby, Kristin, but as you can see, church officials refused to admit us to their offices."

A muffled voice called from the other side of the door, "Go away or we'll call the police."

"No comment, Kristin," she said crisply. "Back to you."

Jewell Newby slammed his fist down on the remote control, which had been sitting on his desktop. The plastic shattered into dozens of pieces, and the channel jumped from the noonday news on Channel 7 to a station showing a large purple dinosaur cavorting with half a dozen children.

"This is an abomination," he thundered. "I thought you told me you had the situation with these people under control. This is your idea of control?"

Cookie Jeffcote tugged at her skirt and blanched. "After the meeting, I tried to talk to Zorn. I offered him a special deal. Special financing. He wouldn't go for it. He's a nut,

Jewell. Just wants attention. I had no idea he'd pull a stunt like this."

A secretary stuck her head in the door. "I'm sorry, Reverend, but it's one of the electricians on the phone. There's a problem at the hotel."

Newby put his hand on the phone and turned back to Cookie. "Take care of this," he said. "I want those people out of my building."

Cookie hurried out of the office.

"Satan is at work at that hotel," he called after her. "You must smite him and all his works."

"Smite your ass," Cookie muttered.

CHAPTER
THIRTEEN

BUTCH GOOLSBY LEANED OVER THE ENGINE of the ailing Mercury. The dentist from Ohio had been livid when he'd brought it back this morning. "This is the worst piece of shit I've ever driven," the guy hollered at Curtis, who did little except nod his head. "It backfires, it stalls. The damn thing leaked oil all over the driveway at the condo we rented; now the manager there wants to keep my security deposit."

Butch didn't like to downgrade the boy in front of customers. Now, though, with Curtis sitting in the driver's seat of the Merc revving the engine like he was told while his father fiddled under the hood, Butch felt some constructive criticism was due.

"Shoulda told that shitbag to take a hike, boy," he hollered over the *pop-pop-pop* backfiring. "Remember this: The customer is never right."

Tammi had propped herself on the service desk, checking on the previous day's rental agreements. "Hey, Butch," she called. "That's deep. Really deep. They teach you that at that Harvard Business School you went to?"

It was on Butch's mind to tell Tammi a thing or two, but instead he concentrated on automotive mechanics, applying the business end of a metric wrench with a tremendous whack to the carburetor head.

The car was humming nicely now, but Tammi had her claws in, and she was enjoying herself. "So I guess we won't be quitting our jobs and moving to the Keys with our winnings from last night, huh? How you two fuck-ups let that Wade guy get away is beyond me. You can just bet that little geek is laughing his ass off at you guys."

Curtis's face was beet red. But it was shame, not anger, that had him in its grip. "I'm sorry, Tammi," he said, switching the engine off and sliding out of the driver's seat. He took a rag and flicked it over the seat. Butch had made him acutely aware of the dangers of oil on the seat of a rental car.

"You been by that Wade's place today?" she asked.

"We went over last night," Butch said defensively. "Right after the cops cut Curtis loose. The kid never showed up."

"What about his old man's house?" Tammi wanted to know. "You said the old man lived over on Snell Isle. Did you morons check there?"

"Yeah," Curtis said sadly. "But there's a big old wrought-iron gate out front. You can't hardly see nothing. And there's private security patrols over on Snell Isle. The guard chased us off."

"Prick," Butch said under his breath.

Tammi slid down off the desk and went over to the soft drink machine. She pressed the Fresca button, banged with her fist twice on the machine's midsection, then retrieved her drink. She opened the can and took a long drink, licking her lips delicately.

"Wade's got that computer program. He owes us money. And we've got what? Nothing."

Butch felt himself doing a slow burn. He took the empty oil can and tossed it in the trash. "Okay, so he gave us the slip last night. We'll get him. Him and the program. We're not done with old Wade-boy yet."

Tammi sipped her drink, unconvinced. Butch Goolsby was full of big plans. Like the time he tried to get her to pull out in front of a Coca-Cola truck and get hit, so she could make a big insurance claim.

"You know what my grandma used to say? She said 'Tammi, if you want it done right, you gotta do it yourself.'"

Cookie Jeffcote scooted over until she was right beside Michael in the front seat of the Continental. "So, where were you last night?" she asked, kissing his ear, letting her hands roam.

"I was at the track," Michael said. "I was gonna call. Honest to God. But Nunz and I had a business meeting. We were supposed to see a guy about a thing, but it got all screwed up."

"What guy?" Cookie said, loosening the knot of his tie, undoing the top button of his shirt.

"Just a guy," Michael said. "He was supposed to sell us something. But when he got there, he didn't have the goods. Then the guy takes off and don't come back. Nunz's salad had croutons, so he got mad, and I had to baby-sit and make nice. Everything was fucked up. I didn't lay down a single bet."

"Talk about fucked up," Cookie said. "You shoulda been in that meeting at the hotel today. Jeezus. I thought those old folks were gonna lynch me when they heard how much Newby's planning to charge for those condo units. Then this fuckin' midget, his name's Ollie? First he tries to get these people to go on, like, strike. Then he goes screaming to Channel 7 that we're puttin' all these old people out on the streets. I'm tellin' you, there's gonna be trouble. Jeezus, I thought Jewell Newby was gonna have a stroke he was so mad. He even threatened to fire me. Like it's my fault about all the bad publicity about this thing."

"Don't worry, baby," Michael said, running his hand up the inside of her thigh. "Mikey's gonna take good care of you today. You're gonna forget all about that hotel and those old folks and Jewell Newby."

"I wish," Cookie said petulantly.

* * *

Michael got them the honeymoon suite at the newest hotel on the beach, the Dorado Palm. After the bubble bath in the heart-shaped tub and a line of coke, Cookie decided to give him a full-body massage.

She had him stretched out nude on towels on the bed, and she was naked, astride him, working her hands across his well-oiled deltoids.

"Hey," he said, turning his head to look at her, "you're really good at this."

"I know, baby," she murmured in his ear. She rubbed a little more. "Who was the guy, Michael?" she asked, digging her fingertips into his knotted trapezoids.

"Huh?" He was blissed-out, relaxed, his defenses down.

"The guy you were supposed to meet at the track last night?"

"Computer nerd," Michael said, letting a long groan escape. "Do that neck thing again, doll. This guy, he's got a computer program that can pick the winners at the track."

"No shit?"

"Yeah, no shit," he assured her. "He's got a girlfriend, knows a lot of inside information, he takes all the information about all the dogs running in a race, feeds it into this computer on some charts he's set up, and the computer spits out the winners. One, two, three. Win, place, and show."

"Cool," Cookie said. "But why's he gonna sell it to you?"

"The little geek doesn't have enough capital to use the program for maximum effectiveness," Michael said. "A two-buck bet, even if it's right eighty percent of the time, don't make you rich."

"Don't I know," Cookie said.

"Anyway, I had Nunz all talked into going partners with me on the deal. We were supposed to meet the geek in the clubhouse last night. Only it's getting late, and the races are about to start. The guy comes in. There's problems.

He don't have the goods. From there on in, you don't wanna know."

"Bad, huh?" Cookie asked, kissing the back of his neck, letting her breasts brush his skin.

"You feel the tension in my back, right?" he asked, his voice muffled. "Nunz was very, very annoyed."

"I'm sorry," Cookie said. She continued kneading and rubbing, losing herself in thought.

"Hey, I read in the paper where a girl got killed at the track last night. Her name was Rosie. Rosie something. She was a tout. A girl tout. You ever heard of one of those?"

The massage had lulled him nearly to sleep. "Uh-huh," he said drowsily.

Cookie sensed he was vulnerable. She slipped off his back and lay beside him, pressing her body into his. "Michael," she whispered. "Can I ask you for a favor?"

"What, sugar? Tell Mikey."

"It's that midget. The one I told you about."

"What about him?"

"He's a troublemaker. He's stirring everybody up down there. The phone didn't stop ringing after that goddamn thing was on the news. Every newspaper, radio, and television station in Florida called. Larry King's producer. Even Oprah! That little bastard."

She started sniffling now, big tears welling up in her eyes. "You could do something about it, Michael. Shut the guy up."

"Me?" Michael rolled his head around to look at her. "You want me to rough up a midget? Get the hell out of town, Cookie. I'm a businessman. I told you that already."

"Just talk to him," she pleaded. "Tell him he better keep his mouth shut. That's all. He's gonna get me fired, Mikey."

Michael sat up to face her. She was kneeling on the bed, naked. Tears were running down her face, down her chest, dripping from the ends of her nipples. Very erotic, he thought.

"Help you how?" he heard himself saying.

"You know," she said, playing coy now. "Take care of him. For me." She ran a finger down his chest, down his belly. He shivered involuntarily. "And Cookie will take care of Mikey."

He rolled off the bed and onto his feet in one swift motion. Now he started dressing. Better get dressed and let his brain start making decisions again. He pulled on his pants and found his shirt on the floor.

"You're good, Cookie," he said, zipping his fly. "But not good enough for me to put a hit on some goddamn Munchkin. I told you before, I'm in sales. Not service. Try somebody else, dollface," he suggested. "Maybe somebody who has to get paid to get laid."

"I'll find somebody all right," she shrieked at his departing backside. "Somebody good. Somebody with balls, unlike you, you dago son of a bitch."

When the door slammed, Cookie sat and thought. Jewell Newby was on to a good thing with this condo scam. She'd done some homework. He thought she was too stupid to read those sales contracts. She knew how he operated. And when the time was right, she'd make her move. Get a piece of his action. With what she knew, he'd have to cut her in. For now, though, she'd have to play dumb. But only until she got things set up just right.

She showered and dressed. She liked nice hotels because they had thick towels and bathrobes and hair dryers in the bathroom. This one even unplugged. She wrapped the cord around it and tucked it in her shoulder bag along with the robe. She took pains with dressing, making sure the coral silk minidress was adjusted just so, that her heavy gold rope necklace and matching earrings hadn't been displaced. Then she applied eyeliner, lip liner, blusher, and cologne. She stood in front of the full-length mirror and sighed.

Then she sat on the bed and reached for the telephone on the nightstand.

"Sun Bay Rentals." The voice was a woman's.

Unfamiliar. Cookie frowned, but she asked for Butch. No, she told the woman, she did not care to say who was calling, just tell Butch it was personal.

The woman put the phone down. Five minutes later Butch was on the line. His voice was wary. "Hello?"

"Hey, Butchie," she said breathily. "Guess who?"

CHAPTER

FOURTEEN

"**G**IBBY?"

It was dark in the El Cap. Dark and cool, with the overhead fans twirling slowly overhead. Truman had to squint hard to see the figure standing beside him at the bar.

Frank Gibhart slapped his rounded belly proudly. "I've put on some weight since I quit drinking. Bet you didn't know me, huh?"

"Oh," Truman said. He frowned. "Gibby, I'm sorry. I clean forgot about that. We can go somewhere else if you like. McDonald's or something."

"Nah," Frank said, pulling out the bar stool next to Truman's. "This is fine. I always liked this place. Sober, it looks even better. I'll drink iced tea. Do they still have navy bean soup on Mondays?"

An Italian family had owned the El Cap Bar on Central for as long as Truman could remember. Years ago it had belonged to a relative who'd been a major league umpire. Various cousins had run the place ever since, but they'd kept all the signed baseballs and bats, the faded black-and-white team photos, pennants, and yellowing newspaper clippings.

Aside from the cold beer and authoritative sports talk, the El Cap was famous for six-inch-thick sandwiches and homemade soup.

Truman took a sip from the pilsner of beer sitting in front of him. "I already ordered it. Ham sandwiches and navy bean soup. Right?"

"Don't tell me you're buying?"

"First round only," Truman retorted. "I'm an old pensioner, you know. Besides, the way I remember it, you always were good at rigging expense-account lunches."

"I learned everything I know from the master," Gibhart said.

Frank Gibhart had been pleased to hear from his old boss. Truman Kicklighter was the last of a breed. A newsman down to the bone. If Truman Kicklighter needed a favor, he had plenty in the bank.

Frank had spent Monday morning working the phones, relishing the opportunity to do some old-time dirt-digging.

Rose, who was married to one of the cousins, brought Frank a mug of iced tea and another beer for Truman.

Frank slid a manila folder toward Truman.

"I saw that piece on the news this afternoon. Hell of a thing. How come you didn't call me sooner?"

Truman shrugged. "Didn't think of it as a story. You know how it is. You're close to something, it doesn't strike you as newsworthy."

They both knew Truman hadn't called his old colleague in the first place because he didn't want Frank, or anybody else, to feel sorry for him. Now, though, Ollie had forced his hand. Maybe it wasn't such a bad thing.

Truman opened the file. "Left my cheaters at home," he said. "Give me the highlights, will you?"

"As far as I can tell," Frank began, "this Church of Cosmic Unity's been in St. Pete for about nine months. They're having services in some old movie theater downtown."

"Must be the Rialto. It's the only one left," Truman said. "What about the head honcho? Name's Newby or something."

"The Reverend Jewell G. Newby," Frank said, relishing

the sound of the names rolling off his tongue. "Age fifty-two. Up until 1987 Newby drove a truck for a wholesale distributor of candy, potato chips, and snack cakes in Dayton, Ohio. That year our man got himself a gilt-edged diploma from a mail-order divinity school out in Laguna Vista. He moved to Plano, Texas, and started an outfit called the Church of the Higher Being."

"That's a religion?" Truman asked. "What do they believe in?"

He had Frank there. "Besides capitalism? Beats me. The church was rolling along pretty good for a while there. But in 1988 he and his wife split up, and the Rev pulls up stakes and moves to San Antonio."

Frank looked down at his notes and frowned. "Things get a little bit cloudy then. For two years, I couldn't find an address, a church, nothing. Then, in 1991, he pops up again. Now he's running an outfit called the Church of Cosmic Unity. He's bought an old Baptist church in downtown San Antonio, and he's packing 'em in."

"What's the scam?" Truman said.

Rose set their plates and bowls in front of them and went to the other end of the counter to watch television. Hot, ham-scented steam rose up and fogged Truman's glasses. He dipped a spoon in, tasted, and sighed. The soup was the same, maybe better than he remembered.

"The scam?" Truman repeated.

"Always the cynic," Frank said, adding pepper to the soup.

"Tell me."

"Well, the church bought up a good bit of real estate in San Antonio. A couple of parking lots downtown, maybe half a dozen foreclosed houses. And church members were being encouraged both to give money and to buy property and deed it over to the church outright."

"Anything wrong with that?" Truman watched the younger man's face. He'd been right to call Frank. Never missed a trick, this guy, and since his drinking days were over, he'd only gotten better.

"You tell me," Frank said. "A cop buddy ran a check. The Reverend Jewell Newby has no record. Not even an unpaid parking ticket. Pays his taxes, seems to report every dime."

"Smart," Truman said. "What else have you got?"

"The Rev likes a warm climate, seems like. After San Antonio he opened a church in Scottsdale, Arizona. Same church name, same game plan. First he rents space, builds up a congregation, and starts acquiring real estate."

"Still nothing illegal or immoral. Right?"

"Not as far as I can tell. The church has a two-hour program on a cable station out there, called *Blessing Time*. I talked to a guy at the station, he promised to send you a videotape."

Frank stopped talking to eat his soup before it got cold. It was coolish outside, high seventies. The bar was nearly empty today. Camilla, the owner's wife or daughter, he didn't know which, emerged from the kitchen and was drying and stacking glasses at the back bar.

After they finished, they traded war stories for a while.

"Got remarried two years ago," Frank said. "She's a great gal."

"Good for you," Truman said.

Frank put his hand on Truman's arm. "I felt real bad when I heard the news about Nellie, TK."

"Thanks," Truman said simply.

Gibby gave Truman a searching look. "So. We've been scooped on this church thing once already. Think there's still anything in it for us?"

"I don't know," Truman said. He motioned for Camilla, asked her to wrap his sandwich half in foil. "Did you check with the law in Arizona to see if everything there is on the up-and-up?"

"No record there either," Frank said regretfully. "There are a couple of callbacks I'm still waiting on, but so far the guy's as clean as they come."

"Slick's more like it," Truman muttered.

"I'm waiting," Frank reminded him.

"Oh." Truman shrugged. "Like I told you. It's early yet. We only got the notice last week. All I know is, the prices they're asking, none of the current tenants can afford to buy. And everybody's got their bowels all in an uproar over it. I'm the fact-finding committee."

"Condo conversion, huh? How much time did they give you?"

Truman tucked the sandwich into his jacket pocket. Camilla brought the check and tucked it under Frank's glass. "I got this one," Gibby said, laying money on the counter.

"Ninety days," Truman said.

"That's all?"

"Doesn't much matter," Truman said. "Unless we can find a way to stop this Newby fella, we'll all be looking for a new address."

Frank looked at his watch and sighed. "I better hit the road before traffic gets backed up on the bridge." He clasped Truman's hand, squeezed it tightly. "Let me make some more calls," he said. "Something sounds hinky."

"That's what I'm thinking," Truman agreed.

CHAPTER

FIFTEEN

Truman eyed the guy leaning against the receptionist's desk, chatting with Yvonne Sweatt. Good-looking, tan. He was vaguely familiar.

Probably somebody from this Cosmic Church outfit, Truman decided, checking out the merchandise.

"Mr. Kicklighter?"

"Yeah?" Truman wasn't usually this rude, but today politeness wasn't in him.

The younger man smiled and held out his hand to shake. "Bobby Roberts. St. Pete Police Department."

"You were at the track. When we found the body."

"That's right," Roberts said. "You know, I went to high school with a Cheryl Kicklighter. Would you be any relation?"

"Her father," Truman said, waiting.

He smiled shyly. "I shouldn't tell you this. I used to have kind of a crush on your daughter. What's she up to these days? She live around here?"

"Yes," Truman said warily. "She teaches kindergarten and she goes to school nights. She's working on her master's degree."

"A teacher, huh? So is she married or anything like that?"

"Cheryl's divorced," he told Roberts. He gave him a searching look. "What was it you wanted to see me about? Or did you want to see me?"

Roberts slapped his forehead. "Hey. What am I doing, going on about old times? Mr. Kicklighter, I'm working on the Rosie Figueroa homicide. There's some questions I'd like to ask you."

The reporter in him came back. "Could I see your badge or something?" Truman asked. "No offense, but you never know."

"Sure," Roberts said. "Can we sit down over there to talk?"

He was pointing at the wicker chairs and rockers in the front window of the lobby. He reached into his inner coat pocket and brought out a badge pinned to a leather case.

Truman peered at it. It was a uniformed officer's shield. "You're not a detective?"

"No, sir. My captain just wanted me to do some follow-up stuff."

They were sitting in the window now, the afternoon sun streaming in on them, showing strong lines of dust motes.

"Like what?" Truman asked. "I thought the D.A. agreed to drop the charges against Mel. Doesn't that mean the investigation is closed?"

"Not really," Bobby said. "There are so many loose ends. My supervisor hates loose ends. 'They'll jump up and bite you on the ass every time,' that's what he always says."

"True enough," Truman agreed. He'd always been a detail man himself. Check everything twice, that was his motto. Saves heartache later on.

"I was at the track that night," Bobby said.

"I remember now."

"Moonlighting," Bobby said. "My ex-wife ran up the credit cards to the max before she took off. That's why I work a second job."

"You meet all kinds of people, working a place like the track."

"I'll say," Bobby agreed. "You name it, I've seen it."

"You knew Rosie?"

"Sure," Bobby said lightly. "Everybody out there knew Rosie. Nice girl. I'll tell you, it was a hell of a shock when I saw who it was."

Truman nodded and said nothing. It was a technique he'd learned as a reporter. Sometimes you found out more by the questions you didn't ask. He had a lot of questions about the murder of Rosie Figueroa.

"Mr. Kicklighter," Bobby said, leaning forward. "Has your friend, Mr. Wisnewski, said anything at all about that night? What he and that girl were doing in that service area? It's restricted, you know, only authorized track personnel were supposed to be down there."

Truman laughed. "Mel thinks he was at Three Rivers Stadium in Pittsburgh, watching Roberto Clemente get a hit off Bob Gibson that night."

Bobby's eyebrows shot up.

"Alzheimer's," Truman said. "I thought you people were aware of his condition."

"We were told that he was confused, possibly senile," Bobby said. "And he really has no idea what he saw or did that night? For real?"

"He's a sick, confused old man," Truman said sadly. "The night he spent in jail damn near killed him. His wife has to put him in a nursing home, you know. The judge made it a condition of dropping the charges."

"I'm sorry about that," Bobby said. "It must be tough for Mrs. Wisnewski. But let me ask you something, Mr. Kicklighter . . . "

"What's that?"

"Okay. Did I understand correctly that you told one of the officers that Mr. Wisnewski went looking for Rosie to buy a tout sheet?"

"That's right. I told it to all your people," Truman said. "Mel went off to buy the damned thing before I could stop him."

"Did Mr. Wisnewski say why he was so anxious to do that?"

"I told you," Truman said, letting the annoyance creep into his voice, "she told Mel last year that she was working on a new system. Something surefire that would mean guaranteed winning picks. Big money. It was all a lot of hooey, but you couldn't tell Mel that. He liked Rosie. He was convinced she was some kind of genius."

Bobby's voice was almost a whisper now. "Did he say anything about a computer program?"

"A computer program? Come on. Where would somebody like this girl get a computer program?"

"Rosie's boyfriend was a computer programmer," Bobby said. "We have information that the two of them had developed some kind of computer program that was eighty percent accurate in picking winning dogs."

"You're serious?"

"Yes, sir," Bobby said. "If your friend Mr. Wisnewski knew about that program, that could have been his motive for murdering her. To get this computer program. It could be worth a lot of money to some people."

"Mel bet two-dollar quinellas," Truman pointed out. "Does that sound like he was a gambling kingpin or something? Look. I told you, Mel is seventy-eight years old. He knows as much about computers as Job's hen turkey. If there really is some kind of computer thing involved, then that's your motive. Find somebody who wanted that thing bad enough to kill for it. Somebody who'd know what to do with it."

"He could take it to somebody who would know exactly what to do with it," Bobby pointed out. "There are computer shops all over town."

"Have you found this computer program?" Truman demanded. "Did they find it when your people took Mel into custody?"

"No. But your friend could have taken it. He could have hidden it somewhere. Passed it off to a partner, maybe. That fenced area leads out to the parking lot. He could have tossed it to somebody on the other side of the fence."

"And then sat down beside the dead girl to wait for the

police?" Truman said, scoffing. "You really believe that cockamamie theory?"

"What about the knife?" Bobby demanded. "And the blood? His fingerprints were all over that knife. Her blood was on his hands and his clothes."

"I never saw Mel with a knife," Truman said. "Pearl says he had a little pocketknife he used to take fishing. But it's in his dresser drawer. She checked. It's right there. You can ask her."

Bobby stood up and straightened the crease in his slacks. "Maybe I will. Is she home right now?"

Butch Goolsby snuck a peek at himself in the motel room window before he knocked. "Lookin' good, Butch," he said. He was a little nervous, but he'd knocked back two or three healthy slugs of Early Times at home, just to take the edge off.

"Butch? Is that you, baby? Come on in. The door's open."

"Baby?"

She hadn't called him baby since she was eighteen years old. Baby?

The room was nice. King-sized bed, big sliding glass doors that opened onto a balcony. You could see the Gulf of Mexico from the doorway, see the waves rolling in, the blue sky and white sand.

"Get whatever you want out of the minibar," she called from behind the bathroom door. "I'll be right out."

Chivas Regal looked good. He fixed it with a splash of water. Then he went out on the balcony and watched the crazy-ass tourists frolicking in the waves. Swimming in April. Christ. It was 80 degrees out, but the thought of getting in that water before July gave Butch goose bumps.

Suddenly she was beside him, kissing his cheek, letting her breast brush up against his bare arm for maybe half a second.

"I'm so glad you came," she said, a sob catching in her throat. "I didn't know who else to call."

She'd been crying.

"What is it, Cookie?"

She turned and buried her head in his shoulders, wrapping her long, tanned arms around his neck, pressing herself tightly to him.

"I'm scared," she sobbed. "I could lose my job. If he fires me, I'll lose everything. My condo, my car. Everything. I'll end up on welfare. Oh my God, Butch, I don't know what to do."

He buried his nose in her hair. She smelled like a flower garden. Her hair was silky, slightly mussed. His hands stroked the bare shoulders, the arms, rested lightly on that tight little ass of hers. Was she wearing any panties? Then the hands moved slowly upward . . .

She slid his hands back around her waist. The horny little creep hadn't changed any. Here she was crying her heart out and he was trying to cop a feel. Better get down to business before he tried to jump her bones right out there on the balcony

"What is it, hon?" he asked, all loving concern. "Tell Big Butch."

She had to bite her lip to keep from laughing at that one. Yeah, she'd called him that, back in the bad old days, when she was trying to sweet-talk him into letting her have her way. He was Big Butch and Little Butch, well, Little Butch was pressing up against her silk dress in a fairly insistent manner. That was Butch's main problem in life. He was always letting Little Butch make his decisions for him.

Cookie wiped at the tears on her face, sniffing loudly.

"You didn't see it on the news?"

"What?" Butch asked, alarmed that she might be referring to the little problem he and Curtis had run into at the dog track.

"Those old people at the Fountain of Youth. They're making all kinds of trouble."

Butch wrinkled his brow. "The Fountain of Youth?"

"The place I work," Cookie said sharply. "Remember, I

told you I'm the office manager? I've been there a year, Butch."

"Oh yeah," Butch said. He remembered no such thing. "The Fountain of Youth. I remember. So what's the deal?"

She told him all of it.

"And the worst thing is, this horrible nasty little midget. Ollie Zorn, that's his name."

"A midget's gonna get you fired?" Butch asked in disbelief.

"He's deranged," Cookie said. "He stood up in this meeting and as much as told me he'd get me fired. And then he tried to get everybody to go on strike. You know, so they won't get out of the hotel during the conversion. And then today he was on the news. He made us look like we were throwing all these old people out on the street."

"Why's that gonna get you in trouble?" Butch asked.

"My boss hates publicity," Cookie said, "especially bad publicity. The little twerp's making the church look bad. That makes me look bad."

"Church?"

Cookie wanted to scream. "The Church of Cosmic Unity. That's who bought the hotel. Reverend Newby, Jewell Newby, he's my boss. He's gonna turn the hotel into luxury condos for church members. But first we have to get these old geezers out of there."

"Why?" Butch still didn't get what had Cookie so worked up.

"Because they're poor!" Cookie shrieked, finally losing it. "They're old and they're poor and they smell funny. We want them out."

"Oh," Butch said slowly. "What do you want from me?"

"I want," she said slowly, through clenched teeth, "you . . . to . . . get rid of that goddamned dwarf!"

Butch smiled. He pulled Cookie closer, let his hands rest right where her panty line should have been. "Is that all?"

CHAPTER

SIXTEEN

"**P**ALM VIEW," TRUMAN REPEATED. "THAT'S the name of this place. I don't see any palms. You see any palm trees?"

Jackleen looked around the reception area. They were sitting on an armless turquoise plastic sofa. There was a glass-and-chrome coffee table, and at a right angle to the sofa, an armless orange plastic chair. The floor was white terrazzo. Fluorescent light overhead gave the room a hard blue glare. The coffee table held back issues of *Modern Maturity* magazine and a display of brochures neatly fanned out over the glass: Managing Incontinence; Estate Planning Tips; Your Role in Elder Care.

"Miss Pearl said there's a garden in the back where the guests can sit in the sun," Jackleen said. "That's probably where they got the palm trees. You can't put palm trees in a parking lot. People run over them. The Publix near my house, all the palm trees are dead 'cause the tourists keep backin' up into 'em. Check that garden out."

"Probably plastic," Truman said, rubbing his arms. "Jeez, it's cold in here. Why do they keep it so cold? These old people hate the cold."

Jackleen rolled her eyes. He'd been bitching and complaining about this nursing home from the minute they set out this morning.

"It smells like pee in here," Truman said. "You smell it?"

She sniffed. "Smells like extra-strength Ben-Gay if you ask me," she said. "Quit fussin', Mr. K. This place ain't so bad. I've seen worse."

"Not me," Truman said. "I already told Cheryl, if I ever get so bad I can't live on my own, I want her to get me a suicide cocktail."

"Hush!" Jackleen said, shocked. "Don't be talking like that. Here comes Miss Pearl now, pushing Mr. Mel in the wheelchair."

When the Wisnewskis came into sight, Pearl pushing the chair slowly, a smile pasted on her wan, worried face, Truman gasped despite himself. "My God," he said.

"Hush," Jackleen hissed from between clenched teeth.

But it was true. They'd found a bed for Mel at the Palm View Personal Care Home on Tuesday. It was only Friday now. Mel wore a pair of blue print pajamas and a bright red bathrobe that seemed to swallow him whole. A blue knit cap sat on his head and he wore thick wool gloves. His cheekbones protruded from thin, fleshless cheeks and his eyes were sunken back into their bony sockets.

"Well, Mel, look here," Pearl said loudly as she approached her friends. "You've got visitors. Truman and Jackleen. Isn't that nice?"

Jackleen bent down and kissed Mel's cheek. "Hi there, Mr. Mel," she said cheerily. "How are you doing today?"

Mel looked anxiously around for Pearl. "Mother?"

"He's doing fine," Pearl said. "He had a big breakfast today, and a nice hot bath, and he's all excited about going on a car ride with you."

"Who's he?" Mel pointed at Truman. "Another spy?"

Pearl laughed nervously. "Heavens, Mel, don't you remember Truman? Your friend, Truman?"

"He's a Russki," Mel declared. "A Commie spy. This place is crawlin' with 'em."

"They let them watch these old movies in the afternoon," Pearl explained. "The men just love the World War Two movies. This morning when I got here Mel thought I was Lana Turner. He pinched my rear!"

"We've got the car right out front," Truman told Pearl. "You coming too?"

"Not this time. I'm having a meeting with Mel's doctor. You all go ahead."

Pearl took Truman's arm and walked toward the front door.

"It's bad, I know," she said quietly. "But he's not in any physical pain, they tell me. He complains about the cold a lot, so I got him the cap and the gloves. I told him you were coming today. He was so pleased."

"But he doesn't know us. He doesn't remember who I am."

"Give him a little time," Pearl urged. "Talk to him about sports like you always do. Remind him of the things you like to do together."

She gripped his arm tighter. "Even if he doesn't remember you, he's thrilled to have visitors, to get out and go for a ride. He can't understand why he has to stay here at night, away from me like this. I come every day, you know that, but he doesn't understand why he can't come home with me. I tell you, Truman, it's almost more than I can bear."

"I know," he said, patting her hand. "You've been a saint."

"No," she said fiercely, shaking her head for emphasis. "I'm no saint. You should hear the way I talk to God at night. Yell at him. Cuss at him. Why? That's what I want to know. Why is this happening to us?"

"Damned if I know," Truman said.

"It would be better if he was dead," Pearl said quietly.

Truman pretended not to hear that.

He trundled Mel into the back of Jackleen's battered old station wagon, then got in beside him.

"Hey," Jackleen said as they pulled out of the Palm View parking lot. "This is just like that movie *Driving Miss Daisy*, only it's all turned around. We got a woman driving two men. What do you think about that?"

"Where are we going?" Mel asked, leaning forward in his seat.

"Where do you want to go?" Jackleen said. "You just name it."

"The track," Mel said promptly. "Let's go to the dog track. I haven't been this year."

Jackleen gave Truman a troubled *what now?* look.

"You don't remember going the other night?" Truman asked.

Mel's brow wrinkled. He glanced down at himself. "That's right," he said mildly. "It's daytime. Why am I in my pajamas?"

"You've been kind of sick, and Miss Pearl wanted you to be comfortable," Jackleen said. "Besides, we're just going for a drive."

"Say, Mel," Truman said, "how would it be if we just drove by the dog track? They don't open till eleven, but we could just look."

"Okay," Mel agreed, "I like the track."

Truman and Jackleen kept up a running conversation as they drove, trying futilely to engage Mel in a discussion of the weather, current events, the passing landscape, even the traffic.

"Look at that clown with the Michigan tags," Truman exclaimed as they headed north on Fourth Street. "He's making a left turn from the far right-hand lane."

Jackleen gave the offending motorist a blast on her horn. "That's telling him, huh, Mr. Mel?"

"Do it again," Mel said, gripping the back of the seat with both hands, as though he were on an amusement-park ride.

Jackleen grinned and laid on the horn for three long blasts.

"Hey, Mel," Truman said, "did you watch that exhibition game on ESPN last night, the Braves and the Dodgers? You know the Dodgers let that bum Strawberry go."

"I watched a war movie," Mel said. "The place where I

live now, we don't see ball games. The Braves and Dodgers? Did the Braves pull it out?"

"By the hair on a gnat's ass," Truman said. "The game was tied two-two right up until the bottom of the ninth. That new kid they brought up from Richmond—Elliott?—hit a two-out double, brought Andrews in. Great game. I think they'll go all the way this year."

Mel's face lit up now, animated as he listened to Truman run down the Braves' lineup.

"I hate to miss the ball games," Mel said. "These old people who live in that place, they like to watch those day-time shows. What are they called?"

"Soap operas," Jackleen said. "You mean you don't watch *Days of Our Lives?*"

"I like ball games," Mel said stubbornly.

"Tell you what," Truman said. "Let's see if we can't get you a TV set in your room. Then you could watch all the ball games you like."

"People come into my room," Mel said. "They come in at night when I'm asleep. They open the cupboards and the drawers and wake me up. But I pretend to be asleep."

"Oh now, Mr. Mel," Jackleen said, "That's probably just the nurses checking to see if you're all right or if you need anything. They're not stealing your stuff."

"They take my clothes," Mel said. "That's why I have to wear pajamas."

Truman stared straight ahead. He couldn't look at Mel.

"Here's the track right here," Jackleen sang out, slowing to a stop at the intersection leading to the parking lot.

Mel pressed his face to the windows. "Let's go in."

Jackleen shot Truman another look. "The matinee doesn't start until twelve-thirty. It's only ten now. How about we drive out to the beach and look at the water. It's a real pretty day today. Would you like that?"

"I'd like a beer," Mel said. "And a cheese dog. That food where I live all tastes like shit."

"We'll get you a hot dog," Truman said, laughing in spite of himself. "The beer might have to wait for another day. Pearl might not like it if we take you back with a snootful.

"We had a good time here at the track the other night, Mel, didn't we?" he asked.

"The other night?"

"Last Friday. When you and I and Jackleen came over here on the bus. The Snowbird Special. You remember that, don't you?"

"We were on a bus," Mel said tonelessly. "It was hot."

"That's right! And when we went inside, you went to look for that girl. Racetrack Rosie. Remember?"

"She sells tout sheets," Mel said. "But I couldn't find her. I got lost. And then Pearl was mad at me. She called the police and they put me in jail for a long, long time."

"Uh-oh," Jackleen said quietly.

"You never found Rosie?" Truman asked. "Never talked to her at all?" He made an effort to sound calm, matter-of-fact.

"Did we win any races?" Mel asked. "I never could find Rosie."

"No," Truman said. "We lost."

"Hot dogs," Mel said suddenly. "I want a hot dog."

CHAPTER

SEVENTEEN

JACKIE SET THE STACK OF PAPER NAPKINS DOWN beside the plastic tray of silverware, then plunked herself down at a table she'd dragged into the doorway leading to the lobby. She liked to be near the sun, and the dining room was dark this time of day.

It was quiet in the afternoon. She was rolling the silverware, humming softly to herself, when Truman came over and sat down beside her.

He reached for a handful of silver and started rolling it into the napkins.

"You're doing it wrong," Jackie pointed out.

He kept on rolling. "You want the help or not?"

"You got a point there," she said. "How come you're not over at the Senior Center? Everybody else was going on that field trip over to Busch Gardens."

"I've been to Busch Gardens," Truman said pointedly.

She put the silverware she'd been rolling into the plastic bus tray. "You're still upset about Mr. Mel, aren't you?"

He shrugged. "It's selfish, isn't it? Looking at somebody else's misfortune and all you can think about is that's how you might end up yourself. And you know what the hell of it is?"

"What?"

"Up until a few months ago, right up until the time Nellie died, I never thought of myself as old. I mean, I knew I was in my sixties. But I felt good. I had plans. We had plans. Then I retired, and before we could do any of the things we planned, she was gone, and none of it seemed to matter anymore."

"What about your daughter?" Jackleen said, choosing her words carefully. "And your grandson. And your friends here?"

"Well, sure. Cheryl and Chip, of course they matter. And Mel and Pearl. But these other folks . . ." He waved his hand dismissively.

"They're old," she guessed.

He smiled sheepishly.

"You know what you need?" Jackleen said, wagging a finger at him. "You need you a job, Mr. K."

"I had a job," he said. "They made me retire when I was sixty-five. Now, I call over to the bureau, just to point out a little mistake, maybe give somebody a lead on a story, they act like I'm some kind of pariah. I called a buddy of mine about this church thing yesterday. You know what the secretary did? She put me on hold. *Me*. I used to be her boss."

"Used to be," Jackie pointed out. "I'm not talking about the kind of job you used to have. I'm talking about giving yourself something to do every day. Something worth getting up for. Worth getting mad about."

"Like what?"

She shrugged. "Can't say. All I know is, my grandmama said a body was born to work. She worked right up until the week before she passed, and she was eighty-two at the time."

"That what you want to do, work right up until the day you die?"

"Maybe," she said. "I've seen people in my neighborhood. Sitting out on porches, hanging out on the corner, doing nothing. Got a dead look in their eyes. I'm not saying I want this job my whole life. I got plans. I'm going back to school, law school maybe, after I save enough money."

"Okay," Truman said, adding his pile of silverware to the pile in the bus tray. "What would you suggest?"

She shrugged. "How 'bout keeping them bloodsucking church folks from kicking us all out of here?"

He shook his head. "Anybody ever tell you you're a nag?"

The front door opened then and a young man wearing navy-blue coveralls, carrying a clipboard and a toolbox, stepped into the lobby and looked warily around.

"There's another one of those workmen. They been crawling all over the place all week long," Jackie said, sniffing. "Looks like they could have spent some money on this place a long time ago instead of waiting until new owners got hold of it."

The young man's cap was pulled down low over his eyes. While Jackie and Truman watched, he strode over to the receptionist's desk, where Yvonne Sweatt was sitting.

"Excuse me, ma'am," he said politely. A long time ago, Wade Hardeson had been raised to be polite. "I'm from Gulf Coast Electrical. Somebody called and wants me to check your circuit breaker and take a look at some of the receptacles in some of the rooms here."

"I never called nobody," Yvonne said, frowning.

"Well, somebody did," Wade insisted. "I got the work orders. Fountain of Youth Hotel, right?" He rattled off the hotel phone number and address. Could have added the number on the hotel's business license too, which he'd memorized at a glance. He could do that with numbers.

"All right," Yvonne said. "New owners must have called you."

"Could you just show me where the circuit box is?" Wade asked. The tile floors and high ceilings made the place an echo chamber. The black chick and the old man were listening to every word he said. "I gotta check that and also the receptacles and switches in some people's rooms. Winkowski, something like that?"

"Wisnewski," Yvonne said. "But Pearl's over at the nursing home right now. Probably won't be back till supper."

"Nursing home?"

"She had to put her husband over at Palm View on Monday," Yvonne explained. "You better come back when she's home."

"Can't," Wade said quickly. "I got four more stops after this. Couldn't you just give me the key?"

"I don't know," Yvonne said slowly. "Pearl might not like somebody goin' in there with her not home."

"Okay," Wade said, giving an exaggerated shrug. "My work order says do it today cuz it might be a fire hazard. I'll tell my boss to tell the new owners you wouldn't let me in."

"Now don't go doin' that," Yvonne said, alarmed. She held up a key bearing a round paper tag. "Here it is right here."

Wade took the key and picked up his toolbox. "Thanks, ma'am."

"You see that?" Jackie asked indignantly. "They're planning on putting Miss Pearl out first thing."

"I heard," Truman said grimly. "Quit nagging."

"That too," she agreed.

CHAPTER
EIGHTEEN

TAMMI STARGELL TAILED WADE TO THE FOUNTAIN of Youth. She didn't hesitate to follow him inside, marching herself over to an empty chair in the window and sitting down.

She looked odd but not terribly out of place in a shapeless flowered muumuu, a pair of old house shoes, a loud striped babushka, and a pair of dark sunglasses. The receptionist stared for a moment, then went back to her magazine.

Tammi was satisfied that Wade hadn't noticed her. She'd been tailing him all day, keeping her own souped-up Firebird well behind the big Lincoln Wade was driving. His grandma's Lincoln, she guessed.

Now he was upstairs, going through somebody's room. She wasn't worried about him getting away with the disk, though. She patted the ugly straw purse she held in the crook of her arm. Her little persuader would help her convince Wade to give her the diskette.

She sat on an armchair near the door, waiting. Tammi was a patient person, if she had to be.

Finding Wade had taken patience, that's all. She'd called the work number he'd put on his rental agreement for the Cutlass, but his supervisor informed her in a bored voice that Wade "no longer works here."

"He's been fired," Tammi shrieked. "I knew it, I just knew it. Here I am, three months gone, and he up and gets fired and disappears. I knew it was too good to be true."

"You're pregnant?" The woman's interest seemed to pick up a little.

"I sure am," Tammi said. "And he was supposed to come over here today and bring me his paycheck. The doctor won't see me unless I pay ahead of time, and I'm nearly out of groceries."

"Have you tried his apartment?"

"He ain't been there," Tammi sobbed. "And I've called and I've left notes. Now what am I gonna do?"

There was a pause at the other end of the line. "You say he was supposed to bring you money?"

"Yesss," Tammi said, sniffing loudly.

"Just a minute."

"You didn't get this from me," the woman said. "He called Payroll two days ago and asked that his last check be sent to Bayfront Towers, care of Mrs. Wade Hardeson Sr. I think it must be his grandmother's condo, because he wasn't on speaking terms with his parents."

Tammi jotted the address down quickly. "Oh, God bless you," she cried. "I'll never forget your kindness. Are you a friend of his?"

"Not anymore," the woman said. "The guy's a lowlife."

Now, first thing this morning, Tammi had parked on the street outside the Bayfront Towers garage, confident that it wouldn't be long before her quarry surfaced.

Sure enough, he'd walked outside around nine o'clock, glanced nervously up and down the street, and then he'd strolled across the street and down a block to one of the seedy old bars over on First Avenue.

After he left the bar, she'd followed him back to the Bayfront. This time, though, he walked into the garage entrance instead of the lobby door. Five minutes later he drove out in what must have been his grandmother's car.

He'd been a busy boy since then. There was a stop at a uniform supply house on Central Avenue. When he came out, Wade was wearing a pair of blue zip-front overalls and a long-billed cap.

Then he'd headed for the tourist court. Tammi had assumed he'd end up there at one time or another. Butch and Curtis had been taking turns staking the place out at odd hours, but so far they'd missed him.

This morning she'd parked her Firebird in an alley that ran behind the last row of tourist cabins, next to the Dumpster. From here she could see all the cabins.

Wade got out of his car and darted to the door of his cabin. He fitted the key into the lock, and she could see him struggling to open the door, but it wouldn't budge.

Tammi smiled to herself. She'd lived this scenario herself not so long ago. It was after the first of the month.

Now he was digging in his pockets, bringing out a wad of dollar bills. He was counting silently. As he walked to the manager's cabin, his shoulders slumped. He'd have to pay the back rent before the manager would let him have his stuff.

When Wade came out of the manager's office a few minutes later, he looked anxiously around the parking lot again, but Tammi wasn't in the car anymore.

With Wade busy, Tammi had decided to take a peek in his cabin. She ran, crouched over, to the back of his cabin.

There were two windows along the back, both partially covered with faded curtains. The first window opened into what was surely a bathroom. All Tammi could see was small black and white tiles and what looked like a pile of dirty laundry.

Next she duck-walked along the back wall to the next window. The screen was gone. The curtain was parted at the center, and if she crouched at just the right height, she could see inside.

It was a bedroom, and it was a shambles. A mattress had been pulled from the box springs, and the bedclothes were wadded up and tossed aside. Drawers were pulled from a cheap pine dresser, and clothes and books seemed to cover every surface in the room.

She heard a key turning in a lock from the front of the unit and ducked back down.

There were footsteps inside, and then Wade was so close she could hear him breathing. She willed her own breathing to stop and inched her head up so it was at eye level with the window.

Wade stood in the middle of the room, not moving. He looked shell-shocked. Finally he opened a small door. A closet. But no clothes remained on hangers. Everything had been thrown on the floor. He reached up to the closet shelf, his hand searching for something, but his hand came back empty.

It wasn't there. He was looking for the diskette, she was sure, but it wasn't in this room, probably not in the cabin at all. Somebody, she told herself, had been in there. Had they beaten them both to the diskette?

"Goddamn." She peeked back in the window again. Wade was standing up now, his face twisted with anger. Then he was striding out of the room. She heard him closing the front door, so she took off herself, toward the Firebird.

CHAPTER

NINETEEN

BY THE TIME TRUMAN GOT DOWN TO THE laundry room Saturday, only one washing machine was available. He cursed but threw in a load of white clothes, some bleach, and detergent. Then he pushed the shopping cart into a corner, took his bleach and detergent, and went back upstairs. It was hot in that basement, too hot to hang around and wait for the spin cycle, that's for sure.

He was irritable, no doubt about it. And he knew exactly why.

His schedule was off. Since he'd moved into the Fountain of Youth, he'd invented a little schedule for himself. Meals at a certain time, walks at a certain time, laundry on Friday nights, dinner with Cheryl and Chip on Sundays, lunch at First Methodist Church on Wednesday.

"Getting to be an old fart. Set in your ways," he grumbled, getting off the elevator on his floor. "Talking to yourself too. Bad sign."

He'd gotten slack about exercising too. Slack, that's what he was.

Truman turned on the clock-radio on his bedside table. WSUN had a Big Band format on Saturday afternoons. This afternoon they were doing girl singers. When Rosemary Clooney started singing "Come On-a My

House," he laid himself down on the worn blue carpet, tucked his toes under the edge of the bed, crossed his hands over his chest, and started doing sit-ups. Three sets of twenty-five repetitions. That was his goal.

By the time Truman was done, he'd heard Doris Day, Helen O'Connell, Margaret Whiting, and the Andrews Sisters. His T-shirt was drenched with sweat and he was gasping so hard he couldn't even whistle along with "Don't Sit Under the Apple Tree with Anyone Else But Me."

When he could breathe again, he toweled off and put on a clean sport shirt.

Now, he thought, with some satisfaction. Now it might be time to do some research.

He looked at his phone. The cost of long distance was astronomical. Once again he missed the days at the bureau, when he could dial anywhere in the world at the drop of a hat and get any information he wanted, on AP's dime, of course. One time he and Gibby had called the American consulate in Peking to settle a bar bet.

Oh well, he thought. He wasn't above a little subterfuge. For the appropriate cause, of course.

Yvonne Sweatt hovered over Truman's shoulder. He was seated at the reception desk, a look of bemused boredom on his face.

"Now, I'll be right back in forty-five minutes," Yvonne repeated for the third time.

"Everything will be fine. I'll be fine," he repeated. "Answer the phone, tell anybody who asks that we don't have rate cards because of the new management, take messages." He tapped the pink message pad in front of him. "I'm all set here. Now go on before I change my mind."

Her already pink face flushed again, she repeated another set of useless instructions and then was gone.

Truman smiled and allowed himself to relax a little. The joint was dead. Everybody was either out doing their

Saturday errands or taking a siesta. It was the time of day Yvonne usually took her break, sneaking away for a quart of ice cream or a bucket of the Colonel's extra-crispy.

He'd sat across from her, pretending to read the newspaper he'd already read at breakfast. Once he looked over at her, caught her glancing for the dozenth time at the big clock on the wall behind her.

"Slow day, huh?" He was all sympathy, all interest.

She sighed loudly. "I'm about to jump out of my skin, I'm so bored."

"Why don't you take a break?" he said innocently. "I could watch the phone, you know. Sort of cover for you."

"No, I couldn't. Absolutely not."

He shrugged, went back to staring at meaningless stock listings.

"You have to take messages, deal with walk-ins, handle emergencies. If the fire alarm goes off, well, it's complicated."

"Has it ever gone off?"

"There's always a first time," she said primly. "I'm the only one here who knows the procedure."

"I understand."

She sighed theatrically. "Still. There are a couple of things I really need to take care of. And you do know all the residents."

"That's true," he agreed.

Ten minutes later she was gone and Truman was dialing information in Scottsdale for the number for the newspaper.

He couldn't remember the name, some suburban daily.

"It's the *Scottsdale Post*," the operator informed him.

The next hurdle was getting past the *Scottsdale Post*'s operator.

"Morgue, please," he said politely.

"Morgue?"

"Your reference department," he said.

"You mean News Data Services?"

"Whatever."

"I'm sorry, but News Data Services is only for the use of the *Post* staff."

"I'm a reporter for the *St. Petersburg Times*," he lied. "Don't you people still believe in professional courtesy?"

It was a time-honored newspaper practice, any working reporter could walk in or call in to any out-of-town newspaper and be given whatever help he needed, phone numbers, access to the paper's morgue, a spare typewriter and phone.

The operator in Scottsdale had to check with her supervisor before she'd connect him. He only hoped they weren't on another line, calling the St. Pete *Times* to check his credentials. He glanced around the lobby to make sure he wasn't being observed.

Long-distance phone calls weren't in his budget for this month. But the Fountain of Youth could afford it. And besides, he was performing a service watching the front desk.

"Sir? I'll connect you to News Data Services now. Miss Peters will be helping you."

Miss Peters sounded bored. It was a Saturday, after all. Downtime for most newspapers, with only a skeleton staff on board.

He told her what he wanted. "Newby," he said loudly. "Jewell G. Newby. Two *l*s in Jewell, Newby ending in *y*. And it's the Church of Cosmic Unity."

"Oh yes," she said dryly. "Everybody here knows how to spell the Reverend Newby's name. What is it you want, specifically?"

"Whatever you've got," Truman said. "He's starting a church here in St. Pete. Bought a retirement hotel, going to turn it into condos for his members. We'd like to know what kind of ministry he ran in Scottsdale. Any problems."

"Let me just call up his file on the computer," Miss Peters said. "Looks like there's a couple hundred citings here. The first entry is, um, late 1991. You want me to start that far back?"

Truman thought about it. Yvonne could come back at any time.

"No," he said regretfully. "I'm on deadline. Could you just hit the highlights? I'm looking for dirt, scandal, the usual stuff."

"You want the highlights of two hundred entries? No way. Look, all I can tell you off the top of my head is that these guys built a big church right out by the mall, and before you know it, the place is full almost every night of the week. And the funny thing is, everybody who goes there, it seems like, is retired. Senior citizens. That's their specialty, their ministry, they call it. I've got a couple of neighbors who think Jewell Newby is the second coming. That church must have two dozen schoolbuses. They're always running the old folks out to shopping or the doctor or on outings. Is that the kind of stuff you're looking for?"

"It's a start," he said reluctantly. "What about the dirt?"

"Just a minute. Let me cross-reference the church with lawsuits. Maybe we'll find something that way."

Truman heard typing. The clicking of computer keys instead of the old clacking of the typewriters they'd used in his day. Still, having computers do the research work in the morgue was an amazing time-saver. No more little brown envelopes full of torn, dusty clippings.

"Okay. Here we go," Miss Peters said, a note of excitement creeping into her voice.

"A family named Sowers filed suit against the Reverend Newby and his church in 1993. They claimed that Newby acted to defraud four family members out of eight hundred twenty-five thousand dollars from their mother, a woman named Arthurene Sowers."

"That's what I need," Truman said. "Could you read me the story?"

"The full text? It's twenty-six inches. Why don't I just fax it to you?"

"Can't," Truman said quickly. "Our fax is out of order. They've had a guy in here working on it all day. How about just reading the important parts?"

"Well, okay," she said, "but if the other line rings, I'll have to get it. I'm the only one here today."

"No problem."

"All right. Looks like this family, Jeffrey C. Sowers, his brother Marvin J. Sowers, and two sisters, Christine Sowers Carter and Annette Sowers Skinner, were the sole surviving children of a Scottsdale woman, Arthurene Sowers, who died here in September of 1992 at the age of eighty-seven. The family, who all live in El Paso, filed the suit. And their mother, Arthurene, had been living in Scottsdale, at a retirement community here called Isla Del Verde, since 1979.

"Some time in the early nineties, our story says, Reverend Newby befriended Mrs. Sowers. She was a loner, not a lot of friends. She'd lived alone here since she retired years ago from a job as executive secretary to the vice president of Arco Oil. And although she supposedly lived pretty simply in a two-bedroom villa at Isla Del Verde, which is pretty posh, by the way, the family claims she was loaded. Forty years' worth of Arco Oil stock options and shrewd financial advice from her old boss."

Truman was writing as fast as he could.

"Let me guess," he interrupted. "Reverend Newby becomes the son Arthurene Sowers already had."

"Close confidant, spiritual adviser, and, eventually, executor of her estate," Miss Peters said. "After she died, the family discovered that over the course of two years, Mama Arthurene had signed over a large chunk of her real property to both Newby, personally, and the church, including the Isla Del Verde bungalow, which was worth two hundred twenty-five thousand dollars, and some undeveloped land out by the Phoenix airport that the heirs claim was worth six hundred thousand dollars. In return for having the property deeded over to him, Newby signed an agreement that stated that he would help her maintain the villa and make himself available to her to take her to the store, to the doctor's office, church outings, or any other place she desired to go."

"That's close to a million dollars," Truman cut in. "just for doing what a compassionate pastor would do for a member of his flock for free. What happened to the lawsuit?"

"Let me scroll the other entries and I'll see."

Truman kept writing notes while he waited.

"You there?" Miss Peters asked.

"Still here."

"It looks like the Sowers family dropped their suit. There's a story here saying that they requested the district attorney to investigate Newby for criminal charges, but after a two-month investigation, they couldn't find enough evidence of criminal intent."

"Too bad," Truman said. "But this is good stuff. You got any more lawsuits against him?"

He heard more tapping.

"It doesn't look like it. Hey. Here's a note appended to the file, though. Somebody from Austin, Texas, requested a copy of some of this Sowers file."

"Another newspaper reporter?"

"It doesn't say so,' Miss Peters said. "The name is Leda Aristozobal. Address is the Texas Department of Revenue in Austin."

"Tax people," Truman said. "I wonder why they're interested in a lawsuit against Jewell Newby?"

"I don't know," Miss Peters said. "Oops. There's the phone. I've got to go."

She hung up before he could thank her.

Truman tried to figure out the spelling of Leda Aristozobal. A tax lady in Texas. Hadn't Jewell Newby gotten his start in Texas? Truman would have to check the notes in his file. He reached for the phone again. He wanted to call information in Austin. See if he could find a home listing for Leda Aristozobal.

"I'm back," Yvonne Sweatt chirped. She was clutching a grease-stained paper sack in her arms, and she was out of breath.

"Any calls?" she asked, obviously waiting for him to vacate her chair.

"Nothing important," he assured her as he vacated her chair.

He was standing waiting by the elevator, feeling just the tiniest bit smug about the scam he'd just pulled.

"I saw that," a voice hissed in his ear.

He jumped a foot in the air.

"Jesus, Jackie!" he exclaimed. "You startled me. Saw what?"

"Saw you tricking Yvonne into leaving you alone with the switchboard," she whispered. People were beginning to straggle into the lobby now, so she had to keep her voice down. "Pretty slick work for an old-timer. What'd you find out?"

The elevator dinged and the doors opened. He gestured for her to enter. "Come on-a my house and I'll fill you in."

CHAPTER

TWENTY

"**H**OLD THE ELEVATOR, HOLD THE DOORS!" a woman demanded.

Truman stuck his foot out and the doors closed on it, then slowly parted again.

Sonya Hoffmayer trundled aboard, holding KoKo in her arms.

The little dog had a good memory. It pricked up its ears when it saw Truman, bared its teeth, and let out a low, menacing growl. Jackleen backed away from Mrs. Hoffmayer and the dog.

"KoKo!" Mrs. Hoffmayer said, pretending to be shocked. She kissed the top of the little dog's head. "We're not ourselves, are we, precious? No, we're not. We're certainly not."

Mrs. Hoffmayer turned to Truman, pretending not to see Jackleen. "One of those awful painters got paint on our little hiney. We've just been to the groomers, and we're not at all happy, are we?"

"Latex, I hope?" Truman said innocently.

"Oil," she said gloomily. "There was nothing the groomer could do but shave." She took the dog out of the basket it was riding in and held it up for inspection. It was wearing a tiny white diaper.

Mrs. Hoffmayer got off on the fourth floor. After she was gone, Jackleen sighed. "Now I know somebody's got a job worse than me."

"What's that?" Truman asked.

"Whoever had to shave that dog's butt," she said.

He'd just begun to fill Jackleen in on the results of his research when there was a knock at the door.

Pearl Wisnewski stood in the hallway, her arms piled high with men's clothes, coats, slacks, and shirts on hangers. Beside her on the floor was a plastic laundry basket full of more neatly folded garments. Pearl's eyes were red-rimmed, but she looked resolute.

"Hello, Jackie," she said. "Here." She thrust the armload of clothes at Truman. "I talked to Mel's doctor this morning. He says Mel's not going to get better. It's a degenerative disease, and he says the advance is rapid. Mel wears pajamas all day in the nursing home, that or a couple pair of those loose elastic-waist slacks. I want you to take these clothes."

Truman transferred the clothes from her arms to his bed. She followed him inside with the basket.

"Isn't this kind of drastic, Pearl? Mel is going to want some of these clothes, I'm sure."

She set the basket on the bed beside the other things. "No," she said simply. "For months now he's only wanted to wear the same clothes over and over again. The doctor says it's a symptom of the Alzheimer's."

She ran her hand over a blue blazer with gold buttons at the cuffs. "Some of these things are like new, Truman. If you can't wear them, give them to somebody else."

"Why the hurry?" Truman asked.

Pearl bit her lip and put her left hand over Truman's. Her wedding band, loose on her hand, clicked against her engagement ring.

She looked ten years older than she had last week.

"He's not going to get better. I've got to face facts.

Every time I open the closet I think of the things we're not going to do together anymore. The places we're not going to go. I'll feel better if his clothes are put to use."

She smiled weakly. "I'm German, you know. A Bierbohm. We don't like to see a bit of waste. Didn't you know that?"

"Sure," Truman said, nodding. "I'll take care of it."

He gestured toward the easy chair by the window. "Have a seat. I was just going to tell Jackie what I've found out about that Newby fella. The one who's buying the church. It's not a lot, but I think he might be involved in something sticky out west where his church started."

But she was already moving toward the door. "No thanks. I've been with Mel all morning. I'm exhausted. I think I'll take a little nap before I go back over there to give him his supper."

When she was gone, Truman stood and looked at the pile of clothes.

He shrugged himself into the blue blazer. It fit all right through the shoulders, but the sleeves were two inches too long. He held up a pair of worn corduroy slacks. Miles too big and too warm for St. Pete anyway. He started working his way through the pile, separating out the few things he thought he could use from the majority that wouldn't fit.

"How about you?" he asked Jackie. "Don't you have a boyfriend? Somebody tall? Some of the stuff's not too bad."

She snorted. "Boyfriend? That's a good one. The last man I dated was like Mr. Mel. He had memory problems too. He kept forgetting he had a wife and two little babies waiting at home for him."

Jackleen got up and went over to the bed. She fingered the fabric of a plaid jacket in Truman's discard pile. "Mr. Mel was wearing this last week when we went to the track. Remember?"

Truman shook his head. "I guess I wasn't paying too much attention to what anybody was wearing. I was too busy worrying that Mel would get lost."

She stroked the jacket. "Lost. Huh. Funny to think about it. Him in a nursing home, hardly knows any of us. So what did you find out while you were minding the switchboard this afternoon?"

He filled her in. "I'm gonna call that Leda Aristozobal person. Even if I have to pay for it myself. But I guess I'll wait till tonight. After the rates go down."

"Hope you find something out," she said fervently. "There's an architect walking around downstairs in the kitchen right now. He's got a clipboard and I heard him telling Cookie they're gonna close the coffee shop in two weeks so they can start ripping out."

Her eyes glinted angrily. "I'd like to rip out her skinny little ass, ʾhat's what I'd like to do. Her sashaying around like she runs the place. She saw me coming in to clock out. You know what she said? 'Girl,' that's what she called me. 'Girl, could you get a cup of hot coffee for our architect?'"

"Ignore her," Truman advised. "We've got to concentrate on other matters."

Jackleen slipped into the plaid jacket. The hem hung nearly to her blue-jean-clad knees, and the sleeves hung loosely, three inches from her fingertips. She pushed the sleeves up to her elbows and flipped the collar up. There was a full-length mirror on the back of the closet door. She stood in front of it, turning this way and that, preening really. The jacket gave her a jaunty, boyish air.

"Look," she said, pleased with what she saw. "Annie Hall."

"Who?"

Jackleen laughed. "Never mind." Her smile faded. "You know, I keep thinking about that dead girl. Rosie. I never saw a dead person outside a coffin before."

Truman had. He didn't bother to tell her you didn't get over it quickly. "I've been thinking about it too. One of those cops came to see me, you know." He snorted. "Thought maybe Mel told me something about why he did it."

"A cop that was there that night?"

"Uniformed cop, not a detective," Truman said. "He

knows my daughter. He said something funny too. The police think that girl was killed because of a computer program."

"What kind of a program?" Jackie asked.

"One that handicaps dogs. Whoever had it could get rich from making the right bets. The cops say this Rosie and her boyfriend came up with the program. And whoever killed her, killed her for that program. It's on a computer disk. Of course they haven't found it."

"Hey," Jackie said. "Remember what Mel told us last week when he went to look for Rosie? He said she had a new system to pick winners. That must have been what he was talking about."

"A computer disk," Truman said. "I'll be damned. Wonder if anybody else out at the track knows anything about the thing?"

"We could go out there," Jackie said. "Walk around, ask some questions."

"Play detective?" Truman sounded dubious. "I don't know." He looked down at the pile of clothes on the bed. Picked up a loud flowered sport shirt. He remembered Mel wearing it to cookouts at the house back when Nellie was alive. He picked the shirt up idly. It smelled like Mel. Like tobacco and some kind of woodsy soap or aftershave. Like Mel used to smell. Not like he did now, not that sour nursing-home smell. The flowers reminded him of the ones on the girl's hat. Roses.

"The newspaper story gave Rosie Figueroa's address. A tourist court off Fourth Street," he said. "I guess it wouldn't hurt anything to go over there, ask the neighbors what they know. Maybe hit the track after that. Just walk around. Ask some harmless questions."

"All right now," Jackie said, grinning. "You think Pearl would mind if I wore this jacket? I really like it."

"Take it," he told her. "Take the whole basket if you want. I got no use for it. And Pearl wants somebody to get some use out of it."

"Just the jacket," Jackleen said, thrusting her hands down into the patch pockets.

Truman bundled the discarded clothes into his arms and plopped them on top of the basket. "We can drop this stuff off at the free clinic," he said as he followed Jackie out into the hallway.

He set the basket down to lock the door.

"Hey!"

Truman looked up at Jackie.

She was holding a small brass key in her palm. "This was down inside the jacket, in the lining. There's a little hole in the pocket lining. It must have slipped through. I better take it back to Pearl, it could be something she needs."

"We'll stop on the way down," Truman agreed.

Pearl turned the key over and over in her hand. "Just a minute," she said.

She went to the dresser and reached inside her pocket-book. When she came back she had a bulky key ring with a dozen or so keys jangling from it. One by one, she held the keys up to the small brass key Jackie had found.

"No," she said, puzzled. "I've never seen this one before. You're sure this came out of that jacket?" She nodded at the plaid coat Jackie had draped over her arm.

"It was down in the lining," Jackie explained. "I felt something hard. I thought maybe it was a button or a piece of change or something."

"Wasn't this the jacket Mel was wearing at the track that night?" Truman asked.

"The police gave me his things back yesterday. They were in a horrible brown envelope marked 'Evidence.' I tore the envelope up and put the jacket with the other clothes to give away. The pants," she said, pausing, her face crumpling, "the pants had spatters. Bloodstains. That girl's blood. I threw them away."

"Never mind," Truman said. He'd thought things over in the elevator. "Never mind. We're going to clear Mel's name, Pearl. Find out who killed Rosie. This key could have something to do with it."

Pearl shook her head sadly. "It won't matter much now, will it? Mel's in that nursing home. I'm here. Alone."

Truman took the key from her. "She was just a kid, Pearl."

When they were alone, on the elevator, Jackie put the jacket back on. "Are we crazy?" she asked. "Thinking we can find out who killed that girl when the police and the district attorney and the judge and everybody else already decided Mel did it, and he can't remember himself?"

Truman took the key out of his breast pocket and looked at it again. "Crazy?" he said. "What's so crazy about asking a few harmless questions?"

They were almost to the lobby door when Truman heard his name being called. He turned around.

Ollie came bounding across the tile floor. He was dressed in a pale yellow sport coat, baggy slacks, and the loudest, widest tie Truman had seen since the forties.

"What's up?" Truman asked.

Ollie favored Truman with an exaggerated wink. "You'll never guess where I'm going."

"You got me," Truman said. "Where?"

Ollie glanced around the lobby to see if anyone could overhear. "Over to Cookie Jeffcote's condo. What do you think about that? Huh?"

"Cookie Jeffcote! What you messing with her for?" Jackie demanded.

Ollie held a finger to his lips. "Shh. It's top secret. I'm not supposed to tell anybody, but I guess you two wouldn't count. She invited me over for drinks. To tell me about the special deal the church might cut some of us on this conversion thing."

"Special deal?" Truman looked dubious. "What special deal?"

"I dunno," Ollie said. He slicked his hair back with the palm of his hand. "But Ollie Zorn was never a man to let opportunity pass him by. No sir." He glanced at his watch. "Gotta go. She lives all the way out at St. Pete Beach and not that many buses go out there Saturday night."

He gave Truman a subtle elbow in the ribs. "I'll give you a full report in the morning."

Jackie watched him hurry out the door. She shook her head. "What you think that's about?"

Truman laughed. "I guess we'll find out tomorrow."

CHAPTER

TWENTY-ONE

WADE HARDESON WAS HUNGRY AND THIRSTY. But he'd had to part with most of the cash his grandmother had given him to pay the back rent and get back into the apartment. And for what? Someone had been there already, trashed the place. The disk wasn't there.

He'd fucked up. Set up a meeting with the mob guy, Mikey, just assuming he'd find the diskette.

There was a shopping center with a brand new Winn-Dixie just a block away. He'd think better after he had some lunch.

Once inside, he got a shopping cart and wheeled it directly to the paper-goods aisle. There he stacked the cart with bulky rolls of paper towels, the largest package of disposable diapers he could find, and an eighteen-roll package of toilet tissue. It made a high white tower, totally obscuring Wade from view.

Then he made his way to the beer coolers. He pulled the cart in front of the cooler door, opened it, and helped himself to a quart bottle of malt liquor. He uncapped it and let the cold liquid slide down his throat. He needed this. It felt like he'd been gargling sand all day.

Moving on to the deli, Wade positioned the cart to shield himself from view again and picked up a half-pound package of sliced honey-baked ham and a tray of sliced sharp American cheese, tucking both under the waistband of his jeans. He was enjoying himself.

Shoplifting smorgasbord, Rosie had called it. If they were broke, which they usually were, they'd make a game of it. Rosie liked shiny new supermarkets, especially the ones with self-serve delis and the hot-entree sections. She got so good at the game, she'd go in, have the clerk fix her a Styrofoam tray of fried chicken, baked beans, coleslaw, and potato salad, and then she'd roam the aisles, eating as she went, stuffing more groceries down her shirt and in her purse. "The fools even give you a plastic fork and knife," she'd said, laughing.

At the bakery, Wade untied a bag of rye bread, slipped four slices of bread out of it, and retied the bag. He reached into a plastic display case, grabbed a chocolate-frosted bismarck, and gobbled it.

Using the paper tower as a shield, Wade worked himself into a corner display of liter bottles of Fresca and Tab and fixed himself two thick sandwiches, which he ate just as quickly.

He was still thirsty, though, so he wheeled the cart back down the beer aisle.

As he was reaching into the cooler again, he spotted something troubling reflected in the glass door. The woman wearing the ugly flowered dress and the head scarf and sunglasses. In-store security?

No, Wade decided. It was the same woman he'd seen at that old folks' hotel. She was way too young to be hanging around a hotel like that. He could tell by her slender calves and ankles. Dynamite legs.

Had he seen those legs before?

Oh yes. The sexy little legs had a vicious mouth that went with the package. Tammi. She was that goon Curtis's girlfriend. And the last time they'd met, he recalled, she'd bragged about having a gun.

Sweat beaded on Wade's upper lip. She was following him. Hoping he'd lead her to the computer disk. He had to get back out to the car, get to Nana's gun in the glove box, pull it on her before she could pull one on him.

He took one last swig of the malt liquor. Cold courage.

The bottle was still at his lips when the crash came. A metal shopping cart full of canned goods slammed into his kidneys, knocking him flat against the metal shelves of the beer cooler.

"Hiya, Wade," Tammi said, flipping up her sunglasses so he could see those icy blue eyes. "Remember me?"

"I don't have it," he said, rubbing at his mouth. The force of the collision made him jab the beer bottle into his upper lip.

"I know you don't," Tammi said, backing the cart up the tiniest bit, to allow her to edge up close beside him and grab his arm. "But I'll bet you know where to find it. Right?"

"I don't," he protested. "Swear to God. It's like I told your friends. Rosie took it. She must have hid it somewhere. I looked all over the cabin. It's not there. Hey—didn't you guys wreck the place?"

"Not me," Tammi said. She dug long nails into the skin of his forearm, enjoying his wince of pain. "Now that you've had lunch, why don't we go outside and discuss the situation?"

"I'm supposed to meet somebody," he blurted out. "A guy who wants to buy the program. He's connected. If I don't show up for the meet, he'll find me and kill me. Then nobody'll get the program.

"I'm the only one who knows where to look for it," he added. "How to use it. It's no good without me."

"That might be," Tammi admitted. She was pinching him now. "I'm kind of thinking you might need a partner. Wouldn't you agree?"

Truman and Jackleen stood on the front stoop of the manager's office. They'd been knocking at the door for five minutes with no response.

Even in the sparse shade of the tall pine trees it was unseasonably hot. Truman mopped his forehead with a handkerchief.

"She ain't home," a voice called from nearby.

He whirled around to see where the voice was coming from.

A boy, maybe twelve years old, sat in the shadows of the next cabin over. His skin was smooth and dark, and his thick black-rimmed glasses rested on chubby cheeks.

"It's her wrasslin' night," the boy explained. "Are you cops too?"

"What makes you—" Truman started.

"Detectives," Jackleen said quickly. "You live here, do you?"

"My aunt Frieda does," the boy said. His voice was deep and hoarse-sounding. "I stay here on weekends. You gonna arrest somebody?"

"Don't know yet," Jackleen said, giving the boy a smile. "Did you know Rosie Figueroa? She lived here too, didn't she?"

"My aunt Frieda knows her."

"What about her boyfriend?" Truman asked. "Did you know him?"

"Uh-huh."

Jackleen went over and sat down beside the kid.

"Tell me about Wade," Jackleen said. "What's his last name? Have you seen him around here lately?"

"I don't know his last name. You want me to ask Aunt Frieda?"

Jackie glanced over at Truman, who gave her a quick nod.

The kid went inside and came back a moment later, aunt in tow.

She was short and skinny. She wore blue nylon running shorts and an oversized man's T-shirt and had the same thick-lensed glasses as her nephew.

"D'Antonio ain't supposed to talk to strangers," she said.

"They cops, Auntie," the kid started.

"Rosie got kilt last week. What y'all want now?"

"Can you tell us anything about this Wade guy?" Jackie asked.

"Rich boy. Drove a Porsche till the repo man come for it. Had some kind of computer job. He stayed drunk mostly."

"What was his last name?" Truman asked.

Frieda peered closely at Truman. "Ain't you too old to be a cop? You got a badge?"

"He's the captain," Jackleen said. "We're plainclothes detectives, working undercover. We don't carry badges undercover."

Frieda considered this. "Wade Hardeson," she said finally. "Rosie was too good for him. She worked her ass off at that track while he'd lay around drinking and messin' with that car of his."

"Have you seen him lately?" Jackie asked.

"No," Frieda said.

"I did," D'Antonio volunteered. "He came this morning. Driving a big black car. He couldn't unlock his door. So he came over here and went to see Miz Irene."

"She probably changed the lock," Frieda said. "You don't pay rent right on time, Miz Irene will lock your ass out in a minute."

"Did Miz Irene give him the key?" Jackie wanted to know.

"Yeah."

"You didn't happen to see what Wade was doing over there, did you, D'Antonio?" Jackleen asked.

The child smiled shyly. "I was playin' spy."

"D'Antonio!" Frieda said sharply.

"Like James Bond," he protested. "I didn't hurt nothin'. When Wade went in there, I snuck up on the porch and peeked in."

"What did you see?" Jackleen asked.

"Nothin'," the kid said. "That place was some kind of a mess. My mama would whip my behind if I made a mess like that. Wade, he be lookin' for something, opening drawers and closets and stuff."

"Did he find what he was looking for?" Truman asked.

"I don't know," D'Antonio said. "That lady in the flowered dress who was sneaking around and looking in the back window, was she a cop like y'all?"

Truman and Jackie looked at each other. "What woman?"

Now D'Antonio was pleased with himself. "She driving a black Firebird. Wearing a funny-lookin' hat on her head, and a big old fat-lady dress, but she had skinny arms and legs like you, Auntie. She go around and peek in the window at Wade. When he come out, she got back in her car and followed him out."

"Have you ever seen her around here before?" Truman asked.

"Nuh-uh."

"It looks like somebody else is after that computer program," Truman told Jackleen quietly.

"That the thing Wade said gonna make them rich?" Frieda asked.

"They told you about it?" Jackleen asked.

"One Sunday Wade be sitting over there drinking beer and me and D'Antonio be out here, cooking hot dogs on our grill. Wade, he come over, mooch a hot dog off of us. Pretty soon Rosie come over looking for him. She say 'I thought you supposed to be working on the computer program.' And Wade, he tell her to shut up, 'cause he's taking a break. And he start tellin' me and D'Antonio about he got a computer thingie can pick all the winners over there at the dog track. I tell him, pick me some winners, I'm sick of poor."

"Did they ever do that?" Jackleen asked.

"Nah. Wade be full of shit," Frieda said. "And I could tell Rosie wanted him to shut his mouth up and quit talking so much."

Truman took the brass key out of his pocket and showed it to Frieda. "Does this look like the key to one of the cabins here?"

"That little bitty key ain't from here," Frieda assured him.

Truman's gaze wandered to Rosie's cabin. Faded curtains hung limply at dust-caked windows. A single beer can lay on its side near the front step. "I wonder if the key is to anything in the cabin."

"You wanna take a look?" Frieda asked slyly.

Truman looked surprised.

"Miz Irene give me the spare, case somebody comes to look at it while she at wrasslin'," Frieda explained. She reached into the pocket of her shorts and brought out a large silver-colored key attached to a bit of yarn. "Y'all find out who did Rosie that way. You hear?"

CHAPTER

TWENTY-TWO

"**T**ELL ME AGAIN WHY WE'RE MESSIN' WITH a midget?"

Curtis Goolsby leaned against the bedroom dresser. He wore a yellow Walkman headset that was in bright contrast to his dark hair.

Butch walked over and wrenched the headset off Curtis's head.

"Ow," Curtis said, rubbing his right ear. "That hurt."

"Maybe now you'll listen," Butch said. "Concentrate. Okay?"

Curtis nodded.

"I told you. He's causing all kinds of trouble for your mama."

"Oh," Curtis said, rubbing his ear again. It really smarted. "But I thought Mama was mad at you," he said. "And you was mad at her. You said she was a low-rent, two-bit—"

"I was mad at her because she sold my gun collection, is all," Butch explained. "But the point is, this son of a bitch is causing your mama all kinds of problems and we got to do something about it."

"Let's just scare him. Tell him shut up or we'll kick your ass."

"An ass-kicking won't do it," Butch said. "Your mama says he's a feisty little sumbitch. He'd just report us to the cops."

"Ain't we supposed to be looking for that Wade boy and that computer thing?" Curtis said, trying another tack. "You said we'd get rich if we got hold of that computer thing."

"We'll get to that," Butch said. "You puttin' money before your mama's best interests?"

He did not bother to tell his son that what was really at stake was a way for him to get back inside Cookie's pants—er, good graces.

"I never killed nobody before," Curtis went on.

"Don't think of it like that. Think about it, like, you're doin' right by your mama. Keeping her from losing her job and having to live in a Dumpster and eat Kibbles'N Bits. Self-defense. Right?"

"If you say so." But Curtis did not look happy.

Butch went on unloading the things from the shopping bag, laying each one carefully out on the bed.

"Okay," he said, pointing to a pile of clothing. "These here are the blue shirts we'll wear with blue pants. So it looks like a uniform. You got blue pants, don't you?"

"I guess."

"Right. Now this here," he said, picking up a large, flat red plastic square, "is the pizza-warmer box. But instead of a pizza, you're going to have a double-barreled sawed-off shotgun inside."

Butch took the shotgun out of the bag and lovingly handed it to Curtis, who flinched, but took it anyway.

"How come I gotta be the one with the gun?" he wanted to know.

"Because I'm the one doing everything else," Butch said. "I'm the one tying them up. I'm the one ramshacking the place and stealing your mama's jewelry and VCR. Plus, I'm the one driving and I'm the one who made the plan and got all the stuff together. Now you want to quit complaining and start listening to the plan?"

"That shotgun's gonna make a big old hole," Curtis pointed out. "Be a lot of blood and stuff. Mama don't like mess."

"Cookie's not going to say a word," Butch promised. "You're going to hit her upside the head with that gun first thing. She'll be out cold. Won't know a thing until she wakes up."

"I can't hit my mama," said Curtis, horrified.

"I'll hit her then," Butch said quickly, and he unloaded the rest of the contents of his shopping bag.

Curtis brightened up when he saw the masks. Black wool ski masks, the kind with slits for eyes and mouths. Butch had finally found them in an army-surplus store.

"Like bank robbers wear. Can I put mine on?"

"No," Butch said, snatching it away. "We got no time for fashion shows. We got to go over this plan to make sure you got it all down."

Jackleen turned the key over to Truman, who buttoned it back in his pocket.

"I sure thought this would unlock something in that cabin, or at least her car. Didn't you?"

"Not really," he said, shrugging. "It doesn't make sense that she'd hide it where they both lived."

"What about a car?"

They raced back to D'Antonio's porch. He pointed to the old blue VW parked under a pine tree, the hood covered with pine needles.

Inside, the car was disappointingly and surprisingly clean. The glove box held a Florida map, a flashlight, a pack of gum, and a lipstick. The trunk was empty too. No sign of computer disks.

"I wonder why she was hiding the disk from her boyfriend, especially if he helped make it," Jackleen said. "And who else is looking for it besides Wade?"

"Whoever killed her," Truman said.

Jackleen got back in her own car. "Want to start at the track?"

"I can't think of anyplace else," he said. "But I still want to talk to this Hardeson boy."

"I'd say he's suspect number one," Jackie said.

"And the woman D'Antonio saw snooping around the cabin today is suspect number two. But who is she?" Truman said.

"I've got an idea," Jackie said. "Remember that cop who came to see you at the hotel last week? Maybe he'd talk to us, let us know what else the police found out."

"Roberts. I doubt he'd tell us anything," Truman said, frowning.

"Didn't you say he was an old friend of your daughter's?"

"Doesn't matter," Truman said. "He won't talk."

"What about if we tell him about the key?" Jackie asked.

"No way," Truman said. "But I'll tell you what. Roberts works at the racetrack as a security guard. Maybe we'll see him tonight."

"Ask him how Rosie got to the track," Jackie said. "And who the woman in the flowered dress is."

CHAPTER

TWENTY-THREE

"**Y**OU THINK THIS GUY KNOWS ANYTHING about computers?" Tammi pulled the dress off over her head and threw it in the backseat. Underneath she wore a black tank top and a brief black skirt. "Like, would he know if you gave him a bogus disk?" she asked, fluffing her hair with her hands.

They were stopped at a light on Gandy Boulevard. Wade had a knot in his stomach. He needed a beer.

"No," he said thoughtfully. "Mike doesn't know shit about computers."

"So how were they going to use it? They got somebody that does know computers?"

"They must," Wade said. "They're not gonna shell out twenty-five thousand dollars just to buy something they can't use. The mob ain't nuts."

"But this Mikey," Tammi kept on. "He's the one you're dealing with. And he doesn't know a bit from a bite in the ass—right?"

"Maybe," Wade said. "What's your point?"

"Give him a fake disk," Tammi said. "How's he gonna

know? You hand it over, he hands you the money, he takes off, we take off."

"And the first time he tries it, I'm a dead man," Wade shot back. "You're crazy, you know that? You don't fuck with these guys."

Tammi was jabbing the back of his neck with the gun barrel. "Here's what we do. You give him a disk. He goes away. We go find the real disk. Or like you say, write another program. When it's done, you call him up: 'Excuse me, I think there's a glitch with the disk you got. But I fixed it and now I'm gonna give you the new improved model. For only another ten thousand dollars. That's a discount.' Right?"

"Rip them off again?" Wade could not believe this chick. Talk about brass balls. Hers positively clanged. Wade wasn't really the ambitious type. That had been Rosie. As far as old Wade was concerned, one good hit at the track was enough for him. The twenty-five thousand Mikey promised was enough of a stake. He'd find the disk or make a new one, hit it big there, at Tampa and Sarasota. Maybe go over to the tracks in Alabama next season.

And there was Marty, up in Lutz. Former jockey, little wrinkled-up old guy he'd met in the bar at the track at Oldsmar Downs, knew everything there was to know about horse racing. Two, three months with Marty, Wade could write a horse-racing program. Horse racing. Now that was a class operation. And you could use it in Europe too. He'd win big here, go over to Europe, travel around. Meet chicks . . .

"Uh-uh," he said, a note of finality in his voice. "You want to get yourself killed, help yourself. I'm gonna try and stall Mikey. Then we go inside the track and find the disk. It can't be hidden that good."

He felt a small cold-steel presence pressing the back of his neck. He wanted to reach over to the glove box, for Nana's gun.

"Do what I tell you, Wade baby, or the last thing you're going to see is your brains splattered on the windshield of this car. Okay?"

They took a quick detour to the tourist court. Wade parked close to the cabin, and they darted inside, locking the door behind them.

He sat down at the table and turned on the laptop. "They didn't mess with it," he said, relieved. "But they took a bunch of my disks."

"Get a blank disk then," Tammi ordered. "You can type some stuff on there real fast. Make it look like the real thing."

"I told you," Wade protested. "It takes hours, weeks, to do this, to make the chart. I can't just—"

"Type," Tammi ordered. "Just type. And hurry up."

"I can't think with a gun pointed at my head. I get nervous."

Tammi crossed her arms across her chest but kept the gun in her right hand. "All right. Now it's not pointed at you. Get moving." She glanced at her watch. "We got thirty minutes."

I need a drink, Wade thought. It was his mantra whenever he was anxious or scared. I need a drink, I need a drink, I need a drink.

Instead, though, he opened a new file, quickly built a makeshift grid, and started typing in the most basic components. Eight dogs, fourteen races. There was no time to do anything approaching a complete chart. Instead, he typed in the most important factors: the dog's grade, the race distance, dog's weight, most recent finishes, and favorite post positions. Typing the numbers soothed his nerves. Numbers did that. Almost as good as a beer.

"Hurry up," Tammi snapped. "Hurry the hell up."

He saw drops of water on the keyboard. It was sweat. His sweat.

Tammi let Wade pull into a convenience store on the way to the track just to shut him up. He went inside and bought a lottery ticket, using his usual numbers, and a liter bottle of malt liquor.

He tucked the ticket in his pocket. He had the bottle half empty by the time he got back behind the wheel of his grandmother's car.

"This better work," Tammi said through clenched teeth.

"You're telling me?"

Michael Streck was right where they'd arranged, in the tenth row from the gate.

Wade parked next to Mikey and got out. Tammi got out too, slowly, giving Mikey a good long look at her legs.

"Who's this?" Michael asked, annoyed.

"His partner," Tammi said silkily.

"I don't like it," Mikey said. "I never said nothing about partners. That's not our deal. You tryin' to fuck with me, kid?"

He opened his sport coat and they saw the grip of the Beretta sticking out of the waistband of his slacks.

Wade gulped. He thrust the computer disk toward Michael. "Here. The disk. See. I told you I'd get it back for you."

A slow smile spread over Mikey's vulpine features. "You sure this is the real thing? I thought you said that other chick took off with it. You found it, or is this some kind of scam?"

Wade laughed nervously. "Come on, Mikey. Look. I made another one. Good as new. Now, uh, about my money."

"You'll get the money," Michael said. "As soon as I'm sure this is the real goods." He opened the car door, got in, had his hand on the door to close it again.

Tammi stepped up and put a delicate hand on the car door.

"The disk works," she said. "But you got to have the raw data to make it work, right, Wade?" She gave him a conspiratorial wink.

Wade's jaw dropped. Why was she doing this to him? Aggravating a guy who was about as friendly as a pit viper.

"I got the race program," Michael said, patting the slick

booklet on the seat next to him. "That ought to take care of it."

Tammi leaned in the window of Mikey's car. "I'm not talking about that shit in the program. I'm talking about the other stuff, inside stuff, that makes our program work. Right, baby?" She turned to Wade for confirmation.

"Well, uh," Wade stammered.

Tammi stood up and smoothed her skirt over her hips. "If you want the blanks filled in," she said, "you gotta pay."

"I'll fuckin' kill you," Mikey gasped, whipping the gun out. He pointed it first at Wade and then at Tammi.

"I don't think so," Tammi said. "I think your bosses want the program. With all the data on it. You kill us, you got nothing." She waggled her fingers at him. "Unless you come up with the money, that disk is all you get. Bye now."

Tammi got back in the car, leaving Wade standing there, mouth agape, like some largemouth bass that had just been landed.

Michael shook his head in disbelief. He looked at the disk in his hand. He had something, but at the same time, he had nothing.

He reached in his jacket pocket, pulled out a roll of bills, money Nunz had given him earlier in the day to make the deal. There were hundreds on the outside, then fifties, then twenties. He peeled off the proper amount of bills and handed it to Wade.

"Here's five," he said. "A down payment. Now let's go find a nice quiet place where you can show me how this thing works."

Tammi leaned across the seat of Wade's car. "We'll go to his place. He'll show you how it works there."

"I don't deal with women," Mikey snarled.

Wade, emboldened now, snatched the money from Mikey's outstretched hand.

"You can follow us in your car," he said, and he ran to his own car, shut and locked the door, and gunned the engine.

Tammi eyed Wade with newfound interest. She took

the gun back out of her purse, but this time she only rested it in her lap. "Let me see the money," she said. "I want to count it."

Wade's fingers raced across the keyboard. He'd added some data categories to the rudimentary chart on the disk, now he was filling in the blanks from the racing program Mikey had brought along. Some dogs he recognized from other races he'd previously handicapped.

Hot Flash, the number seven dog in the third race, he definitely remembered. She was a big brindle female out of the Bainbridge kennel, a dog Rosie always favored on a five-sixteenths mile race, and she'd had six firsts already this season. He weighted the chart in her favor under a catchall heading he called "star power."

Hot Flash looked a good bet, but there was so much information he didn't have: the stuff Rosie picked up in her rounds of the kennels, the trainers, vets, and lead-out boys, that was the data that made the difference. If only . . . never mind. He pushed the thought from his head.

Michael stood behind him, watching, impressed. The kid knew handicapping. This thing would be a gold mine.

Tammi had gone out for beer, taking the five thousand dollars with her. Wade wished she would get back. He glanced at his watch again. It was nearly seven. "These are the only races I'll have time to do if you want to make the daily double," he said. He didn't need to tell Mikey that to win the daily double, you had to pick the winners of the first and second races, in exact order. He liked the odds for tonight; if Michael played his picks, he was liable to do okay. He'd also doped out the super trifecta and the Big Q. They were all races with big payoffs.

He pushed the enter button and waited. The laptop made quiet whirring noises and the screen saver came up, a graphic of three racing greyhounds. When the screen came back, the chart had numerical rankings attached to each of the six races he'd handicapped.

He typed the print command, and Michael stood, arms folded, glowering at the machine as it spat out the play sheet.

By the time Tammi got back, the printout was nearly finished. Wade was already marking up Mikey's race program. He didn't want anybody at the track seeing his chart or the data on it. Wade was conscious of a deep, bone-jarring sense of dread. He was exhausted. A nervous wreck.

Mikey snatched up the computer disk and the printout as well as his marked-up program.

"Don't get lost," he warned them. "This is like a test run. If it works, you'll get the rest of your money. If not, you'll get dead."

Wade snapped the lid of the laptop shut. "Bet only the races I've marked, and bet the way I suggested too," he said. "Like in the fourth race, you need to box a trifecta. Don't just buy a two-dollar quinella ticket, because it won't come in. Understand?"

After the screen door slammed shut behind Mikey, Wade stood up, stretched, and began gathering up his papers.

"Where do you think you're going?" Tammi asked.

"Out of here," Wade said. "Your boyfriend and his buddy are still out there looking for me, right?"

"Right," Tammi said absentmindedly. She took the pistol out of her purse again.

"You can go back to your grandma's for now. But I'll take the computer. Security deposit. You better hope he wins tonight."

"I know," Wade said gloomily. "I know."

CHAPTER

TWENTY-FOUR

"**J**UST A MINUTE."

Truman stopped and pulled his billfold out of his pocket.

He thumbed through his senior citizen discount cards: Winn-Dixie, Eckerd's, Steak and Shake. Finally he pulled one out. The American Association of Retired Persons card. That one was golden.

"Here it is."

Jackie kept on walking. She was impatient to get inside, start looking. Truman caught up with her at the admission window. She'd paid her money and gotten the token that would let her through the turnstile.

Truman pushed the AARP card through the slot in the window along with a dollar bill.

The cashier, a heavy-set black man with a gleaming bald head and a too-tight red blazer held up the card. He frowned. "What's this?"

"AARP card," Truman said. "Members get fifty percent off at Florida attractions."

"Not this one." He shoved the card back through the slot.

Truman pushed it back again. "I've used it at Busch Gardens and Disney World and Silver Springs. They never give me no trouble."

He heard whispering behind him. Two young couples stood there, money in hand, eager to get inside and blow it all.

Jackie edged up to Truman's side. "It's only a buck, Mr. K. I'll pay it. C'mon, okay? We got a lot of ground to cover."

"Hey, man, can we go ahead of you?"

Truman scowled but stepped aside to let them by. Then he stepped up to the window again.

"You again?" The cashier had his hand on the phone. "I told you, buddy, it's two bucks. No discounts. No exceptions."

Jackie pushed two dollar bills through the slot in the window. The cashier smirked and flipped a token through the slot.

She tugged at Truman's sleeve. "Can we go in now?"

"I want his badge number," Truman muttered.

"Later," Jackie promised.

They walked down the concrete runway toward the grandstands. It was nearly five; the matinee crowd was slowly drifting out and most of the evening crowd had yet to materialize. Here and there knots of casually dressed people stood around looking up at the closed-circuit television monitors watching taped replays of the matinee races.

Others sat on the rows of green-painted wooden benches, hunched over racing programs. Workmen with wooden pushbrooms swept drifts of betting slips, beer cups, programs, and hot-dog wrappers into irregular piles along the fence.

Truman and Jackie walked over to the rail separating the grandstands from the track. On the infield, a gardener slowly pushed a fertilizer spreader.

"What now?"

"We start looking," Truman said. He was gazing out at the sky. It was brilliant blue. Ribbons of orange and pink streaked along the horizon, and occasionally a seagull swooped and landed in the tall sabal palms at the edge of the infield. It was cooler now. A slight breeze made the hairs on his forearms stand up.

Mel would like this, he was thinking. He always liked to be early to things, ball games, the track. He liked to watch batting practice, liked to watch the dogs prance by on their walk-out.

Jackie was talking. "Mr. K? Let's go talk to some of the cashiers. Maybe one of them knew Rosie."

The first they asked, an older man, just shook his head when they asked about Rosie. "Saw her around," the second one said. "But she never bet with me." He turned to the cashier in the booth next to his. "You ever know that tout that got killed last week?"

"Rosie," the cashier said. He was young, maybe twenty-two, and Hispanic. "Marion knew her," he said. "Ask her. Next level up."

Marion was studying the racing program, bifocals balanced on the tip of her nose.

"Rosie was a cute kid," Marion said. She was pudgy, looked to be in her fifties, but her skin was smooth and unwrinkled. "Rosie was superstitious. Thought I brought her good luck." She frowned. "Not so good the other night, huh?"

"You saw her?" Truman asked.

"Just for a couple of minutes. She was in line in back of a high roller, Billy from Philly. One of my regulars. Billy was taking his time, shooting the breeze, and I noticed Rosie looked nervous."

"Did she talk to anybody else?"

"Not that I saw. When she finally got up to my window, she had a piece of paper with all her bets for the night, like a kind of chart."

"Is that how she usually made her bets?" Jackie asked.

Marion shook her head. "Rosie bet one race at a time. Always the same way. I told you, she was funny about that kind of stuff. The other night it was different. I'll tell you something else, too," Marion offered, "she had a lot of money that night. Mostly twenties. It was the most money I'd ever seen her with."

"Did she make the bets?" Truman asked.

"No," Marion said. "She got spooked. Yanked the paper back, put the money in this little nylon zipper pouch she wore around her waist, and took off running."

"Did you see who she was afraid of?" Jackie asked.

"No." Marion sighed. "Poor kid. Hell of a thing, that was."

"Getting killed like that," Jackie agreed.

"That too," Marion said. "I saw the first three picks before she jerked that paper away. All of 'em winners. Long shots, too. She would have made a pile if she'd gotten those bets down."

"First three races all winners and all long shots," Truman said slowly. "Was Rosie always that accurate?"

Marion shrugged. "She knew dogs pretty good. Rosie won some and lost some. But I never saw her bet every race like that. I guess it was the first night for her new system."

"You mean the computer program?" Jackie asked eagerly.

"Yeah," Marion said. "Her and that boyfriend dreamed it up. Rosie thought it was gonna make them rich."

"Did you know her boyfriend?" Truman asked.

"Wade? I never saw him. From what Rosie said, he was supposedly the one who knew computers."

"Hey!"

Truman and Jackie turned around. A short bald man dressed in pastel-yellow Bermuda shorts and matching knit golf shirt had a handful of cash in one hand and a large lit cigar in the other.

"You people having a prayer meeting here or something? Let's get going, okay?"

"Hold your horses, Al," Marion said. "They were just leaving.

"Sorry," she said in a low voice. "That's another of my

regulars. He's a good tipper. I can't afford to piss him off."

"That's okay," Truman said. He paused, took a dollar bill out of his pocket, and pushed it across the window toward her. "For your trouble," he said.

"No problem," she said.

"One more thing," Jackie said. "Did you tell the police about seeing Rosie that night?"

"I left early that night," Marion said. "Had a fierce migraine. After I read about what happened in the paper, I called the cops." She rolled her eyes. "Big deal. They switched me from one line to another. Finally I got the homicide detective's office, one of those voice-mail systems. I finally just hung up."

"Nobody ever called you back?" Truman asked.

"Come on, come on," Al said. He pushed up to the counter and started counting out bills.

"Never heard from nobody," Marion said. "Sorry. I gotta work now."

They had to rap on the glass doors of the Derby Club to get someone to let them in. Finally a red-jacketed waiter appeared at the door. "We don't open till six," he said, starting to walk away.

"Wait," Truman called. "I need to ask you something."

The waiter came back and unlocked the door, holding it ajar.

"We're trying to find out something about the young woman who was killed here last week. Rosie Figueroa. She was a tout, worked the entrances all the time. Maybe you knew her?"

The waiter shook his head. He was middle-aged, thin, with a thick mustache and muttonchop sideburns. "I saw the girl's picture in the *Times*, but no, I didn't know her."

"Could she have been up here in the restaurant last Saturday night?" Jackleen asked.

He shrugged. "If she was, I didn't notice her. That was Snowbird Special night: four thousand tourists, all of them wanting the eight ninety-nine early-bird special. What a nightmare!"

"I can imagine," Truman said.

"Besides that, the only thing out of the ordinary was that security got called to drag some suspicious character out of here. Somebody said the guy had a gun."

"A guy with a gun?" Truman asked. "What was he doing?"

"Just standing there glaring, like a tough guy," the waiter said.

"What did he look like?" Jackleen wanted to know.

"Big guy. Maybe six three, two forty, two fifty. Muscular-looking. He wasn't dressed to come in here— our customers have to wear a coat and tie—so he stood outside by the elevator."

"But he didn't pull the gun or threaten anybody?"

"Nah. Nothing like that."

Truman took the key out of his pocket and showed it to the waiter. "Does this look like the key to anything around here?"

"Why?"

"We're detectives," Jackie said. "We think it might have something to do with the murder."

"It looks kind of familiar," he allowed. "But I don't know why."

"Would it fit anything up here?" she asked, looking around the deserted three-tiered dining area.

"Take a look," the waiter offered. Truman and Jackie followed him across the room to a service bar. The waiter bent down behind the counter. "Can I try it?" he asked, holding out his hand.

Truman handed it over. A second later the waiter stood up and handed it back. "Sorry. No good."

With Jackie and Truman following behind, the waiter tried the key in the kitchen meat locker, a storage room where extra glassware and linens were kept, the mop closet, and the employee rest rooms.

The waiter seemed disappointed at his failure.

"Seems like I've seen a key like it. But I can't think where."

"Thanks anyway," Truman said.

On the club level, business had started to pick up. All the seats at the curving bar were filled, and another dozen or more people sat at tables. It was dark in the bar. Ceiling-mounted televisions and red-shaded candle lamps at the tables provided most of the light.

"Let's ask the bartender," Truman suggested.

"Never seen it before," she said, glancing up from the lemons she was slicing.

"Are you sure?" Jackie pressed.

"I've got three keys for this bar," she assured them. "None of them look like the one you got."

By the time they got down to the grandstand area, people were streaming through the turnstiles.

"You know what?" Jackie said. "We forgot to show the key to Marion."

"You're right," Truman said. They walked back over toward the cashier's line. At least twenty people were in Marion's line.

"She must be everybody's lucky teller," Truman said.

"Let's come back later to talk to her," Jackie suggested. "I want to look for that cop friend of yours."

"My daughter's," he reminded her.

They found Bobby Roberts down by the bleachers. He stood with his back to the crowd, scanning the rows of benches for something or someone.

"Bobby?"

Roberts whirled around, smiled broadly when he saw who was standing there.

"Hey, Mr. Kicklighter. How you doing? You gonna win some loot tonight?"

"Haven't even doped out my picks yet," Truman said, suddenly realizing the truth of the statement.

Bobby leaned in closer, putting an arm around the older man's shoulder. "Put a little something on the three-six-eight in the fourth," he said. "I was talking to some people today, say it's a sure thing."

Truman pulled his change purse out and extracted two bills. "I'll do just that," he said. "Thanks for the tip."

"Say, if you're not betting, what are you doing here?"

Truman saw he was looking pointedly at Jackleen.

"Bobby, this is my friend Jackleen. She works in the restaurant at my hotel. She was with me and Mel last week."

"Doing a little sleuthing, eh? Return to the scene of the crime?"

"Sort of," Truman admitted. "We were wondering, do you know anything about a woman, a blond woman who could have been mixed up in this thing with Wade Hardeson and that computer disk?"

"A blonde? No. Why?"

"We went over to the tourist court where Rosie Figueroa lived today. A kid told us he saw Wade going into the cabin this afternoon. And while he was inside, this woman, she drives a Firebird, she comes up and she's peeking in the windows, watching him."

"That right? The kid see anything else?"

"Nothing important," Jackleen said. "We were wondering something else too. Rosie's car has been parked at that place all week. It hasn't been disturbed. We were wondering how she got here."

"Carl, one of the guys at the valet parking, saw her getting off a city bus about six-thirty, something like that."

"Half an hour before post time," Jackie said thoughtfully. "Plenty of time to hide something."

"Whoa now, folks," Bobby said sternly. "I understand you wanting to clear your friend's name. But you can't go around messing with evidence. You do that and you'll hurt your friend more than help."

"All right," Jackie said. "I guess we sort of got carried away."

"No problem," Bobby said, relaxing. "Say, Mr. Kicklighter, did Cheryl tell you I looked her up? We had dinner the other night. Heck of a nice kid, that grandson of yours."

"What?" Truman's mind was somewhere else. "Oh, uh, no, I haven't talked to her. That's nice."

Bobby's eyes flicked toward something behind Truman.

"Whoa. Gotta go. There's a couple of high school kids at that hot-dog stand over there, buying beer. Fake ID probably. Lemme go explain the law to them. See you folks later."

Jackie's face was glum. "Oh well. No sense hanging around here, right? You got any other ideas?"

"Yeah," Truman said, holding up the two dollar bills he was still clutching. "I got an idea. Let's go play that tip Bobby gave us. At Marion's window. Then we go down to that loading area where they found the girl's body; see if we see any locked doors down that way."

"But that cop just said—"

"The hell with him," Truman said, waving his hand dismissively. "That's what's wrong with this generation of yours. You never learned to question authority."

CHAPTER

TWENTY-FIVE

THERE WAS A NEW GATE, CHAIN METAL, SIX FEET tall with a heavy-duty padlock blocking off the rampway to the area where they had found Mel, sitting beside Rosie's body.

"This gate wasn't here last week," Jackleen said. She tried to put the key in, but it stuck, and she had to wrestle to pull it back out.

"Is there another way down there?" Truman wondered.

"Beats me. I know there was a fence around the area where the dogs were locked in their trucks, and that led out into the parking lot," Jackleen said. "I guess we could go outside the track, walk around till we see it."

"We'll check it on the way out," Truman said. "But I'll bet the outside gate'll be locked and double-locked now."

"Let's try to talk to Marion," Jackleen suggested.

The redheaded woman smiled when she saw them. "You folks still here?" She was breaking up a roll of quarters, putting them in her cash drawer.

Jackie held up the key. "We found this and we're thinking maybe she got killed for it. Does it look familiar to you?"

Marion took the key and looked at it.

"Hey," a voice behind them said. "You people mind? It's only a couple minutes to post time and I got bets to put down here."

Marion handed the key back. "Looks like any other key," she said. "I can't talk. My supervisor's standing over there, watching me."

Reluctantly, Jackie and Truman moved away from the windows.

"Can we eat now?" Jackie asked. "We've been on the run all day. I'm really, really hungry."

"Okay," Truman said. "Let's get a hot dog down there on the mainline, watch a couple of races. Then we can start looking again."

Mr. K's energy was a marvel to Jackie. Here he was, what, sixty-some years old, and he never seemed to tire out. Her own sorry behind was dragging and here it was barely nine o'clock.

"No. I want to sit down and eat. Get me a cold beer," she said. She added quickly, "My treat."

He started to refuse, but she insisted. "You drove," she said.

"Just a sandwich then," he said, relenting.

They found a table in the fourth-floor lounge, ordered club sandwiches and two beers, and sat back to watch the third race.

Jackleen produced a racing program from her purse and began studying it.

"Where'd that come from?" Truman demanded.

"I found it on the counter in the ladies' room," Jackleen said. "I guess somebody got fed up and went home early. Look. Somebody had all their bets planned out."

"If they went home this early, they were losing," Truman said. "I played the race that cop told me about and lost. I'll watch, but I'm not playing any more tonight." He crossed his arms over his chest to demonstrate his resolve.

Jackie dug down in her pocketbook and brought out a small zippered change purse. She counted out the crumpled ones and the quarters, nickels, and dimes. "Sixteen dollars," she announced.

Their sandwiches arrived and Jackleen nibbled at hers while poring over the program, her pen poised on the race form.

Truman ate half his sandwich in five quick bites. He was hungrier than he'd realized.

Bored, he began looking around the room. For a lounge, it was well lit—so people could study their programs, he assumed.

The crowd was a mixed bag but ran heavily to casually dressed retirees like himself. Here and there were tables with younger couples and there were some college kids too, down for spring break. Sitting at the bar were the serious players, hunched over their programs and drinks, a blue haze of cigarette smoke swirling above their heads.

"Okay," Jackie said, slapping her hand on the tabletop. "Quinella box, seven-four-five. Here goes nothing."

"You're nuts," Truman said. "Why don't you take that money and flush it down the toilet instead?"

Jackie was up and moving toward the betting windows.

When she came back she fanned the betting slips in front of Truman's face with a flourish. "Marion said it's a long shot, but she likes it." Then she held the tickets to her lips and kissed them lightly. "That's for luck," she said.

The bell rang and the mechanical rabbit took off with eight greyhounds in hot pursuit.

"Seven-four-five," Jackie chanted, squeezing her eyes shut and crossing her fingers on both hands. "Come on, seven-four-five."

A moment later Truman was standing up, shouting at the television screen. "Seven-four-five, seven-four-five! Yes!"

"I won?" Jackie was startled, looking around for confirmation. The numbers flashed on the tote board.

"I won," she screamed. "Thirty-eight dollars!"

"Beginner's luck," Truman said. "Take the money and run."

"No way," Jackie said. She pointed to the program. For the sixth race someone had penciled in "trifecta key-8-over-1-4-7."

"What's that?" Jackie asked, showing the notation to Truman.

"Three trifecta tickets betting the eight-one, eight-four, and eight-seven combinations," Truman said. "Fool's bet. Cost six bucks, too."

"I can afford it," she said, her eyes sparkling with excitement. She fairly danced back from the betting windows, ticket in hand.

"Marion says that Sunny Gal, the eight dog, is a long shot with twenty-two-to-one odds. I could win forty-six dollars if she comes in."

"Or lose the six bucks," Truman pointed out.

Jackie couldn't watch the race. She covered her eyes with her hands and poked her thumbs in her ears to shut out the shouts from the others in the bar. "Come on, eight, come on, eight," she chanted over and over.

She was still chanting when Truman reached over and shook her shoulder.

"It's over," he said. "That eight dog of yours was a bum. Hardly made it out of the box before he was over in the infield, sniffing the flowers."

"Oh," Jackie said glumly. "Oh well."

"Sorry," he said.

Truman was standing up now. "Come on," he said, pulling her chair out. "You won one and lost one. You came out ahead. Let's get out of here before you lose both our shirts. We've got work to do—remember?"

"You're right." She tore her losing tickets in half and put the bits in the ashtray on the table.

CHAPTER

TWENTY-SIX

COOKIE JEFFCOTE POURED A CAPFUL OF BUBBLE bath into the tub. The stuff was forty-two dollars a bottle and usually she . . . . The hell with it, she thought, emptying the whole bottle under the tap.

Bubbles frothed up and over the side of the tub. She giggled and stepped in, sinking into the hot, scented suds up to her chin. She raised the champagne glass and took a long, deep sip.

"To me," she said aloud, raising her glass in a toast.

Tonight was the night. Butch would take care of Zorn and then she'd be in a position to deal with Jewell Newby. She'd been doing some calculations. Her share could be worth close to a million.

She thought briefly about Butch. Her bathwater was steaming hot, but she shivered at the memory of those grease-stained hands roaming over her body.

Butch could become a problem, she realized. But nothing she couldn't handle.

She'd made him tell her his plan, fearful of another of his monumental screwups. But actually, the scheme should work.

She'd made vague promises to Ollie Zorn about "special consideration" in return for his cooperation.

He'd practically drooled all over the floor when she'd suggested meeting at her condo. Men, they were all the same, young or old, tall or midget, they all wanted the same thing.

Butch had an alibi all planned out: He and Curtis were to get themselves into a brawl at a bar out on Treasure Island, allow themselves to be tossed out, and go on to another bar.

Cookie, the only witness to the unfortunate incident, would say the killing happened at exactly the time Butch and Curtis were getting shitfaced down the beach at Shacky's. There would be no neighbors to contradict her, because the condo on one side of her was empty—its Canadian owner still up in Ottawa—and old Mrs. Fuller, on the other side, was deaf as a post.

It was nine now. She sighed. Zorn would be here soon. She would order takeout from the Chinese place down the street when he got there. She had plenty of booze on hand. She wanted the little twerp good and drunk by the time Butch and Curtis arrived.

When the door buzzer rang, she sat upright in the tub, spilling some of the champagne. What the hell? She'd told Zorn it would be a late-night meeting.

The buzzer rang again and Fluffy, her Pekingese, went nuts, barking and yipping and throwing himself against the door. Cookie threw on a short satin robe and matching satin mules and hurried to the door. If Butch was early, the plan would be ruined.

She scooped Fluffy up into her arms and jerked the door open. "You idiot—"

Michael Streck stood on the other side of the door, his suit jacket hitched over his shoulder, a bottle of champagne in his hand. A slow, self-satisfied grin on his face.

"Hey now, doll," he said, when she'd grabbed him and jerked him inside the condo and shut the door. "Thought I'd come by for a little visit."

Fluffy growled and bared his teeth.

"Shush, sugar," Cookie said, patting the dog's bow-tied topknot. "This is mama's friend Michael." She took a deep breath. "Baby," she cooed. "I didn't mean to yell at you, but you know, I wasn't expecting you. And these god-damned neighbors are all so nosy. Well, I'm always glad to see you, you know that, but you should have called, honey."

Michael set the champagne bottle on the table in the foyer. He pulled her to him, untied the robe sash, stood back, and took in the view; her skin still pink from the bath, bubbles clinging to the curves and folds.

"Why so jumpy?" he drawled. "Let's celebrate."

She set the dog down gently on the floor. Michael's hands were all over her now and despite the voice in the back of her head that screamed "Caution, caution," Cookie found herself responding in kind.

"What are we celebrating?" she asked.

Michael reached into the inside breast pocket of his jacket and pulled out a fat packet of bills.

"The big score," he said, chuckling. "Remember that thing I mentioned, the thing Nunz wanted me to get for him and the boys? The guy delivered tonight, and I tried it out. Works like a charm."

He peeled off ten hundred-dollar bills and tucked them in the pocket of her robe. She shrugged out of it, laid it on the arm of the loveseat, and led him by the hand to the sofa.

He sat there, amused, while she walked, naked, to the French doors and pulled the curtains shut. Then she went to the wall switches and flicked the lights off, one by one. He was being so sweet and generous, she couldn't chase him off.

When she joined him on the sofa, he was struggling out of his shirt.

"Let me," she said, nuzzling and unbuttoning at the same time.

"I almost forgot," he said, taking a tiny tinfoil-wrapped

package from his shirt pocket. "Another present—to get you in the mood."

She was already in the mood. But she drew a line of powder on the glass-topped coffee table and snorted it all.

They made love on the living room sofa, with Fluffy barking like hell every time Cookie screamed or moaned.

"Just a minute," Michael said. He got up, picked up the snarling Pekingese, and groped his way in the dark to the French doors, then opened them and threw the dog out onto the terrace.

"Hey," Cookie said, struggling upright. "You'll hurt him." She glanced at the glowing clock on the VCR. It was almost ten. Jesus. She had to get herself straightened up. If Zorn walked in now, the whole deal would be ruined.

She stood up and put on her robe. "You gotta go, babe. I'm supposed to have a business meeting. Somebody from the Fountain of Youth is supposed to come over in a little while."

Michael picked up the slacks he'd tossed on the floor. Another tinfoil packet fell out. "Oops," he said, holding it up so she could see it. "I forgot about dessert. Relax, Cookie, it's early yet."

Ollie looked out the window of the bus and back at the luminous dial of his wristwatch. Ten after ten! He fumed silently. He'd been on the damned bus for nearly two hours. And before that he'd spent another hour on the wrong bus, gone all the way out to the Veterans Administration Hospital in Gulfport before discovering his mistake.

He'd had to go all the way back downtown to Williams Park to catch another bus. And after all that he'd forgotten to get a transfer, so he had to pay full fare again. Full senior citizen fare, but still.

Now his stomach was growling. The newsstand had been busy today, so busy he'd only had time for a package of cheese crackers and a chocolate soda for lunch. He hoped Cookie Jeffcote was a good cook.

He glanced out the window. Rows of high-rise hotels and condominiums lined both sides of the street, but he couldn't make out any street numbers because the buildings were set so far back from the road. He stood up and walked unsteadily down the aisle of the bus to the driver.

"I'm looking for the San Souci condominiums," he said politely. "Fifteen thousand Gulf Boulevard. How far away are we?"

"Far away?" The woman laughed. "Mister, we passed that ten minutes ago. Big pink building on the right."

"Passed it?" Ollie said shrilly. "We passed my stop?"

"What am I, a mind reader?" she asked. "You want off here?"

"Right here," Ollie said. "And listen here. You drivers need to be more courteous to senior citizens. We pay your salary, you know."

The driver slammed on the brakes, watching with grim satisfaction as the tiny man caromed off the back of her high-backed seat and into the empty seat in the next row.

They were late. Five minutes. Curtis had insisted that they put a real pizza pie inside the thermal case, in case they got stopped. "We can leave it there. The cops will go looking for a real pizza man."

"Keep your head down," Butch said quietly as they entered the condo lobby. There were closed-circuit cameras in the lobby aimed at the elevators. They'd worn baseball caps pulled down low.

In the elevator Butch whipped the ski mask out of his shirt pocket. Curtis followed suit.

"You know what to do?" Butch demanded.

Curtis nodded. He was busy pulling his mask over his head. It was hot. The wool was itchy and the eyeholes, they must have been made for a Chinaman or something. They were too close together. He twisted the mask to the

right and to the left. But he could see out of only one eye-
hole, no matter how he moved it around.

"Daddy," he said urgently, "I can't—"

The elevator stopped moving and the bell dinged softly.
Six times. They were there. The door slid open. Butch put
his foot out to keep it open. He felt a rush of adrenaline. It
felt right. Everything was worked out to the last detail. Hit
the apartment, pop the midget, get the money and jewelry
and VCR. Deliver the pizza, that's how he thought of it.
Get rid of the shotgun and clothes and then head for
Shacky's.

He took a deep breath and glanced over at Curtis, who
was fumbling with his mask and muttering something.
Butch couldn't tell what he was saying because the mask
muffled his speech.

"Let's do it," he said.

Three steps out of the elevator, four steps to the left.
He peered around the elevator doors. The hall was
deserted.

"Come on," he hissed, grabbing Curtis's arm.

They were in front of the door. Butch pulled the baseball cap off and stuffed it in his pocket. The mask went on.
Itchy. Hard to see. He rang the doorbell, held the thermal
pizza box in front of him.

"Pizza man," he said loudly.

Cookie stirred on the sofa. The room was dark, its contents dim and spinning around. Jesus! She'd done two
more lines of coke and drunk half a bottle of champagne.
She felt dizzy. Nauseous. And there was that insistent
buzzing in her ears.

Then she heard it. Muffled, but distinct. "Pizza." Oh
God, oh God! What time was it? Where was Ollie Zorn?
She couldn't remember him coming in, didn't remember
when Michael left.

The door buzzed again. "Pizza," the man called again.
She stumbled toward the light switch, banging her knees

on the edge of the coffee table. Goddamn, that hurt. They'd wake up the whole fucking building at this rate. She found her robe, clutched it around her waist, and opened the door.

"Cut it out," she whispered. The masked men on the other side pushed her aside. For a moment there the terror of seeing them made her forget. She started to scream.

What the hell was Cookie doing? She wasn't supposed to scream. It wasn't in the plan. Butch whipped out the sawed-off shotgun and thwacked her across the back of the head. The scream died in her throat and she crumpled to the floor.

"What the hell?"

Michael Streck walked into the living room from the bathroom; the light spilling from it barely illuminated the darkened room. He was dressed only in his boxers, and there were two masked men standing over Cookie. "What the fuck?" It was a hit. Nunz had sent someone to whack him.

His Beretta was in his pants. He dropped to the floor, groping for them.

"Look, Daddy," Curtis said, awed. "He's crawling. Begging us."

Butch kept his eye on the man on the floor. Pretty tall for a midget, but then Cookie always did exaggerate.

Michael found the Beretta and stood up.

"He's got a gun," Curtis screamed.

Butch raised the twelve-gauge, pumped, and fired.

Blam. The first shell hit the glass coffee table, shattering the top and sending a shower of shards shooting into the air.

Michael screamed. Bits of glass pierced his face, chest, hands, and neck. "What the fuck?" He wiped the blood out of his eyes, pointed the pistol again.

Butch fired a second time. Michael was knocked backward, into the sliding glass doors, a gaping, grapefruit-sized wound in his chest. Now Fluffy was barking, yipping frantically, throwing himself again and again against the blood-spattered glass.

"Did you get him?" Curtis asked, whipping off the mask.

Butch already had his mask off. "I got him," he said grimly. "Turn on the light. Let's see if Cookie's okay."

Curtis stumbled around the room for a moment, feeling his way along the wall for a light switch. He stepped over the dead man and found a bank of switches on the wall near the French doors. With a single motion he flipped them on, bathing the room in harsh white light.

Butch and Curtis looked down at the dead man. Late thirties. Dark-haired, lean body. Definitely not a balding midget in his sixties.

"Uh-oh," Curtis said.

CHAPTER

TWENTY-SEVEN

"**H**EY," JACKLEEN SAID, NUDGING TRUMAN. "Look at that."

They were working their way toward an exit gate, caught in a throng of like-minded racegoers who'd found that their luck had run out.

"Look at what?" Truman's feet hurt, and his head throbbed. The whole night had been a wild-goose chase, he decided.

Jackie pointed to a woman ahead of them. She wore a red jacket and carried a set of clothes on hangers, draped over her back.

"That's the same kind of uniform Marion was wearing," Jackie said. "And she's carrying street clothes."

"Spell it out for me."

"Lockers," Jackie said, barely able to contain her excitement. "She works here, and she's carrying her street clothes, so she must have changed into her uniform here. In a locker room."

Jackie took out her key chain and jangled it, holding aloft a small silver key. "It's to my locker at the hotel," she said. "The waitresses have a little locker room off the kitchen. It even has a shower. Doesn't my key look like Mel's key?"

They were outside the track now, in the parking lot. The high-powered streetlights made it bright as daylight. Truman took the brass key out of his pocket and held it up against Jackleen's. They were of approximately the same size and thickness.

"I'll be damned," Truman said. He turned around and looked at the turnstiles. "You think we should go back in and look some more?"

"They probably won't let us back in," she said reluctantly. "But we can come back tomorrow. I'm only working the breakfast shift."

"I thought the place was closed Sundays."

"Didn't you see all the signs inside?" Jackie asked. "They don't have live racing here tomorrow, but they broadcast races from other tracks around Florida on those television sets all over the place. They have off-track betting. That's what that big satellite dish is for."

Truman shook his head in disapproval. "You'd have to be a pretty hardcore gambler just to come over here for that."

They'd reached Jackleen's car. She handed him the key ring. "You drive, huh? I'm beat."

He got in and looked for the seat belt, but there wasn't one. "I'm supposed to have lunch with Cheryl and Chip tomorrow, but I can meet you out here after that. Say two o'clock?"

"No problem," Jackleen said.

He started the engine. It turned over, wheezed, and died. Truman frowned, switched the ignition on again, and repeated the process.

"Give it a little gas," Jackleen suggested, her eyes closed. "It's kind of temperamental."

"It's a piece of crap," Truman said, but he pumped the gas pedal, turned the key, and the engine fired, sending the car lurching forward.

* * *

Butch poured out a tall glass for himself. He set the pitcher down and tossed the beer back, draining it in one long gulp. He paused, belched loudly, and poured a second mug.

"What about me?" Curtis asked.

Butch tossed back another mug of beer and belched again. "Better get your own pitcher, boy. My nerves are shot to hell."

Curtis stalked over to the bar. The bartender, a tall, skinny man with Harley-Davidson tattoos on both his ropy forearms, regarded Curtis with friendly amusement.

"Hey there, buddy," he greeted Curtis. "You and old Butch out tomcatting around without that cute little girl-friend tonight?"

"Uh, yeah," Curtis said with little enthusiasm. "Me and Daddy been out drinking. Gimme another pitcher of Bud, will you, Lamar?"

Lamar drew the beer. "Y'all pretty thirsty tonight, I see."

"You don't know the half of it, Lamar," Curtis said.

He took the full pitcher and walked carefully back to the table, trying hard not to slosh any beer on his shoes. They were the only pair of sneakers he had left now. Butch had made him throw out his favorite Nikes, along with the clothes and the twelve-gauge. After they'd left Cookie's condo, he'd stripped and changed in the truck.

Butch drove a ways down Gulf Boulevard, toward Treasure Island, one of the string of tiny Gulf beach com-munities that went from Pass-a-Grille, to the south, all the way up to Clearwater on the far north end of Pinellas County. It was cool tonight and only a few tourists strolled along the sidewalks in front of the high-rise hotels and condo towers that lined the beach.

They crossed over a humpbacked bridge at John's Pass, the cut between Tampa Bay and the Gulf that had been carved out by a long-ago hurricane. The last remnants of a once-thriving commercial fishing industry clustered around John's Pass. Most of the fishing now was done from charter-fishing outfits catering to tourists who wouldn't know a snook from a snapper.

Butch pulled the truck around in back of Mayhall Seafood, the biggest wholesale-seafood distributor on the beach. A long, shabby dock stretched out from the Mayhall seawall into the bay and three shrimp boats rode the tide there.

Wedged between the back of the Mayhall processing plant loading dock and the seawall stood a row of huge, stinking Dumpsters. Seagulls dipped in and out of the open containers of rotting effluvia.

Curtis swallowed hard to keep from gagging. Butch handed him a blue work bandanna. "Tie it on over your mouth and nose," he said grimly. "And pitch this stuff in the Dumpsters." He handed Curtis the black vinyl garbage bag with the clothes and shotgun.

Curtis shook his head, tears welling up in his eyes despite the protection of the bandanna.

"Do it," Butch said, the tone of his voice implying violence. "Come Monday, they load this shit up on barges and tow it out to the ship channel and dump it. Nobody's coming near this shit that don't have to."

When Curtis came back to the truck, brushing at imaginary fish scales, Butch got out. He opened the tailgate and jumped in, kicking a paint-spattered canvas tarp aside. "Get the feet," he told his son.

It was slow, heavy work now. They'd wrapped the body of the dark-haired stranger in garbage bags from Cookie's kitchen, then wrapped it again in an Oriental rug from the foyer of the condo. They used the service elevator to take the rolled-up rug out to the truck. With a length of chain wrapped around it, Butch promised the body would sink to the ocean floor like a rock.

Before they left the condo, Curtis had knelt down and touched the back of Cookie's head. "She's got a big old bump and there's blood," he reported, his face anxious. "You reckon she's all right?"

Butch's face darkened. It didn't take a rocket scientist to

see what had been going on here. Cookie naked as a jay-bird, the dead guy in his underwear. Cookie had screwed him again, but he hadn't had nearly the fun the dead guy had.

While Curtis was wrapping the body, Butch had ran-sacked the place, filling a pillowcase with jewelry and cash. He'd found five thousand in cash in the dead guy's billfold, along with his driver's license. His name was Michael Streck, and he lived in Tampa. Another thousand turned up in the pocket of Cookie's robe. He decided to pass on the VCR. Too heavy.

Passing Cookie on the way out of the bedroom, he managed to give her a swift, soul-satisfying kick in the ass.

Curtis hadn't wanted to leave his mama lying there, naked like that; it was indecent. But they had to get out of there. This way it looked more like a robbery. Now they were establishing their alibi.

Back at the table, Curtis set the pitcher down on the table, sloshing just a little over the sides. The beer ran out onto Butch's lap.

The older man jumped up, his face reddened and twisted with sudden rage. "Son of a bitch," he yelled. "You did that on purpose." He took the full pitcher and dumped it all out on Curtis's head.

"Daddy," Curtis hollered, "don't—"

Now Butch was shoving him, head-butting, yelling about how he wasn't gonna take no more. He knocked Curtis to the floor and flung himself atop him, slapping and kicking him like a man possessed.

Curtis tried to deflect the blows, but Butch kept slug-ging away. Suddenly, though, Butch was gone. Curtis peeked through his hands and saw Lamar, dragging Butch away, toward the bar's open front door. In the next minute he was back, jerking Curtis up by the front of his beer-soaked shirt.

"Hey, Lamar," Curtis protested. "Don't be tearing my shirt, man, this is my good shirt."

But Lamar shoved him toward the door, propelling him

further with a swift powerful kick that sent Curtis reeling out the door, leaving him sprawled in a heap on the sidewalk outside Shacky's.

He looked up, dazed and bleeding. Butch was standing, leaning really, against the cinderblock wall, wiping at his bloody lip.

In the distance, they heard the wail of a siren, saw the glow of whirling blue lights atop a series of speeding police cruisers, and the fleeting flash of red from an ambulance.

Butch held out a hand to Curtis, helped him up off the sidewalk. He looked thoughtfully at the retreating lights of the emergency vehicles.

"Bad wreck on the bridge, maybe," Curtis offered.

Butch shook his head. "Don't think so, son, I don't think so."

CHAPTER

TWENTY-EIGHT

CHERYL WAS CRACKING EGGS INTO A BLUE MIXING bowl, humming to herself. She poured in some milk and began whisking the mixture. "Turn the bacon, will you, Dad?"

Truman put the scissors down on the kitchen table and held up a small scrap of paper. "Fifty cents off on peanut butter," he said triumphantly. "That's a dollar off on double-coupon day." He moved to the stove, picked up a fork, and began flipping the sizzling slices.

"We don't eat peanut butter, Grandpa," Chip said, looking up from the word puzzle he was working on the funny pages.

"Don't eat peanut butter? What do you take to school for lunch?"

Cheryl and Chip exchanged a knowing look. "He gets a hot lunch at school, Dad."

"Isn't that expensive? Your mom used to fix your lunch, honey. Peanut butter and jelly—"

"Oatmeal cookies and an apple," Cheryl recited. "I know, Dad, but Chip doesn't like peanut butter. Besides, his lunch is free."

"Like food stamps? Welfare?" Truman's long, thin face knotted up in disapproval. "No Kicklighter has ever been on the dole before and we're not starting now." He reached into his pocket.

Cheryl dipped the slices of bread in the egg batter, then placed them carefully on the griddle on the front burner. "Put your money away, Dad," she said calmly. "It's not just Chipper, and it's not welfare. The majority of the kids in his school qualify for a free lunch, so they go ahead and give it free to everybody. It cuts down on paperwork and it keeps the really needy kids from being stigmatized."

"Stigmatized!" Truman muttered. "It still sounds like the dole to me, and I still don't like it." He went back to his coupon clipping.

By the time Cheryl slid his plateful of French toast and bacon in front of Truman, he had a fat pile of clippings neatly arranged by category. Cheryl kissed the top of his head. "Thanks, Dad," she said, tucking them into the pocket of her shorts.

She set a jug of orange juice on the table, poured out three glasses, and sat down. The sun streamed in through the kitchen window, bathing them in a honey-colored light.

Chip poured a river of maple syrup on his toast and took a big bite. "Hey, Mom," he said, chewing away, "did you tell Grandpa about your date last night?"

She blushed. "Chipper! Don't talk while you're eating."

Truman raised an eyebrow and sipped his juice. "A date, huh? How come I wasn't consulted about this matter?" He was secretly glad to hear it.

"It wasn't a real date," Cheryl insisted. "But actually, you were consulted. Bobby Roberts came over yesterday afternoon. He said you've been trying to help the police come up with some information about that poor woman they say Mel killed. We watched an old movie on cable and later he invited Chipper and me out for pizza."

"He paid, so it was a date," Chip said, grinning.

"You went along. So it was not a date," Cheryl said.

"Sounds like a date to me," Truman told Chip in a conspiratorial whisper. "You like this fella?"

"He's okay," Chip said.

"So what's happening with the church thing at the hotel, Dad?" Cheryl said, wanting to change the subject.

Truman thumped a black plastic cartridge he'd set on the kitchen table when he'd arrived.

"They're tearing the place up, got everybody in an uproar," Truman growled. "Ollie was supposed to go meet that Cookie Jeffcote woman last night to talk about some special deal. Hah! This here," he said, gesturing to the box, "came in the mail yesterday. I want you to play it in your VCR for me."

"Sure," Cheryl said. "What is it?"

"It's a tape of the television show this Reverend Newby does."

The three of them trooped into the tiny living room. Cheryl popped the videotape into the VCR and they sat back to watch.

The broadcast opened with a huge American flag fluttering in the breeze in a bright blue sky. Then the camera moved back to reveal that the flag flew in front of a huge warehouse with a two-story cross affixed to the front. Organ music swelled, and the words "Blessing Time with the Reverend Jewell G. Newby of the Church of Cosmic Unity" appeared on the screen.

Now the camera was inside the church. A tall, distinguished-looking man stood in front of a flag-draped podium. He looked nothing like Truman's idea of a television evangelist. For one thing, Jewell Newby was downright boring-looking. No greasy, pomaded patent-leather pompadour, no flashy suits or diamond-studded pinkie rings. With his graying blond hair, conservative white shirt, and blue blazer, the Reverend Newby looked like an IBM sales rep or maybe a CPA.

His voice was pleasant and sincere. Newby read from the Bible, his selections heavy on New Testament readings that reflected his "gospel of prosperity."

That's what he called it too. "Jesus wants you to be happy. He wants us to be blessed," Reverend Newby said. "Doesn't the Lord tell us in the book of Leviticus that 'you shall inherit the land of milk and honey'?"

After an uplifting hymn Truman didn't recognize, Newby read aloud from letters written by faithful viewers, numbering and detailing the many blessings the Lord had showered upon them since their conversion to the Church of Cosmic Unity. The tape ended with a brief but fervent appeal for funds "to continue the Lord's work."

"He's not so bad," Cheryl mused. "I mean, at least he doesn't pretend he can heal everything from cancer to postnasal drip by slapping somebody on the forehead. All in all, I thought he was pretty low-key. What about you, Dad?"

Truman shrugged. "There's a woman with the Texas Department of Revenue sniffing around, looking into Newby. I want to talk to her. Find out if Reverend Newby has been playing games with church money. And frankly, I don't give a good goddamn for somebody who's selling a line to old folks living on a fixed income."

He stood up and went into the kitchen, with Cheryl tagging along behind. Truman opened a drawer. "Where's your screwdriver? I'll fix the porch light before I leave. I'm meeting Jackleen at the dog track at two."

Cheryl's face colored slightly. "Oh, Dad, thanks. Don't worry about it. Bobby fixed it yesterday. It works fine now."

"Bobby says he's gonna take me for a ride in his police car sometime," Chip said. "And I can push the siren button and talk on his radio."

"He said maybe," Cheryl said gently. "Maybe."

The phone rang.

She picked it up. "Dad? It's for you. Ollie Zorn."

CHAPTER

TWENTY-NINE

"**Y**OU SEE THIS?" OLLIE ASKED, HIS VOICE RISING in indignation. "See what they've done to Pearl? They're trying to scare us into leaving. And that's not all. Last night someone beat up Cookie Jeffcote. Damn near killed her. I'm the one found her. Thought I'd have a heart attack. Now they're attacking us in our own rooms. I'm calling the cops and then I'm calling that TV station again. This church outfit wants to kill us."

"Calm down," Truman said, looking around the room, trying to make some sense of the confusion. "Tell me what happened."

"She won't go to the hospital," Dotty Milas said, shaking her head in disapproval. "You talk to her, Truman."

He sat gingerly on the edge of the bed. "Pearl?"

Pearl Wisnewski's face was shockingly battered, bruises around both eyes, her lip was cut and swollen, and her neck was ringed with more bruises.

"What in God's name happened?" Truman asked.

Pearl managed to open one eye. "Someone knocked on the door. They . . . hurt me. Wanted something. A disk?"

The room had been ransacked. Dresser drawers lay on

the floor, their contents strewn about; the closet door was ajar, with clothes tossed everywhere; pictures had been smashed on the floor.

"Who was it?" Truman asked, bending down close to Pearl. "Did you see who did this to you?"

"A man," Pearl whispered. "Had a hat pulled down over his face. He kept shaking me, hitting me. I told him I didn't have a disk."

"We were supposed to go to church together," Dotty volunteered. "She must have thought it was me knocking."

"Did you see the guy?" Truman asked.

"No," Dotty said, clearly disappointed. "Well, maybe just the back of him as he opened the door to the stairwell. He wore navy-blue pants and a shirt the same color. That's really all I saw."

Dotty brushed a lock of hair back from Pearl's forehead. "She was on the bed here, trying to pick up the phone when I came in. Poor soul. Truman, tell her she needs to go to the hospital."

Pearl shook her head slightly. "I'm all right," she said, her voice barely audible. "Just need rest. Maybe some aspirin."

Truman took her hand. It was cool to the touch, and the pulse in her thin wrist seemed weak.

He picked up the telephone and dialed 911. "No more arguing," he said firmly. "You're going to the hospital."

Dotty Milas rode in the ambulance with Pearl. Ollie decided to ride in the car with Truman.

"Something's going on here," Ollie said. "You should have seen Cookie Jeffcote last night. I tell ya, I thought the girl was dead. Blood everywhere, broken glass. And now why would anybody want to beat up someone like Pearl? They didn't even take anything." He eyed Truman suspiciously. "What's this about a disk?"

Truman bit his lip. If word got out about the computer disk, the cops would want to know why he hadn't come to them with it.

"Some crazy rumor about a computer disk," he said finally. "I don't really understand it myself. Supposed to be hush-hush."

"Come on," Ollie said scornfully. "Waddya take me for? What's going on, TK?"

"I'm not sure yet," Truman said. "But I may know something by tonight or maybe tomorrow. It has to do with that girl that got killed. Rosie Figueroa. It's just a theory. Nothing I can talk about yet."

"You'll tell me as soon as you know something? I'll keep my mouth shut, TK."

"Right," Truman said.

Cookie Jeffcote gingerly touched the bandage that covered the back of her head. Even the lightest pressure from her fingertips sent waves of pain radiating through her head. Her face was swollen, her eyes caked with the remains of smeared mascara.

The Reverend Jewell Newby smiled tenderly down at her, took one of her hands, and squeezed ever so gently. "You gave us all quite a fright," he said softly. "Feeling any better now?"

She touched her head again and hot tears began spilling from her eyes.

"They cut my hair. Those bitches cut my hair."

Jewell Newby frowned. "You're alive, Cookie. Surely that's all that matters. The Lord delivered you from a certain death."

She fixed him with a cold stare.

"You let them cut my hair, you bastard. Why'd you let them cut my hair?"

The events of the previous night were still hazy. She remembered Michael showing up unexpectedly, and then the next thing she knew, the masked men were forcing their way into the condo and beating her with that shotgun. Her head hurt like hell, still.

When she woke up the midget was standing over her,

screaming and screaming and screaming, wild-eyed with terror. It was Ollie Zorn.

"*Oh my God!*" he kept screaming. "*Oh my God!*"

She remembered ambulance sirens. Someone was leaning into her face, talking about a concussion. And then this big, butch-looking nurse had taken a pair of shears and lopped off her hair.

They sedated Cookie after she swung and connected to the nurse's chin, screaming she'd kill the bitch. And when she woke up her glorious red hair was gone, her scalp shaved clean as a baby's butt.

"I'll never forgive you for this," she said, glaring at Newby.

"Me?" Newby looked befuddled. "I came as soon as the hospital called. Why, there's a prayer chain working for you right now."

"Fuck your prayer chain!" Cookie hissed.

"I'll call the nurse. I think your pills must be wearing off."

Cookie reached out and grabbed him by the cuff of his shirt. "Listen to me, you asshole. This is all your fault. You told me to shut Zorn up. I tried to shut him up. It was supposed to look like a robbery gone bad. Now we've got real trouble. And if you think I'm taking the fall for this thing, Rev, you better think twice."

He froze. "What the fuck are you talking about?"

So she told him. She told him what she knew about his real estate schemes, and about Michael, and exactly what she wanted.

When he was gone, she got up and hobbled to the door to lock it. Her right hip was bruised and sore as hell. She picked up the phone and dialed. It rang six, seven, eight times.

"You moron," she said. "You killed the wrong guy."

Butch Goolsby did not wait to hear the rest of her invective. He knew most of it by heart anyway. He pushed the disconnect button. Then he yanked the cord out of the wall jack and crawled back into bed.

CHAPTER

THIRTY

TRUMAN PUSHED HIS AAA AUTO CLUB SENIOR citizen discount card through the slot in the cashier's window.

The cashier was young and Oriental, with an easy smile. "Sir? We don't take discount cards. Sorry."

Truman feigned surprise. "Really? I used it just last Sunday; supposed to be a dollar off on Sundays, on account of no live races."

The girl glanced around, looking for someone to consult. But hers was the only ticket window open.

"You're sure?" she said in a voice that said she wasn't.

"Positive," Truman said, pushing six quarters through the slot.

The girl gave him his card and a token, and Truman went through the turnstile, feeling a bit better about the day.

The doctors at the hospital had said Pearl would be okay. The cops were interviewing her when Truman left.

"I'll stay with her," Dotty Milas insisted. "You go on."

Someone had attacked Cookie Jeffcote in her home and Pearl in her room at the hotel. Maybe Ollie was right.

Maybe someone at the church was trying to force them all out.

He was leaning against a wall, considering the possibilities.

"Sir?" A female employee dressed in red blazer, black slacks, and a white shirt stood at his elbow, frowning. She had a track ID pinned to her left breast. "I'll have to ask you to come with me."

"I just—"

He did a double take. The "employee" was Jackleen Canaday.

"I'll be damned," he said, looking her up and down. "I could have sworn you were track security. Where did you steal that getup?"

"The word is borrowed. My cousin Twyla? She works at a dry cleaners. Seeing that woman yesterday gave me the idea. So you think it looks okay?"

"I was ready to surrender. How'd you get the track ID card?"

"Easy. There's a check-cashing place, over near that liquor store down the street? They got a photo booth and a laminating machine in there. I just made a picture ID and typed the word *security* real big on it. Been faking IDs since I was in junior high."

"You misspelled 'security.'"

She put a hand over the badge. "I'm not planning on letting anybody else get close enough to my boobs to read it. Let's get going."

He told her the news about Pearl and Cookie Jeffcote as they went down the ramp toward the mainline and betting windows.

"That's awful," she gasped. "Somebody knows we're getting close to that computer disk, Mr. K. We gotta find it before anybody else gets hurt."

It wasn't nearly as crowded today, a fact that made them both nervous. "You're sure I look real?" Jackie repeated.

"Act real and you'll be real," Truman said. "Let's see if Marion is here today. Maybe she could try the key for us."

One of the cashiers told them Marion had Sundays off. "Okay," Jackie said. "Where do you suppose the employee lockers are?"

"Turn around," Truman said quietly. "Walk quickly, down toward the beer stand over there."

"Why?" Jackie said, but she was moving as she talked.

"Because a real security guard was giving you the once-over," Truman said. "And he was staring right at your chest."

They stood in a cluster of thirsty customers for a tension-filled moment, saying nothing, willing the crowd to keep them camouflaged.

"Okay," Truman said finally. "He's gone. There's a door, over by the instant teller machines, marked 'Employees Only.' Try that one."

Jackleen took a deep breath. She squared her shoulders and walked briskly toward the door. And briskly back to Truman's side.

"Chicken out?"

"Gimme the key," she said. "You ever see some of the places I snuck into when I was a kid? Shoot. This is a piece of cake."

This time she opened the door and went through it. Truman stood in front of one of the television sets and tried to act interested in what was being broadcast—harness racing from a track at Palm Beach. Every few seconds he glanced over at the door.

He'd been watching for five minutes when he saw one of the female tellers at one of the betting windows approach the door, open it, and go in. Truman felt his pulse quicken.

Two minutes passed. Finally Jackie emerged. Truman caught her eye. She shook her head, then motioned for him to follow her.

She was walking rapidly up the stairs toward the second level when Truman caught up with her. "No good," she said. "The key fit in the lockers, but it wouldn't turn."

"So we're on the right track," he said. "But in the wrong place."

"I had an awful thought," Jackie told him. "What if she put it in one of the men's lockers?"

"I guess if you can play dress-up, so can I. Where do you want to try next?"

"The Derby Club," she said.

They caught the elevator up to the Derby Club. A hostess was stationed near the door. She asked if they wanted a table for lunch.

"Uh, no," Truman said. "We'll just sit at the bar, thanks."

When they were out of earshot of the hostess, Jackie whispered, "I see an unmarked door over there, near the kitchen. I'll check it out, and if that doesn't work, I'll go back in the kitchen."

"Don't take so long this time," Truman said. "My nerves aren't what they used to be."

"Get a drink. Watch the races on TV. I'll be right back."

Truman sat down at the bar and ordered a beer. "You like horses?" The bartender was standing in front of him, polishing glasses.

"Nah. I just like to get out of the house. How about you?"

"They're okay," the bartender said. He was short, nearly bald, with four or five springy wisps of black hair protruding from his scalp. "What I really like is jai alai."

"No kidding," Truman said. "I never went to jai alai. Years ago, when I first moved down here, somebody told me it was rigged."

"Used to be it was rigged. Now they got all kinds of state guys watchdoggin' it. I tend bar over there at the Tampa fronton, during their season."

"Good money?" Truman asked idly.

"Not bad," the bartender was saying. "A different class of people over there, those Cubans, you know what I'm saying?"

Truman had no idea what he was saying, but he nodded gamely.

"And then there's them damned Canadians. Come down here in October with a hundred-dollar bill and a clean shirt and never change neither one all winter long."

"Hah, hah," Truman laughed. The bartender rambled on, stopping every so often to fill a drink order for one of the waitresses, in between times regaling Truman with stories about ignorant jai alai fans who didn't know jackshit and couldn't talk English.

Truman had drained his glass and was considering fleeing to the men's room to escape when he saw a familiar streak of red moving toward the elevator doors. Jackleen turned and flashed him a hundred-watt grin. He hurried over to her side.

"I got it," she whispered. "I got the disk."

CHAPTER

THIRTY-ONE

MEL WISNEWSKI LAY ON HIS SIDE IN THE BED, a thin blue cotton blanket pulled up to his chin. His eyes were tightly shut.

There was a nurse in the room. Bustling around, talking to him, calling him by his name, as though she knew him.

"We'll get this straightened out and you'll feel better," the nurse was saying. She opened the cupboard and rifled through the clothes.

He tried to tell her "Go away." But he knew he was mumbling.

The nurse was thin and blond, not one of the nice black nurses whose thighs made a rubbing noise when they walked and who sometimes came and sat by the bed and talked softly with him.

She was jerking clothes off the hangers, throwing them on the floor. Not straightening things at all. Then she moved to the dresser. The noise was so loud. He opened one eye and peeked. She took his clean socks and underpants and pajamas and dumped them out on the floor and pawed through them. Mel was embarrassed. He did not want this woman touching his things.

She did the same thing with all the other drawers in the dresser and then she attacked his nightstand, spilling a glass of water.

Mel moved his mouth to tell her to go away, to leave him alone.

She shook him by the shoulder. "Mel!" she said sharply. "Pay attention, Mel. Did you take something from Rosie? A disk?"

Mel squeezed his eyes shut tight.

"Look at me, Mel," she said angrily. "I'm talking to you. Where did you put it? A disk? A little square of plastic. Did you hide it?"

Her nails dug into his shoulder blades, cutting the paper-thin skin. "Where is it, dammit?" she said, her breath hot in his ear. "We'll hurt your wife. Is that what you want?"

A single tear ran down his cheek, followed by another. He shook uncontrollably. "Go away," he tried to say. "Leave me alone."

Now she was pinching his ear, squeezing, he felt it would pop like a grape.

"I want that disk, Mel," she hissed. "And if you don't give it to me, I'll hurt you. Hurt you bad."

There was a knock at the door then and the rattling sound of bottles on metal. "Mr. Wisnewski," a cheerful voice called. "Are you dressed? Can I come in?" It was the nurse who brought him Jell-O.

The bad woman sucked in her breath. He opened his eyes just a crack. She moved quickly toward the door, pushing it open, hard. Then she was gone, and he was crying. His ear hurt. Where was Pearl?

Cookie rattled the door so hard the whole trailer shook. "Let me in, Butch. I know you're in there, you lowlife scumbag maggot."

A woman riding by on an adult tricycle stopped pedaling and watched, open-mouthed.

Cookie took off one of her spike heels and hammered at the glass panel. "I'll break the goddamned glass," she screamed.

The woman gasped and started pedaling again.

Cookie whirled around and looked for another weapon. The yard of the trailer was weed-strewn, with dirt ruts. A long-abandoned tire swing hung from the branch of a pine tree, the only tree in the whole lousy trailer park as far as Cookie could see.

She stepped off the crude wooden landing and scooped up an armful of pinecones from under the tree, dumping them on the landing in front of the door. She got out a small gold cigarette lighter.

"I'm gonna set this goddamned cheese box on fire," she hollered. "I'll smoke you out if I have to, you sorry son of a bitch."

She was bent over, holding the lighter to one of the pinecones, when she heard the door being unlatched. Cookie kicked the pinecones aside and threw open the doors.

The inside of the trailer was dark and rank-smelling. After her eyes adjusted to the dim she saw Butch. He sat at a plywood dinette table. A cigarette burned in the ashtray. He was unshaven, his thinning dark hair uncombed. He was dressed in a pair of grayed-out white Jockey shorts and an equally dingy pair of sweat socks. He squinted in the half-light. And he held a .45 aimed at Cookie's chest.

"Shut the door," he said quietly. "The light hurts my eyes."

She pulled the door closed but didn't take her eyes off the gun.

"I want my money back," she said, her voice level.

He picked up the cigarette and inhaled deeply, coughing on the exhale. "What money?"

"The money you stole from me last night, you bastard. The money you took off Michael. There must have been at least five thousand. Give it back. Or I'll go to the cops."

"And tell them what?" Butch said, coughing.

He'd quit smoking months ago, but the first thing he'd reached for when he was finally ambulatory this morning was a cigarette. He'd found a half-pack of Kools in a jacket pocket. They tasted like roach droppings. He'd smoked them all, one after the other, saving just this one for the moment he'd been expecting.

"So. Michael's dead?"

"You could say that."

Cookie thought about things. Her discussion with Newby had been brief but profitable. They would be partners, in a business sense only. Maybe, she thought, he would be willing to deal with Butch.

"Give me back the jewelry," she said finally. "You can keep the money. But I want the jewelry back. It's no good to you. You can't pawn it for anywhere near what it's worth."

"Probably not," he agreed again.

"Just my Rolex and the diamond ring then. Please?"

She edged a half-step closer.

"Ah-ah-ah," Butch said, waving the pistol. "Mother, may I?"

"Give me the ring and the watch, Butch. Give them back and I swear to God I'll never say a word about what happened last night. So far the cops just think it was an assault and robbery."

Butch laughed. "You ain't sayin nothin' to nobody, Cookie. Where's the murder weapon? Better yet, where's the body?"

"You dumb-ass," Cookie said. "You'll get caught. You always do. The cops will find the body and the gun. Face it, Butch. You're a screwup. And you know what else? Michael was connected. Yeah, big-time connected, with the Gianni family. Sallie Gee's boys are gonna come for you. And if they don't catch you, the cops will."

Butch stubbed the cigarette out in the ashtray and yawned. "Wanna fuck?"

She turned on her heel and stalked out, one hand holding onto the wig.

"Is that a no?" he called after her.

* * *

"Hurry up," Truman said, gripping the back of Cheryl's chair. "Can't you make it go any faster?"

Cheryl Kicklighter swiveled around in her chair to face her father. "Calm down, Dad," she said. "The computer has to run an anti-virus program. It takes a minute or two."

Her voice echoed weirdly in the empty classroom. Cheryl didn't own her own computer. But she did have the key to the media lab at Bay Point Elementary School, where she taught.

"You mean computers get sick?"

"People plant deliberate problems in programs sometimes. It screws everything up," Cheryl explained. "The anti-virus program tracks them down if they're there."

She punched some buttons and the screen began to fill with a grid full of names and numbers. "It's some kind of chart," she said. "Is that what you were looking for?"

Jackie leaned closer to get a better look. She pointed to a line on the chart. "This is it, Mr. K. See this name, Kinda Kinky? I remember it ran the night we went to the track with Mel."

Truman followed her finger down the chart. "Looks like some kind of numerical ranking is assigned under different categories, but they're abbreviated. I can't make heads or tails of it." He felt let down.

"It's numbered," Jackie pointed out. "This is the first race. Are there other races on here too?"

Cheryl tapped another key. "I'll scroll down."

The next race appeared on screen, eight dogs, each one ranked one to five in six indecipherable columns. Cheryl tapped the button, held it down, and the screen scrolled through fourteen charts. The last four charts were incomplete.

"Fourteen charts, fourteen races," Jackleen said. "This is what Rosie Figueroa got killed over."

"And this is what put Mel Wisnewski in jail, and in that pisshole of a nursing home," Truman said bitterly.

"And Miss Pearl in the hospital," Jackleen added.

"But these charts are only good for those specific dogs that ran on that one night," Cheryl said. "Why would someone break into Pearl's room, beat her up like that, to get a program that predicts race results that are more than a week old?"

"For the charts themselves, the program, the system, whatever you call it," Truman said. "Somebody's convinced this thing is important enough to kill for."

"Somebody like Rosie's boyfriend, that Wade guy," Jackleen said. "Or that blond woman, the one who was following him around."

Cheryl knit her brow and chewed her bottom lip. "Dad, don't you think you'd better turn this disk over to the police?"

"Not yet," Truman said stubbornly. "I want to see how it works."

"What?" Jackie said. "I thought we were just gonna get it and give it to the cops."

"The chart and the ranking system," Truman said. "They're standard from what I can tell. All we need is somebody to help us fill in the blanks. Somebody who knows greyhounds, knows how to handicap 'em. That's what we need."

"To do what?" Jackleen demanded.

"To try it out. You said it yourself, it must be good if these guys were willing to kill to get it. All I want is one shot; one shot to see if it works. A day at the races. Then we'll turn it over to the cops."

"You're crazy," Jackie said.

But she was already calculating how much cash she could round up. How much was in the tip jar she kept in her bedroom closet? A hundred, maybe more?

CHAPTER

THIRTY-TWO

THE FOUNTAIN OF YOUTH WAS A BATTLEFIELD under siege. Workmen battered the old plaster walls of the lobby with sledgehammers, spewing the fine white dust everywhere. In the corner, behind the reception desk, an electrician on his knees snaked coil from a new receptacle box toward the desk, where a telephone lineman waged war with the receptionist.

"Dr. Mandelbaum promised me," she said. "He promised he would never touch my switchboard."

The lineman set his metal toolbox on the floor with a loud thud. "Listen, lady," he said. "I got a work order right here. It says we put in a new BelTron 2000 system, call waiting, auto answer, auto dial, you name it. That thing you got is a dinosaur. It goes."

Tammi and Wade picked their way gingerly through the debris in the lobby and into the coffee shop, where the campaign had yet to advance.

They took a table close to the door and ordered coffee and cherry pie from a thin, horse-faced girl with a ponytail and thick ankles.

"The old guy's not here," Tammi said after searching

the room. "I saw him at the nursing home, when he went to visit his buddy. He's skinny, maybe five-six, got funny-looking red hair."

"Is that the girl?" Wade asked in a low voice, nodding toward the back of their departing waitress.

"No," Tammi said, her eyes sweeping the coffee shop, looking for the young woman who'd accompanied Truman to the track. She spied Jackleen coming through the swinging doors of the kitchen, a pot of coffee in her hand.

"That's her," she said, lowering her head. "Don't stare."

Wade averted his eyes. For the next thirty minutes the two of them sipped coffee and nibbled pie and watched while Jackie buzzed about from table to table, most of them filled with elderly women.

"Let's go," Tammi said finally. "We can come back around six. They've missed the matinee. If they're going at all, it will be tonight."

"You've got the charts?' Jackleen asked anxiously. "You're sure?"

Truman patted the pocket of his tan windbreaker. "Right in here. How much money did you bring?"

Jackleen gulped. "One hundred and sixty dollars. All my tip money, plus a little bit I had stashed away for some new work shoes."

He looked around to see who might be listening in. Only half a dozen people were scattered about in the lounge. They'd gotten to the track early, claimed a seat in the fourth-floor lounge, and ordered beers.

"Four hundred bucks," he whispered. "My rent money."

"No!" Jackie said, her face registering her alarm. "You can't be gambling your rent money, Mr. K. What happens if we lose?"

He shrugged. "You've seen what they're doing to the hotel. These church bums could throw us out in the street any minute if they want to."

Truman opened the race program and laid it out on the table next to one of Rosie's charts.

The program print was tiny, nearly illegible. He ran his fingers across the columns in it. "Look," he said, jabbing his finger at a line of print. "This is for finishes: how many times the dog has finished in the money. The computer chart has something labeled F, maybe that's what it stands for."

Jackie leaned over and stared at Rosie's chart. "This all might as well be a foreign language. Martian, maybe. I just don't see how you can decide what dog can win based on all these numbers."

Truman was looking idly around the room, waiting for Jackie to calm down. A woman entered the lounge, sat down at the bar, and started chatting with the bartender. Her auburn hair shone in the dim light.

"Maybe she does bring luck," Truman said.

"Who?"

"Rosie's friend. Marion."

She was sipping a glass of iced tea and smoking a cigarette. The blond bartender was the same one Truman remembered from the last time.

He sat down beside her. "Remember me?"

She narrowed her eyes. "Oh yeah. Dick Tracy. You still looking for clues?"

"We found one," Truman said. "But we could use some help. Could I interest you in a business proposition?"

"It's my night off," she said, shrugging.

She brought the iced tea and the ashtray to the table. Jackie smiled brightly at her and gave her the charts.

"Well, well. Rosie's sysem." Marion ran a practiced finger down the columns of the first chart. "Looks good." She read in silence for a moment, turning the pages, studying the grids.

"Rosie knew breeding," she said, taking a puff of her cigarette. "She weights the charts that way. She knew the trainers and kennel people too."

"We don't know how to fill in the blanks on the charts," Jackie said meekly.

"I do," Marion said.

Her pencil flew over the stack of papers, scratching out numbers, adding and subtracting for differing variables. A cloud of smoke hung over the table. "Too bad we don't have a laptop," she said, not looking up from her calculations. "My math's lousy."

At one point she chuckled softly to herself. "Old Rosie liked the big black dog, all right."

"What's that?" Jackie asked.

"Breeding theory. Mostly only old-timers believed in it, but Rosie could be old-fashioned like that. The idea was, a male black dog has an edge over other dogs. Especially a big one. Black dogs are dominant, so the theory goes, and more likely to be lead dog in the pack. In a race, the other dogs will get out of the way and let the lead dog run."

Jackleen's eyes widened. "For real?"

"That's what some people think. Rosie thought so."

Truman picked up his program and looked at the listings for the first race. "Here's one, Smoochie Boy, black, male, weighs seventy-seven pounds. What's the chart say?"

Marion studied her notes. "That's the eight dog? Just using the basics of her system, I'd say the eight dog's good at least to place."

She did some quick calculations. "Quinella box seven-eight-three. You're gonna play the daily double, right?"

"What's that?" Jackie asked.

"That's where you pick the winners in the first and second races and you bet both before the first race," Truman said.

"There's a dog in the second race, Cavalier Cad, number seven, charts out good, according to Rosie, and it's a long shot too, eight to one odds. Let's do a seven-one-three box," Marion suggested.

Truman raised an eyebrow. "You sure?"

Earlier he had brushed aside Jackie's worries about risking too much. Now when it came time to put his money down, he felt a rush of misgiving.

"It's Rosie's call," Marion said, shrugging.

The tourist wore baggy white jeans that hung from his hips and a loud flowered shirt. He walked casually by Truman's table, then quickly back to a table in the corner.

"They got it," he announced.

Tammi pushed her sunglasses down on her nose. "You sure?"

"They're my charts," he said. "The ones we did for the first night. They had to have the disk to print them out. They've got my fuckin' charts," he said with gritted teeth.

"Shut up," Tammi said. "Look—the old guy's going up to make his bets. Get in line behind him, see what he bets. Bet the same."

"I thought we were gonna get the disk away from him," Wade complained. "It's mine. I want it back. The Festival of States race is this Saturday. It's the biggest betting pool of the season. I gotta have it by then. Besides, they got the charts, but they don't mean a thing unless you're a handicapper. Rosie used her own codes. No way a couple of neophytes like those two know what they're doing. Besides, I got my own picks."

"You really are an idiot, you know that, Wade? See that woman there with them? She must be telling them how it works."

"That Marion? So what?" Wade said indignantly. "She sells tickets. That's all. They're my charts."

"Forget it," Tammi said, getting up. "I'll do it myself."

She arrived at the betting window just in time to see Truman collect his tickets and walk off.

Tammi took the glasses off and smiled engagingly at the cashier.

"I'll bet what that gentleman who just left bet."

The cashier shook his head. "Can't do it," he said. "Against the rules."

She pushed a ten-dollar bill across the counter toward him. "It'll be our secret."

The cashier took his thumb and forefinger and flicked the bill back at her. It fluttered in the air and landed on the floor at her feet.

"You have a bet to make?" he asked. "I've got customers waiting."

Tammi gave him a venomous look. "I'll remember you."

"You do that," he replied.

She stepped away from the window and looked around in time to see Wade walking away from another ticket seller. The bell announcing post time rang before she could call out to him.

Wade was pouring himself another beer from the pitcher when she got to the table. Betting slips poked out from the breast pocket of the shirt. She felt herself fill with sudden, white-hot rage.

"Next time I tell you to do something, you do it," she said savagely. "Or you won't have to worry about Butch and Curtis. Because I'll personally take care of you."

He took a long gulp of beer. "Okay. No big deal."

Another bell rang. The lead-outs put the greyhounds in their starting boxes and scrambled off the track. The mechanical rabbit went whizzing by and seconds later the dogs burst from the start in a flash of color and noise.

Tammi wasn't watching the dogs. She was watching the three figures at the table across the room.

"Look at Smoochie Boy," Marion said. "Did you see the way he exploded from that turn?"

Truman's eyes were glued to the track, and to the big black lead dog. He'd bet the 7-8-3 as she'd suggested. He and Jackleen had decided to pool their funds, with Truman matching her hundred and sixty dollars.

"Put the rest of that rent money away," Jackleen

begged. "If they bounce you out of the Fountain of Youth, you ain't coming to stay with me."

At the betting window he'd put twenty-four dollars of their money on each of the first two races, and then, he'd pulled a crisp twenty-dollar bill from his hip pocket and bet an 8–7 perfecta.

Now the dogs were coming down the straightaway. Truman's concentration wavered for a moment. The eight dog had led the whole way, with the three dog, Who's Voodoo, in a white blanket, only inches behind, on the inside rail. Truman was looking for the seven dog. Where was the green and white blanket?

"Bayou Gal," Jackie screamed, pumping the air with her fist and hopping up and down.

"Is that the seven?" Truman asked.

"Right there," Marion said, pointing. "She came out slow, but she's gaining, see her coming up on the outside?"

Truman looked where she pointed. Bayou Gal, a sleek brindle female, was inching her way up the pack. But there were still two more dogs between her and Who's Voodoo.

"Watch her," Marion said. "Look what she's doing." With only yards to go before the finish, Bayou Gal poured on the speed, moved inside and, at the last possible moment, thrust her neck forward in a desperate rush to the finish.

"My God," Truman said, stunned. "We won."

He looked up at the tote board to be sure. The lighted numbers blanked out for a moment, then flickered on again. Win eight. Place seven. Show three.

Marion smiled serenely. "Not bad."

Truman looked around for Jackleen. She had her head down on the table with her hands covering her ears. He reached over and pried the hands away. "It's all over," he said gravely.

"It is?" Her face fell

"We won," Truman shouted. "By God, we won."

Jackleen looked from Truman, to Marion, to the tote board.

"*We won!*" she screeched.

Truman looked at the tote board. "We won two hundred and eight dollars," he said, grabbing Jackleen's arm. "See that?"

"Good old Rosie," Marion said.

The lead-outs brought eight more dogs onto the track to parade past the crowd.

"What are our numbers?" Jackie asked. "I want to see what our dogs look like."

Marion put on a pair of bifocals and started working the charts again. "Can somebody get me another iced tea?"

They developed a routine. Each race Truman made the bets while Jackie went for more iced tea and beer. During the race, Jackie kept her eyes shut. They put their winnings in an empty potato chip basket in the middle of the table.

"Don't tell me how much we've won," Jackie begged. "I can't stand it."

Truman pointed to the overflowing basket. "Would have been more if that damned K's Infidel had come out of the box like he was supposed to in the sixth."

Marion looked guilty. "We only missed the seventh by a hair. If it hadn't been for the photo finish, we would have cleaned up. And I don't know what happened to Palooka Joe in the ninth."

She stole a quick look at her watch. "Sorry, folks," she sighed. "I've got to go. My mother takes her medicine at ten and she forgets if I'm not there."

"We better go too," Truman said. "Quit while we're ahead."

Jackie looked disappointed. "All right," she said.

Truman counted the money, putting it in three stacks. He pushed one stack toward Marion.

"Poor old Rosie," Marion said, smiling sadly. "She was never this lucky when she was alive." Her eyes met Truman's. "What will you do with the computer disk?"

"Give it to the cops," Truman said. "This was a one-shot deal."

"Too bad," Marion said. "Saturday is the Festival of States race."

"That's a good one?" Jackleen asked.

"Biggest program of the year," Marion said. "It's a stakes race, so all the winningest dogs of the year race that night. The best dogs bring out the big bettors and big crowds. The more people bet, the more money you can win."

"Mr. K?" Jackie said when Marion was gone. "How much?"

"Our share? Roughly six thousand dollars."

"Oh my God," Jackleen said. "Oh my God."

Tammi stood up and looked down at Wade with a look of pure loathing. He was slumped over on the table, glassy-eyed and mournful.

"Let's go get the disk," he mumbled. "Gimme the gun."

"Shut up," Tammi said. By her own reckoning, the old man and his friends had cleared at least a couple thousand. Halfway through the night, when it was clear just how useless Wade was, she'd made up her mind about a plan of action.

"I'm out of here," she announced.

"Hey," Wade protested. "Wait for me."

She took a dollar bill from her purse and slapped it down on the table. "Take the bus."

CHAPTER

THIRTY-THREE

JACKLEEN OPENED HER EYES, YAWNED, AND SHIFTED in her seat. She looked out the window at the passing scenery. The streetlights flickered off. Six-thirty and it was still nearly pitch dark outside.

Mama had taken the car today. She had to get to work at Publix by 4 A.M. to start baking pies, and Jackie didn't like her having to walk to the bus stop alone so early in the morning.

Her stop was coming up. She yanked the bell cord and stood up. The bus heaved to a stop, shuddered once, and the pneumatic doors flung open.

Jackie picked up her tote bag and stepped off the bus.

The street was quiet, deserted. Stores on this block wouldn't be open for two more hours yet. She shifted her tote bag to her right hand and started walking the half block to the hotel.

Someone grabbed her, rudely, from behind. An arm clasped tight around her neck, so tight it lifted her off her feet. She tried to scream, tried to kick, but now she was being dragged off the street, into the alley.

The alley was dark and smelled of urine and rotted

garbage. She was choking, gasping for breath. Her attacker's free hand roamed over her, touching her pockets, now ripping at her tote bag.

For a moment the pressure around her neck relaxed a bit. She tucked her chin forward and sank her teeth into the big hairy forearm.

She bit down until she tasted warm salty blood.

Her attacker screamed in pain, but kept yanking at her arm, the one holding the tote bag. She let go of it suddenly and her attacker released his hold on her for a second.

It was all the time she needed. She whirled around and saw him for the first time. He was tall, maybe six-three, white, clean-shaven with brownish hair and an arm that was now dripping blood. Jackie moved closer and he grabbed her around the neck again. She jerked her knee upward with all the force she could muster, into his crotch.

He howled in agony. She took off running and didn't look back until she was inside the lobby of the hotel.

Out of breath, she collapsed into an armchair to try to catch her breath. She was still sitting there, trying to collect her wits, when Mr. Wiggins, the dining room manager, came looking for her.

"There are three tables full on your station," he said, in that snippy tone of voice he had. "Are you planning on joining us today?"

"I was mugged," Jackie gasped. "Just now. A block from here. A man grabbed me as I was getting off the bus. He dragged me into an alley."

Mr. Wiggins raised one eyebrow. "You weren't hurt?"

"No," she said, shivering. "Just scared."

"Good," Mr. Wiggins said. "I suggest you get to your station then. You can call the police and report the attack after the last seating."

He hurried away. The thug who'd attacked her hadn't hurt her, but Jackie was hoping he'd have some stitches in his arm to remind him of her. He had her tote bag, but not her wallet, which was at home.

Then it struck her. Her shoes. Her eighty-five-dollar,

brand-spanking-new white work shoes that she'd bought with her racetrack money. She looked down at the broken-down loafers she'd worn on the bus. "Shit."

Truman finished his deep knee bends and looked at the clock on his bedside table. Only 7 A.M. The sky outside was still plum-colored and streaked with pink and yellow. He opened his window and stuck out his head, and looked way, way off to the right, so that he could see the glimmer of Tampa Bay in the distance. There was a slight chop on the water this morning.

Beautiful day coming, he thought with satisfaction.

He knelt down on the floor and slipped his hand down in the space between the wall and the radiator, bringing out a brown envelope. The disk was still there and so was most of the money. He took out a twenty and wedged the envelope back into its hiding place.

It made him uneasy, keeping the cash in his room like this, but he didn't feel right about putting it in the bank yet, either. He didn't plan on keeping the money for long, anyway. They'd decided yesterday: one more trip to the track, to try to win enough money for the down payment on his unit. The Festival of States race.

He put on a sweater, locked his door, and headed downstairs.

Ollie had just finished unlocking the pull-down door at the newsstand when Truman strolled up.

"Pearl's coming home this morning," Ollie announced, pushing a box of HavaTampas across the counter. "The doctor put her on some new blood pressure medicine. Haven't seen you around lately."

Truman pushed the cheap cigars away. "No thanks. Let me have a box of those Cubana Selectas, will you?"

Ollie had to stand up on his stool to reach the shelf where he kept the expensive stock. "They're twelve dollars a box," he said, raising his eyebrows.

"I know," Truman said. He selected a *Sports Illustrated*

and plunked it facedown on the counter, adding a package of razor blades, a pack of gum, and a ladies' magazine. The gum was for Mel, the magazine for Pearl.

"Swimsuit edition, eh?" Ollie said coyly.

"Good story in there about spring training," Truman said.

He collected his change and started for the door. He wanted to stroll around the block, smoke one of those cigars before breakfast.

"You hit the lottery?" Ollie asked. "Sure are throwing money around good all of a sudden."

"Got four numbers right this week," Truman lied. "Decided to treat myself."

"Thought you and me were gonna have a talk," Ollie said, leaning over the counter, getting right up in Truman's face. "Thought you were gonna tell me about that computer thing."

Truman felt his face flushing. "Computer thing?" He glanced down at his watch. "I've got to be going. I'm making some phone calls, a little research on the Church of Cosmic Unity. I'll look you up this afternoon. All right?"

He hurried for the door.

The last thought that entered his mind was this: Have to be more careful.

A second later he heard a loud bang, accompanied by a metallic grinding noise. Turning, he was confronted with a blur of shiny black paint and a gleaming chrome bumper. The bumper nicked his thigh. Truman leapt sideways, slamming up against a brick storefront.

He turned to scream at the driver, but all he saw was a flash of blond hair as the car fishtailed back off the sidewalk and onto the street, taillights glowing in the dawn shadows.

Ollie was on the sidewalk now, breathless with excitement. "Jesus Christ, Truman," he said. "An inch closer and that crazy broad woulda mowed you right down. You okay?"

Truman looked down at his leg. His slacks were ripped

on the left knee where the bumper had grazed him, and there was a sharp stinging. A dark stain was spreading on the fabric. His right shoulder hurt, too, from where he'd banged up against the brick storefront.

"Did you get the license number?"

Ollie looked shamefaced. "Geez, I'm sorry. It was all so fast."

"Never mind," Truman said. "I'm all right. Shook up a little, that's all."

"Goddamn crazy women drivers," Ollie said, shaking his fist at nothing in particular. "They'll kill us all. You wanna go back in the stand while I call the cops?"

"Cops? What for? There's nothing they can do. I'll see you later, Ollie."

He limped off down the street.

CHAPTER

THIRTY-FOUR

TRUMAN UNLOCKED THE DOOR AND WENT INTO his room.

"What the—?"

His neat-as-a-pin, everything-in-its-place room looked as if it had been hit by a whirlwind.

He shut his eyes and leaned against the doorjamb. He was drenched in sweat, exhausted. His knee was throbbing.

He limped over to the radiator and slipped his hand down in the space in back of it. The envelope was there. The cash and disk were still inside. He took the disk out, then put the envelope with the cash back in its hiding place. Was it worth it? he wondered. Maybe it was time to call the cops.

He hefted the mattress back onto the boxspring, grunting at the effort, and sank down on the bed. The phone rang.

"Mr. Truman Kicklighter?" The voice was a woman's, faint over the long-distance lines.

"You'll have to speak up," Truman said irritably.

"Can you hear me now?" She was almost shouting.

"I'm not deaf," he said. "You can tone it down a little."

"Sorry," she said. "Listen, my name is Leda Aristozobal. I live in Austin, Texas—"

"And you're interested in Jewell Newby and the Church of Cosmic Unity," Truman said, sitting up now. "How the hell did you find me? I've been meaning to call you."

She laughed. "I called the newspaper in Scottsdale to get them to send me photocopies of their files on Newby and the woman mentioned that she'd talked to you. Um, she was under the impression you worked for the *St. Petersburg Times*. But I called there and they said they didn't have a reporter by that name."

"I lied," Truman said briskly. "That a problem for you?"

She chuckled. Her voice was deep, faintly accented. "I admire tenaciousness. Maybe we could help each other."

"You work for the Texas Department of Revenue, that right?"

"That's right," she said.

"You folks know your Reverend Newby's church bought the hotel I live in here in St. Pete, don't you?"

"I figured he was up to something there," Ms. Aristozobal said. "Let me guess. They're converting it to condominium units. Right?"

"The Fountain of Youth Residential Hotel," Truman said. "That's the name of it. It's no Ritz, but it's cheap and it's comfortable and there's quite a few of us here who're going to be out of a home if Newby's condo scheme works."

"I'm sorry about that," she said.

"What kind of tricks has he been up to out there in Texas?"

"Same kind of thing," Ms. Aristozobal said. "He bought a small apartment complex here in Austin, over near the University of Texas campus. He kicked out the tenants, mostly students and older people, and converted it to condos for—quote—church members."

"Is that illegal?" Truman asked.

"Not in and of itself," she admitted. "But the way

Reverend Newby conducts his church business raises some interesting questions about his church's tax-exempt status."

"Oh?"

"He's since bought a shopping center and a little restaurant near campus," Ms. Aristozobal told him. "Quite an empire he's building. And, you know, the State of Texas wouldn't mind collecting taxes on some of that. If we can prove it's a profit-making enterprise he's running rather than a bona fide religious organization."

"Don't know if there's much I can tell you," Truman said. "I don't know anything about the church itself. I know nobody's tried to recruit us to join."

"You're not rich enough," she said. "I was sort of hoping . . . Oh well," she said briskly, "I wish you luck."

"Hold on now," Truman said. "Can't you give us some ammunition to keep him out of our hotel?"

"Like what?"

"I don't know," Truman said, feeling hopeless. "They've already started knocking down walls and messing stuff up. The lobby looks like a demolition derby. We've had some crime too. A neighbor was attacked in her room this week. Guy just walked right in the hotel."

"He's already starting with the nuisance stuff, huh?"

"Nuisance stuff?"

"Construction. People bothering and harassing tenants. It's a game he plays—a game designed to make the tenants give up and vacate before they're legally obligated to do so," she said.

"Can we do anything to stop it?" Truman asked.

"Depends on how good your lawyer is," she said. "Your tenant group has hired a lawyer to fight it, haven't they?"

"There was some talk about that," Truman said. "Tell you the truth, I've been kind of preoccupied, don't know if they did or not."

"I can't give you any advice myself," Ms. Aristozobal said. "It would be a conflict of interest. But if I *were* to give you some advice, it would be to check out those church services. And have your attorney contact your state's real estate commission or revenue office. See if Newby's meeting all Florida's regulations for tax-exempt status."

"I'll do that," he said gratefully. "Thanks a lot, Ms. Aristozobal."

"For what?" she asked. "I didn't give you any advice."

Curtis was taking inventory, counting cans of motor oil and air filters and alternator belts and singing some moronic song about an achy-breaky heart. Butch was sitting with his feet up on his desk, watching the five o'clock news.

"Hey," Butch said suddenly. "Shut up. Listen to this."

The news anchor had on her "this is serious, folks" look.

"And in Treasure Island," she said, "authorities from the State Environmental Protection Division said they are holding a barge containing fish waste from the Mayhall Seafood Company.

"Authorities seized the barge last Monday, with an estimated three tons of rotting fish waste aboard, charging that Mayhall was illegally dumping waste in the Gulf of Mexico.

"The barge has been tied up at a Florida Marine Patrol dock at Treasure Island since last week. Residents of the area have complained about the stench, but the state says the barge is evidence."

"You hear that?" Butch was on his feet, highly agitated. A vein in his forehead was bulging. "You hear what they're saying?"

Curtis sniffed. "I don't smell nothing."

Butch sat back down and buried his head in his hands. "It ain't just mullet heads rotting on that scow down there, boy. They got a dead Mafia guy buried in there with all those fish guts too."

"You mean . . . the place where we dropped the you-know-what?"

His father nodded. Then he stood up and got the truck

keys. "Let's go," he said resignedly. "We gotta go take a look at that Florida Marine Patrol dock, see what's what."

It took Truman two hours to get his room back to some semblance of order.

He finally decided to take a break. He'd just lain down on the white chenille bedspread and closed his eyes when the whine of an electric drill started up, right outside his door.

He got up and opened the door. A workman stood on a ladder, fiddling with one of the ceiling fixtures in the hallway.

"Do you mind?" Truman said irritably. "People around here like to take a rest in the afternoon."

"Too bad," the worker said, applying his drill to the fixture's cover. "I got a work order."

Truman slammed his door. He thought of the conversation he'd had with Leda Aristozobal. "Nuisance stuff," she called it.

Now he was fighting mad. He dialed the AP bureau number in Tampa.

"Gibby? Truman Kicklighter here. Listen, remember that talk we had about the outfit that's trying to take over my hotel?"

"Hotel?" Frank Gibhart sounded vague, distracted. "Oh, yeah. That preacher. Sure. You let me know if anything comes of that. Okay?"

"Something is coming of it," Truman said. "I just talked to a woman who works for the Texas Department of Revenue. This guy's got a whole empire going. Wants to make our hotel a link in the chain. And he's pulling dirty tricks now. Deliberately harassing people. Letting security go to pot. We've had two break-ins just this week."

"I'll look into it, Truman," Gibhart said. "Call you next week."

Truman was left looking at the phone in his hand. The brush-off. He knew it well. Had given it to well-meaning pests hundreds of times over the years. "We'll look into it." Hell.

He went to the sink in his bathroom, washed his face, and wet a comb before applying it to his hair.

It was Wednesday night. He'd seen a flyer posted in the lobby advertising services for the Church of Cosmic Unity at the old Rialto Theater at Seventh and Central. He had a sudden hankering for religion.

CHAPTER

THIRTY-FIVE

THE OLD GLASS-ENCLOSED BOX OFFICE THAT stood in the black-and-white-tiled lobby of the Rialto was empty, the glass shattered by what looked like a BB. A faded and torn Coming Attraction poster showed Julie Andrews romping through an Austrian meadow.

The lobby was jammed. It was an odd crowd for any-place except St. Petersburg. Nobody looked to be any younger than sixty. As usual, men were a strict minority. It was a blue-hair, white-shoe, walker-and-wheelchair crowd. Truman decided that even in St. Pete he had never seen such a collection of the aged and infirm.

People were filing slowly into the auditorium, taking programs from a woman dressed in a white blouse and red skirt.

Others were milling around a table that held a scale model of something that looked suspiciously like the Fountain of Youth Retirement Hotel.

But this building had pale gray stucco on the outside and a tasteful carved plaque proclaiming it to be Jerusalem House. A diagram showed where the clinic, the pharmacy, and the "assisted care living area" would be. A photograph of a unit showed cozy living/dining room combinations, galley kitchens, and bedrooms with sitting rooms. A far cry from Truman's spartan bedroom/bath.

The only young person Truman saw in the room stood beside the display, hands clasped in front of him, a wooden smile on his lips.

The man held out a hand as Truman approached. "Hello! I'm Reverend Newby's son, Jewell Jr. But everybody calls me Jim. Get it, Little Jewell, Gem?"

Truman peered at the model. "Some operation you've got here."

"Every inch of it will be first-class all the way," Jim said. He picked up a light gray folder from a stack on the table. "Would you like to see our prospectus?"

"I'd love to," Truman said. He opened the folder and looked at the contents. There was a letter from Newby, a glowing description of the project, floor plans, and letters of endorsement from residents of Newby's other "senior environments" in Scottsdale and San Antonio.

"No price list?"

Jim frowned. "Reverend Newby likes to discuss financial matters with prospective residents on a one-to-one basis," he explained.

One of the "hostesses" stepped into the lobby. Overhead lights flickered on and off. "Services are beginning," she called.

Jim gestured toward the auditorium. "Will you be joining the service, Brother . . . ?"

"Kicklighter," Truman said. "I'm looking forward to it."

The house lights had already been dimmed. Truman found his way to a seat on the left side, squeezing past two plump women who had stationed themselves on the aisle, leaving the inner part of the row empty. Now he remembered why he'd quit going to church.

A banner was pinned to the faded red velvet curtains on the stage. In bold red script it said "JESUS LOVES YOU—YES HE DOES!"

From the back of the theater, a tape was switched on. It

was a tinny recording of a gospel choir singing "Amazing Grace."

Audience members struggled to their feet. They were singing lustily, clapping their hands, faces alight with joy.

A shaft of light emitting from the projection room broke the darkness. Truman turned around in time to see the Reverend Jewell Newby bound through the lobby doors. He strode down the center aisle of the auditorium, stopping to shake hands, pat someone on the back, lean over and kiss the occasional wheelchair occupant, like the patriarch at a giant family reunion.

The recording looped back and started again and everyone stayed there, standing and singing and clapping their hands raw until the Reverend Newby clambered onto the stage.

Now the music faded and a single blue spotlight picked out the spiritual leader of the Church of Cosmic Unity.

Since it was a midweek service, Newby had opted for a casual "folksy" look, crisply pressed khaki slacks and a short-sleeved plaid sport shirt. A thick gold watch gleamed on his wrist.

The blue light made Newby's thick wavy hair look like platinum, his teeth like pure white marble. He was, Truman thought, perfect for this old theater and this particular audience. He was a matinee idol.

Someone came out on stage and clipped a tiny body mike to the collar of Newby's shirt. He looked out at the lambs in his flock and gave them a dazzling smile.

"Are you ready for *bless*ings?" he asked.

"*Yes!*" the crowd called back.

"Are you ready for a message of *un*conditional love?" he asked.

"*Yes!*" the lambs answered.

"Good," Newby said, bowing his head and closing his eyes. "Now let us pray for the prosperity our Heavenly Father so wants us to have a share in."

After the prayer Newby launched into a heartfelt sermon that started with the biblical tale of the prodigal son.

"'How could I not kill the fatted calf?' the father asks the jealous older son. 'For he was lost and he is found. He was dead, but now he is alive.'

"And the message," Newby emphasized, "is *love*. *Un*conditional *love*. Our father's *un*conditional *love*. And the love he *commands* us to have for one another.

"You," Newby said, stretching his hands out to the audience, pointing here and there in the crowd. "You are the church family. You, Emma Rauscher, you, Hattie Mae Squires, you, Harry Ballard, you, Caroline Crouch, you are family. You matter. You are not alone. Jesus loves you. *We* love you."

Now Jewell Newby was joined onstage by Jewell Jr., who took a pointer and waved it at a five-foot-high chart. The words "Jerusalem House" were at the top of the chart. There were columns for "Gold Plan" and "Silver Plan" and "Platinum Plan" and "Apostles." Each column was marked in gradients and none was below the halfway mark.

Jim Newby held the pointer under the Apostle column.

"We have a new apostle tonight," he said, beaming. "Let's have Sister Jeannette Boynton stand up for a love offering."

A tall, elegantly coiffed woman in the front row stood slowly and gave a brief, queenly wave before sitting back down. The crowd stood, clapping and cheering, for a long time.

Truman recognized the name Boynton, if not Jeannette Boynton. The Boyntons were an old Pinellas County pioneer family. Founders of banks, hospitals, and a fortune that, from what he'd read, grew larger every year. He didn't know what Jewell Newby's apostle plan entailed, but he was willing to bet the price didn't come cheap.

Fifteen more minutes were spent giving love offerings to half a dozen members who'd signed up for various plans, although no other apostles were recognized.

Then Newby's face grew grave. Miss Cookie Jeffcote, the church's "vice president for marketing" had been the victim of an unfortunate accident. He urged the audience to remember her in their prayers, as he did every night and morning.

Vice president, Truman thought. Cookie had gotten a promotion.

There were more announcements. A free bus trip to Sea World would leave the church on Friday. Sign-up sheets were available in the lobby for the church shuttle bus to take church members to the doctor's office, grocery, or drugstore. And everyone was invited to the covered-dish supper Friday night at Reverend Newby's home.

Then another tinny recording began, this one of "What a Friend We Have in Jesus." Father and son Newby waved to the crowd, then disappeared behind the curtains.

The lights came on again and Truman saw that the old movie house was filled with excited chatter, laughter, a general feeling of shared community. Jewell Newby, Truman thought, had pulled the old water and wine stunt. He'd taken a roomful of strangers, the elderly, the infirm, the isolated, and made them feel unique. Special. Of course there was a price for that. But Newby's lambs were obviously eager and willing to make their own love offerings.

The walk back to the hotel was uneventful. But for every five steps he took, Truman looked back over his shoulder, searching for a blonde in a black sports car.

CHAPTER

THIRTY-SIX

"**M**RS. SKINNER? ANNETTE SOWERS SKINNER?"

"This is Carl Skinner. Her husband. I'll get Annette."

Truman waited for what was surely five minutes. Long distance to Albuquerque, New Mexico.

"Hello?" A woman's voice. "Who's calling, please?"

"Truman Kicklighter here," he said. "I'm a reporter for the *St. Petersburg Times*. I'm working on a story about Jewell Newby."

A grim laugh. "Newby, huh? He kill some rich old lady down there?"

"What?" Truman said, startled.

"He killed my mother," Annette Sowers Skinner said. "For the money. The land. You knew about that, right?"

"I knew your mother deeded the land over to him," Truman said. "But no charges were ever brought against him. Isn't that correct?"

"We couldn't prove anything. But up until that last year, Mama was healthy as a horse. Mean as a snake, too. We never knew anything was wrong until they called to tell us she had died."

"What were the circumstances of her death?" Truman asked.

"Circumstances? There were no circumstances. Newby said he was at her house, having Bible study with her, and she keeled over. By the time we got to Scottsdale, all we had of our mother was her ashes."

"He never notified you of her death?"

There was a pause. "We aren't what you'd call a close family, Mr. Kicklighter. My parents were divorced years ago, and Dad got custody of the kids. Mother's job was her family."

"And she'd had no health problems that you knew of?"

"Not until Newby got his hooks into her," Annette Skinner said.

Everybody in St. Petersburg knew that the Boynton family was represented by the city's oldest blue-blooded law firm, McGowan & Young. Old man McGowan and old man Boynton had partnered up in lucrative land deals back in the twenties, and McGowan & Young's offices took up two floors of the Boynton building.

The receptionist at McGowan & Young was reluctant to let Truman talk to Jock McGowan.

"Tell him it's about Jeannette Boynton giving her inheritance to a church that meets in an old movie theater," Truman suggested. A minute later the secretary rang him through.

"Mr. Kicklighter?" Jock McGowan's voice was louder than necessary. "What's this about Jeannette Boynton?"

"You ever hear of an outfit called the Church of Cosmic Unity?" Truman asked.

"No," McGowan said. "Should I have?"

"If I were you I'd look them up," Truman said. "Since Jeannette Boynton pledged her share of the Boynton estate to them this week."

"What's that?" McGowan said sharply.

"Write this down," Truman said. "The Reverend Jewell

Newby. If anything happens to Jeannette, you'll be signing over a lot of Boynton family assets to that joker."

"What's your interest in this, Mr. Kickligher?" McGowan asked.

"Newby's church bought the hotel I live in. The Fountain of Youth. Plans to turn it into some luxury retirement home for his church members. I'm a journalist," Truman said. "Did a little checking and I found out Reverend Newby has a history. His flock runs to a particular kind of sheep, one that's easy to fleece, old, lonely, and wealthy. That's how he likes 'em."

Truman gave McGowan Annette Sowers Skinner's phone number, and Leda Aristozobal's number too.

"We'll look into it immediately," McGowan promised. "Just between the two of us, Mr. Kicklighter, I'm the executor of Benson Boynton's estate, and I've been concerned about Jeannette for some time now. She's always been the odd duck of the family. Never married. Been living alone in that old wreck of a mansion for years. She'd be ripe picking for any kind of charlatan who happened along. I'm grateful for the information, Mr. Kicklighter. Mighty grateful."

By the time he'd finished with his phone calls, Truman had begun to feel a glimmer of hope. He sat back on his bed to enjoy the newspaper he'd been too busy to read earlier in the day.

When the phone rang, he jumped for it.

"Dad?" Cheryl Kicklighter's voice was quavery.

"What is it? What's wrong?"

"Did you pick Chip up after school today?"

"No. Didn't he come home?"

Now Cheryl was crying, gasping for breath. "Called his friends . . . the neighbors. Dad, he's not anywhere. Could you come over here?"

"I'm on my way," Truman said. "He probably just stopped to play. You know how little boys are. Did you try the park?"

"Hurry, please," Cheryl begged.

Together they drove every possible route from the school to the house. They checked the park, empty lots, convenience stores, then cruised the streets of the neighborhood, Cheryl calling the boy's name again and again until she was hoarse and dry-eyed from crying.

"I'm calling the police," Truman told her.

"He's only ten," he told the dispatcher. "And it'll be dark soon, and it's not like him to worry his mother like this."

The patrol cars cruised the neighborhood again, calling Chip's name over a loudspeaker. Officers fanned out, knocking on doors.

Neighbors came out of their houses and stood in their neat yards, looking over at Cheryl's own neat yard, with the football next to the front door and the red bicycle lying on its side near the garage.

When the call came, the voice was low, indistinct. "We have the boy. We want the computer disk. Leave the cops out of it. We'll call again with directions." There was a click and then the dial tone.

Truman wanted to throw up. "Cheryl?"

She came hurriedly into the kitchen. "Was that the phone? News about Chipper?"

"He's been kidnapped," Truman said, taking his only daughter in his arms. "It's all my fault."

When he finished telling her the whole long story, it was dark out. She turned on every light in the house and made another pot of coffee. Neither of them could eat.

Someone was knocking at the door. Cheryl went to answer it.

It was Bobby Roberts, still dressed in his white and green uniform.

"I was out on a traffic call," he said, taking Cheryl's hand in his. "I came as soon as I heard it on the radio. Is there anything I can do?"

Cheryl looked at Truman questioningly. He shook his head ever so slightly.

"He'll be all right," Bobby was telling Cheryl, still holding her hand. "Kids that age wander away all the time. Especially boys. It's dark now, he'll probably come running in for supper any minute."

"No," Cheryl said slowly, still not believing it herself. "He's been kidnapped. Somebody has my son."

"It's true," Truman said dully. "They just called. They have Chip."

There was another knock on the door, and this time it was the patrol officers. Truman told them about the call and one of the officers called headquarters. "There's a detective on the way," he told Cheryl.

Within ten minutes the detective, a short, round-faced man named Matt Carmichael, was sitting in the living room with them.

Truman repeated the whole story, leaving out only one detail, the part about how he and Jackleen used the disk to win six thousand dollars.

"We were afraid to tell the police," Truman said lamely. "I guess we were naive to think we could find out who really killed Rosie."

Cheryl had been standing with her back to them, staring out the window into the darkness. She turned around.

"When they call back, tell them we'll give them the disk. The disk, money, whatever they want. I just want my son."

Truman looked stricken. "I don't have the disk."

Carmichael sighed. "Where is it?"

"I decided things were getting dangerous," Truman said. "I put it in an envelope and mailed it."

"*Mailed it where?*" Cheryl shrieked. "My God, Dad."

"I sent it to Ollie at the newsstand," Truman said. "Nobody would think of looking for it there."

"When did you do this?" Carmichael asked.

"Tuesday," Truman said. "Day before yesterday. Tomorrow's Friday. It ought to be there by then."

The telephone rang. Cheryl looked panicky. "What if it's them?"

"Let your dad pick it up," Carmichael said. "Try to keep them on the line."

Truman dashed into the kitchen, followed by the others.

"Hello," he said, slightly out of breath.

"Have you got the disk?" It was the same voice as before.

"No, not right now," Truman said. "I'll have it tomorrow."

"You don't get the kid till we get the disk," the voice said. It was impossible to tell whether the caller was a male or female.

"I don't have it," Truman said. "I mailed it someplace. To keep it safe. It won't be delivered until tomorrow."

"Get it or the kid dies," the caller said. "We'll be in touch."

At some point during the night a police electronics expert arrived and hooked up call-tracing equipment to the phones.

Neighbors came and went with sandwiches and casseroles and loving words and anxious expressions.

Carmichael left briefly, and when he returned he was accompanied by a tall, thin black man named Kenyon. He was an FBI agent. Truman never did catch his first name. He told Kenyon his story, told him about the blonde and the man who grabbed Jackie and the one who'd assaulted Pearl and how someone had searched Mel's room at the nursing home.

Carmichael was dispatched to pick up Jackleen.

Jackie looked miserable as she recounted the story. She kept glancing at Cheryl. "I'm so sorry," she told her. "So sorry." Truman gave her a warning glance; she left out the part about the money.

"It doesn't matter," Cheryl said. "I just want my boy."

By midnight, they were all numb with fear and exhaustion.

Bobby Roberts left reluctantly, promising to return the next day after his shift. Carmichael took Jackie back home.

Kenyon stayed in the kitchen where he could be close to the phone. Cheryl insisted on sleeping in Chip's bed. Truman lay down on the living room sofa, vowing to stay awake until the kidnappers called again.

When he awoke at dawn the numbness had worn off. He looked in the mirror in the bathroom and saw someone he didn't recognize. An old man. Useless, defeated. He'd intended to shave and shower. Instead he dressed and dragged himself into the kitchen.

Kenyon and Cheryl sat at the table drinking coffee. The morning newspaper lay on the table between them.

"It's in the paper," Cheryl said.

MISSING BOY FEARED KIDNAP VICTIM the headline said. There was a color photo of Chip. The story had most of the details right. Except for the motive. "Police refused to divulge the kidnapper's demands," the story said, noting that Chip's mother was a divorced schoolteacher and that his grandfather was a retired reporter.

"A polite way of saying we're too poor to pay a ransom," Truman said.

They moved through the morning like sleepwalkers.

By daylight, a knot of people had gathered on the street in front of the house. Cars drove by slowly. There were reporters and photographers, mobile satellite vans from the television stations.

At eleven, Carmichael got a telephone call and left, saying he'd be back. He returned with a familiar-looking manila envelope.

"Picked this up at the main post office," he explained.

Gingerly Truman took the envelope and opened it. The seal had already been broken. He looked up, surprised.

"We made copies of the disk," Carmichael said. "Kept the original for evidence. It's identical in every way to the original."

"We'll hand this over to the kidnappers and they'll let Chip go?" Truman asked.

The men looked at each other and shrugged. "Maybe," Kenyon said. "They're calling the shots. It's up to them.

When they let us know about the pickup, we'll start planning. We'll get the boy back."

"When they call," Carmichael reminded Truman, "ask to speak to Chip. Ask how he is. And make sure they tell you exactly where the pickup is to be. Get them to repeat it if you can."

"It's been in all the papers. All over the news," Cheryl pointed out. "Won't they know the police are involved?"

"Yeah," Carmichael said. "But do it anyway."

Each time the phone rang that morning, they all jumped nervously. Each time Cheryl got the caller off the line as fast as possible.

At 11:25 the kidnappers called. Truman picked up the phone.

"Listen up," the caller said. "Tomorrow, 11 A.M. You stand on the northeast corner of Beach Drive and Third Avenue. Alone. No cops. You'll hear from us. Got that?"

Truman was scribbling furiously. "Wait. I want to talk to Chip."

"He's asleep." There was nothing else except the dial tone.

"Is he okay?" Cheryl asked. "Did you talk to him?"

Truman rubbed his eyes with his fists. "I'm sorry," he said. "They said he was asleep, then they hung up."

Kenyon took off the headset that had been plugged into the kitchen phone so he could listen in. He picked up the phone the police had installed the night before and dialed a number.

"Get anything?" Kenyon asked the person doing the tracing. He listened for a moment, then hung up.

"That's what I was afraid of," he said. "All that static on the line. The call came from a cellular phone."

"What's that mean?" Truman asked.

"One of those portable phones, like the ones housewives carry in their purses and drug dealers carry in their cars," Carmichael said.

"Can't they trace calls from one of the those?"

"Not if it's stolen," Kenyon said. "And this one was."

"Tell me what they said," Cheryl demanded.

"The pickup is set for 11 A.M. tomorrow at the northeast corner of Beach Drive and Third Avenue," Kenyon said.

"Tomorrow? Christ!" Carmichael said disgustedly.

"What?" Cheryl asked anxiously. "What's wrong?"

"The Festival of States parade is tomorrow," Carmichael said.

"Oh my God," Cheryl said. "I'd forgotten about the parade."

"You wouldn't if you were a cop," Carmichael said grimly. "Starting at 10 A.M. that corner is right on the parade route. There'll be almost four hundred thousand people lined up shoulder to shoulder along Beach Drive. Streets will be blocked off, every cop in town has traffic detail."

"Northeast corner of Beach and Third," Truman repeated, trying to picture it. "That's Little St. Mary's."

"A church?" Kenyon asked.

Carmichael cracked a smile. It was the first one anybody had seen in the house in nearly twenty-four hours.

"It's a bathroom," Carmichael explained. "Sixty years ago this builder had a beef with St. Mary's Church. You know, the big redbrick one on Fourth Street South? Something about unpaid bills. I heard they stiffed the guy. So a few years later he's hired to build restrooms for the city right there at Beach Drive at the foot of the Municipal Pier. He builds the most beautiful civic outhouse you ever saw—an exact miniature of the church."

"You're kidding," Kenyon said. "I've never seen it and I've been here for two years now."

"You'll see it tomorrow," Carmichael promised. "Up close and personal."

CHAPTER

THIRTY-SEVEN

IT HAD BEEN YEARS SINCE TRUMAN HAD SEEN A
Festival of States parade. When Cheryl was a kid, he and
Nellie went every year. They sat on the same corner every
year, outside Mastry's Bar and Grill, ate the same ham
sandwiches, and cheered for the same beauty queens. They
loved the bands and elaborate floats—but Cheryl always
covered her ears when the Hernando de Soto Festival float
came into view, bristling with savage buccaneers and a live,
booming cannon.

Today they were on a different corner, but Cheryl was
with him, clutching his hand as tightly as she had when she
was eight. The corner was thronged with people; they'd
had to jostle their way through the mob, even at 8 A.M., to
claim a spot on the curb.

"Dad, I'm scared," Cheryl confessed. Her hand in his
was sweaty, or was it his hand? It was ten-forty-five, almost
two hours into the parade. Dark clouds had threatened rain
around nine, but mercifully the clouds scudded off to the
west and the sun burned its way through the morning
mists. Now it beat down mercilessly, eighty-seven degrees
already.

Truman squeezed Cheryl's hand. "It'll be all right, honey. We've got company, remember?"

Standing right next to them, wearing a sunbonnet and loud plaid shorts, was a female police detective named Mindy. There were more plainclothes detectives lurking around inside and outside Little St. Mary's. Across the street, wearing a fishing vest and carrying a long-lens 35mm camera and a press badge, was Matt Carmichael.

Kenyon, the FBI man, had passed by twice, pushing a shopping cart loaded with stuffed animals, bags of cotton candy, and helium-filled balloons.

There were still more cops stationed up and down the parade route. "Oh," Cheryl said, glancing to her right. "Don't look, Dad, but Bobby's right there."

"Where?" Truman asked, glancing around.

"I told you not to look," she chided him. "He's standing on the curb. He's got on a white baseball cap and he's carrying binoculars."

"Look," Truman said, pointing up the street. "Here comes the Shriner units. Remember how much you used to love their funny cars and all the clowns?" Under his breath he muttered, "I see him now."

Cheryl snorted. "As I recall, you were the one who was so enthralled by those silly Shriners. You used to threaten Mama that you'd join the Shriners just so you could drive one of those go-carts."

"Hey, Dad," Cheryl said, nodding slightly to their left. "Didn't you say Jackleen was supposed to work today?"

Truman turned and saw Jackie standing half a block down, staring intently at the passing unit, which consisted of eight old rattletrap Model A pickup trucks loaded with members of a hillbilly band. The cars bucked and snorted, backfired and spewed black smoke all over the street, drawing screams of laughter from the crowd.

"She was supposed to work, but I knew she'd be down here," Truman said. "She feels as bad as I do about the whole thing."

"It's five of," Cheryl said, glancing down at her watch.

"I can't take this. I really can't. Do you think they'll bring Chip with them?"

"They might," he said. Secretly he figured if the kidnappers made good on their promise, they would leave Chip somewhere else. A parade with four hundred thousand witnesses was just too risky.

"Think about something else, honey. Hey. You know, we've never brought Chip down to this parade, have we?"

"Not since he was a baby," Cheryl said sadly.

"Next year, what say we do it? Bring him down to Mastry's, sit on the curb together?"

"I'll make the ham sandwiches," Cheryl said, attempting a smile.

They heard a sudden roar then and the hillbilly unit gave way to a battalion of motorcycle-riding Shriners. The riders wore jeweled red fezzes, red jackets, and rode the biggest, loudest Harley-Davidsons Truman had ever seen. Slowly, they rode in and out of fancy formations—stars, interlocking circles, pinwheels.

From out of nowhere three dozen red-wigged clowns on mopeds swarmed the street. The clowns buzzed in and out of the motorcycle formations like small, annoying gnats, riding inches away from the powerful Harleys, then veering away only seconds before a collision. The street filled with the thick white smoke from the motorcycles' exhausts.

Next the clowns launched an assault on the crowds lining the streets, careening toward a throng and screeching to a heart-stopping halt right at the curb, pitching handfuls of candy and phony foil doubloons, causing adults and children to spill onto the pavement to grab for the treats.

Truman bent down to pick up a piece of candy at his feet.

"The disk, man, gimme the disk." A moped-riding clown sped up alongside Truman, so close he could see the cracks in the clown's white pancake makeup.

He heard Cheryl gasp, and without thinking he held out the disk. A moment later the clown disappeared into the smoke-filled street, joining three dozen other identical clowns on wheels.

Truman turned to the plainclothes detective beside him, but she was gone, running into the street, trying to get closer to the clown unit.

Carmichael, across the street, had seen the exchange take place through the long lens of his camera. He was sprinting along the other side of the street, trying vainly to keep up with the unit, which was moving in a ragged formation rapidly down the block.

Now Kenyon came running past, his shopping cart abandoned.

"Where's Chip?" Cheryl cried, her voice cracking. "Where is he?"

Bobby Roberts rushed over. "What happened?" he asked. "I couldn't see anything. One of those Harleys nearly mowed me down."

"A clown. On a moped," Truman said, craning his neck to see up the street. "He took the disk. Carmichael and Kenyon are following them."

By now the motorcycle unit was a distant hum. The parade finish line was two blocks down the street.

Two police motorcycle units roared down the street past Truman and Cheryl, sirens blaring, lights flashing.

"I'm going to see if they need any help," Bobby said, dashing off.

Cheryl buried her head in Truman's shoulder. "What happens now?" she asked.

They had agreed to meet under the banyan trees in Bayboro Park, near the parade finish line, by no later than eleven-thirty. They had to fight their way through throngs of people, packing up to leave.

The streets were clogged with traffic, all of it at a standstill. Uniformed traffic cops tried vainly to unsnarl the mess, and frustrated motorists sat in their unmoving cars, honking horns out of boredom.

Carmichael was standing under the banyan tree, gulping water from a cup when they arrived. His face glowed beet red and his shirt was drenched with sweat.

"We lost him," he said glumly. "Kenyon didn't want us getting too close, afraid we'd spook the guy. We followed that clown unit all the way to the finish line, right down by the Yacht Basin. You know how many guys they got dressed in those clown outfits? Forty-two."

"Lost him?" Cheryl said incredulously. "What does that mean?"

"We did find the guy who owned the moped, locked in one of those motorcycle trailers," Carmichael said. "Guy nearly died of heat prostration too. It must have been over one hundred fifteen degrees in there."

"Did he see who stole the moped?"

"Nah," Carmichael said. "Those guys have been up, drinking beer, partying, since 7 A.M. Our guy went behind his trailer to take a leak, somebody hit him on the head. Next thing he knows, he's in his skivvies, minus his costume, locked inside the trailer."

Kenyon walked up now, mopping his own sweat-streaked face with a handkerchief. "We found the moped," he reported. "It was abandoned behind a construction trailer a few blocks from here. They're processing it now for prints."

"The clown wore white gloves," Truman said.

"Figures," Kenyon said. He put his hand on Truman's shoulder. "We need to get you and your daughter back to her house. They've got what they want now. They know that the longer they keep Chip, the riskier it is that they'll get caught."

Cheryl's face was pale, drained of emotion. "They'll call now, right, Mr. Kenyon? To tell us where Chip is?"

"Hey, Mr. K!" It was Jackleen, jogging toward the group, a tall plastic drink cup in each hand.

"I brought you a drink," she said as she drew closer. "Y'all like blueberry Slu—"

She was almost beside them when her foot caught something and she tripped.

Truman reached out and grabbed her arm to keep her from falling, and twenty ounces of icy blue ooze sloshed down his shirtfront.

"—pees?" Jackleen righted herself and looked at the empty cup, then at Truman. His shirt and trousers were covered with Slurpee. "Oh no," she gasped.

Kenyon handed Truman his handkerchief, and Truman dabbed ineffectively at the mess.

"I'm so sorry," Jackie wailed.

"Look at this," Truman said, annoyed. "This stuff is sticky as hell." He looked at Jackie. "Can you give me a ride back to the hotel so I can change?"

"Sure," she said. "I'm parked in a lot two blocks away, shouldn't take any time to get there."

Kenyon glanced down at his watch. "We'll take you home, Cheryl. They could call at any time. Mr. Kicklighter, should we send someone to the hotel to get you?"

"I'll be right there," Truman promised. "Jackie can bring me."

"Hurry," he said when they were out of earshot of the others.

"I said I was sorry," she said. "Your fault anyway, it was your foot I tripped over."

"We're not going back to the hotel," he said when they were in the car, moving into traffic.

"What?"

"Those cops lost the clown," Truman said. "The kidnappers aren't going to just hand Chip over. I've got an idea."

"What?" she said warily.

"Take me back to that tourist court," Truman told her. "I want to see if Wade's been back there. Maybe he's got Chip."

"You're crazy," she said, but she did as he said.

They parked near the manager's office. "Now what?"

Jackie said. "That guy might have a gun. You think of that?"

Truman scanned the horseshoe-shaped courtyard. On the porch next to the manager's office he saw a familiar face.

"Hey there, D'Antonio," he said, getting out of the car.

The boy looked up from his paperback novel, *Encyclopedia Brown*.

"Y'all the police," D'Antonio said, getting up and coming up to them.

"That's right," Truman said. "Have you been playing James Bond again, D'Antonio?"

The child looked warily around. "Y'all won't tell my auntie?"

Truman and Jackleen promised.

"Wade been back here and now he got a girlfriend," D'Antonio said. "That blond lady, the one with the black car? She come back over here and Wade be with her. They got another white dude with 'em too."

"When was this?" Truman asked eagerly.

The child screwed up his face and thought. "This week. After I saw y'all."

"Did you look in the window?" Truman asked.

The child gave them a conspiratorial grin. "Uh-huh. Wade be typing on that computer, and the others be yelling at him, telling him to hurry up."

"Say, D'Antonio," Truman said. "You haven't seen them with a little boy, have you? A blond-headed little boy?"

"Nah," D'Antonio said. "They ain't been back since then. I been watching too."

Truman's face sagged with disappointment. "All right." He reached in his pocket. He brought out one of his old business cards, scribbled out the office number, and wrote in his number at the hotel. "If you see them again, you call me, okay? It's really important. Can you do that?"

D'Antonio nodded eagerly. Truman took out a five-dollar bill and handed it to the child.

They were in the car, getting ready to leave, when D'Antonio ran up to them. "Hey, mister," he said, showing them the back of his hand, the numbers written there in fading blue ink. "I wrote down that white lady's license plate number, like the crime dog say on TV. You want that?"

He found a pay phone at a convenience store nearby and sent Jackie in with money to buy him a clean T-shirt.

"Gibby?"

"Hey, Truman," Frank Gibhart sounded concerned. "I heard about your grandson. What the hell are you mixed up in over there?"

"Can't talk right now, Gibby," Truman said, glancing down at his watch. "I'm calling in another favor, Gibby. You still got a friend at the Department of Motor Vehicles?" He crossed his fingers.

"Yeah," Gibby said. "I know a guy."

"I need a license plate run," Truman said. "I never needed anything more, Gibby. You understand?"

"It's about Chip, isn't it?" Gibhart said. "TK, this is horseshit. You're not a reporter anymore. You let the cops handle this. Or you'll get yourself and the kid killed."

"The cops already bungled it," Truman said tersely. "You gonna do this for me or not?"

"Give me the tag," Gibby said. "And a number where I can reach you."

Jackie came out of the store with a paper sack. "It's all I could find," she said apologetically.

Truman took out the T-shirt. It was a sleeveless muscle shirt, bright pink. He shrugged, pulled the stained sports shirt off, and put on the muscle shirt. There was a cold can of Coke in the bag, too.

"I thought you might be tired of Slurpee," she said.

He took a pull on the Coke, then got back out of the car and again headed for the pay phone.

By the time the phone rang, he'd finished the Coke.

"Is the car a black '93 Firebird?"

"Something like that," Truman said.

"It's registered to a Tammi Stargell. The address is out on Sunset Beach, 1662 Harrell Avenue. Right off Gulf Boulevard."

"All right," Truman said shakily. "I know where that is. Little dinky houses. I covered a drug bust out there once. Okay. One more favor, Gibby?"

"What the hell," Gibhart said. "You gonna give me an exclusive when this all comes down?"

"Sure," Truman said. "You got a current crisscross directory?"

"Yeah."

"Look up that address for me," Truman said.

He was gone another five minutes.

"House belongs to somebody else," he said. "Owner's name is Mary Ellen Ahlert."

"That neighborhood, the Stargell woman probably rents from her," Truman said. "There a phone number in the crisscross?"

Gibhart gave it to him.

"I owe you, Gibby," Truman said.

"Take care," Gibby said. "Don't be stupid."

Truman dropped a quarter in the slot and dialed the number. It rang three times.

"Hello?" A woman's voice. Truman hung up and raced for the car.

CHAPTER

THIRTY-EIGHT

"I NEED A GUN." TRUMAN SLID INTO THE FRONT seat of the Nova.

"A gun? What you need a gun for?"

"I know where they're keeping Chip. It's that blond woman, the one who tried to kill me. He's out in a house on Sunset Beach."

Jackie signaled and pulled out into traffic. "That's what the police are for, Mr. K. You let them handle this."

Truman gestured to the backed-up traffic at the light just ahead. "I called Cheryl's house. They're not there. Must be stuck in this damned traffic."

Jackie shook her head. "Call the police department. They got other cops."

Truman snapped his fingers. "Ollie. He's got a gun. Keeps it under the cash register. Take a right here."

"This ain't right," Jackie said, but she pulled to a stop in back of the newsstand.

A minute later Truman was back, carrying a newspaper folded in half.

He unfolded the paper and showed her a tiny nickel-plated pistol. "It's only a .22," he said regretfully. "But it's loaded."

"Now what?"

"Sunset Beach," Truman said. "Go out Central Avenue."

She drove for a while. "I could stop at a phone booth. You could call."

Truman's jaw was set. "They let that clown get away. You saw it. No, I got Chip into this, I'll have to get him out."

"Lord." Jackie sighed. "You got a plan?"

"I'm thinking," he said. "Just let me think."

Jackie maneuvered the car through the snarled downtown traffic and Truman laid his head against the back of the seat.

Once they got past downtown, it was a straight shot out Central Avenue toward the beaches.

"Can't you go any faster?" Truman griped.

"Any faster, the transmission might fall out."

They crossed the Central Avenue Causeway, looked out and saw the sailboats skimming along the bay.

"I'd like to learn how to sail," Jackie said dreamily. "When I get rich, I'll have me a sailboat. Sail all over the place, go places in the Caribbean. All that kind of stuff."

"Sailboats go too slow," Truman said. "I want a speedboat."

They were at Treasure Island now. "Turn left here," he said. "Sunset's a couple miles down. We're looking for Harrell Avenue."

"You got that plan worked out?"

"I need to see the place first. Figure out where they're keeping Chip. I don't want him getting hurt."

Sunset Beach was the smallest, cheapest, most laid-back of the Gulf Beach towns. A collection of bars, seafood restaurants, and mom-and-pop motels.

"Slow down," he instructed her. "Here's Harrell, right here."

The houses were run-down, little more than shacks, set close together on tiny sandy lots.

"There's the house. Sixteen sixty-two. Drive on past," he said. Two houses down from the pink concrete-block house there was a For Sale sign in the yard. The front door of the house had a real estate lockbox hanging from it.

"Pull in this driveway right here."

Jackie pulled the Nova into the driveway. "There's a pay phone in front of that Majik Market back on Gulf Boulevard," she said. "Those cops will be at Cheryl's by now. Wondering where you went."

"We'll just look around. Then we'll call the cops. Okay?"

"Now you're talking," Jackie said.

They got out of the car and Truman stuck the .22 into the waistband of his jeans. The backyard of the empty house was a jungle. Overgrown grapefruit and orange trees, oleander bushes, and bougainvillea. Flies buzzed around rotting fruit on the ground. A shaggy hedge of sea grapes ran along the west side of the property.

Truman peered around the hedge. The backyard of the next house over was littered with junk, old cars, washing machines, bicycles, and lawn mowers, all of it layered with rust and festooned with a yellow-flowering vine. The centerpiece of the junk montage was an old motor home that rested on deflated tires, like a kneeling elephant.

Truman and Jackleen tiptoed into the yard, hiding behind the motor home.

"What if somebody's home here?"

"Hush!" Truman whispered.

He peeped around the edge of the motor home. Another sea grape hedge ran along the side of the junk house, but through the leaves Truman could see bits and pieces of the pink house.

It had a concrete-block garage, and from the rear the bumper of a shiny black car poked out. There was a large boat in the yard, a weather-beaten Chris-Craft, maybe twenty-eight feet long, sitting on jury-rigged wooden scaffolding.

In the middle of the yard, stretched out on an aluminum

chaise longue planted in the middle of a plastic wading pool, was the blonde.

She wore a tiny black bikini and her oiled hide gleamed in the sunlight. She was reading a thick paperback novel.

Truman scooted back to the cover of the motor home.

"She's there," he said. "The woman who tried to run me down. Sunbathing. The black car's there too."

He glanced in the direction of the pink house. "Chip's in there. We've got to get him out."

"We got to call the cops is what we got to do," Jackie whispered.

"By the time they get here anything could happen," Truman said. "Look, go over to the house. Ring the doorbell. See if she'll answer it."

"And what if she does? What if that country boy that tried to throttle me is in there?"

"Scream your head off. Run like hell. You're young, you can outrun those two. But I think she's alone."

"You think. What are you gonna be doing?"

"If the girl gets up and goes in the house, I'll go in the back way. Try to surprise her, put the gun on her, make her take me to Chip."

"I don't like it," Jackie said.

"Just try to distract her, that's all. Can you do that?"

"You're gonna get us both killed," Jackie said. But she walked around the front of the house.

Truman took the gun out of his waistband. It fit snugly in the palm of his hand. His sweating, trembling hand.

Five minutes passed. He kept his eyes on Tammi Stargell.

"Excuse me, ma'am?" The voice startled Truman. He peered around the hedge. Jackie was standing in the back-yard. What was she doing?

Tammi Stargell sat up on the chaise longue. She squinted in the bright sunlight, then reached for her sunglasses.

"How'd you get back here? What do you want?"

Jackie flashed a bright, well-meaning smile. "I was looking at that house for sale, the one two doors down. I was wondering, do you know how much it is? It's a cute little house."

Truman stood up straight, poised to sprint into the yard.

"Do I look like a real estate agent?" Tammi snarled. She reached down under the beach towel on the chaise longue and brought out a large black .38. "Where's the old man?"

It was now or never. Truman rushed at her, grabbing for her gun hand. But she was slippery, greasy from the suntan oil. His hand slid right off. She whirled around and chopped the .38 down on his forearm, sending his .22 sailing off into the sand.

She herded them inside the pink house at gunpoint.

"You tried to get cute," she said. "People like you ought to know better than to get cute."

"Where's my grandson?" Truman asked, looking around the kitchen. A box of Trix cereal stood on the counter.

"He's around," Tammi said casually. She picked up an oversized black T-shirt and slipped it over her head, holding the gun aimed at both of them.

They heard the sound of a car pulling into the gravel driveway outside.

Truman glanced out the jalousie window and saw a green-and-white police cruiser roll to a stop inches from the rear bumper of the black car. He tensed, wondering what Tammi would do.

"In there," she said, motioning to a hallway leading from the kitchen. "Quick."

She forced them into a small darkened room. It was a living room, but the only furniture was a sofa, a television, and a stationary exercise bike.

"Over there," she said, pointing with the gun to the sofa. "Now. And not a word out of you."

A car door closed outside. They heard footsteps coming

from the back of the house. The kitchen door opened. More footsteps, slow but steady.

Jackie held her breath, wanting to scream for help, but Tammi's gun was pointed right at her chest.

The footsteps were coming down the hall. Tammi held the gun steady.

"What have we here?" Bobby Roberts, still in his police uniform, stood in the doorway, looking amused.

"Got a little surprise," Tammi said, going over to greet him. She gave him a long, lingering kiss, daring Truman and Jackie to move.

"How long have they been here?"

"Just a few minutes."

Bobby walked over to Truman and looked down at him. "You couldn't stay out of it, could you?"

Truman glared back at him. "I could say the same thing of you."

Tammi laughed. "Did you really think lover boy here had the hots for that daughter of yours?"

"I thought he was one of the good guys. I can see I was wrong."

"Sticks and stones," Bobby said lightly.

"We called the cops before we came out here," Jackie said. "They're on their way. Right now."

"Don't think so," Bobby said. "I've been listening to the scanner. Even called over to Cheryl's house. They're all sitting around waiting for the phone call."

He glanced over at Tammi. "You take a look at the disk? Everything check out okay?"

"Looks fine," Tammi assured him. "Wade baby's been busy all afternoon, filling out the charts. We're all set."

"You take care of him?"

"Oh yeah," Tammi said. "Everything's under control."

Bobby walked into the kitchen and came back with a steak knife and a length of clothesline. While Tammi held the gun, Bobby tied their hands behind their backs.

"Get dressed," he told Tammi. "I'll take care of them."

* * *

"Where's Chip?" Truman asked through clenched teeth.

"I'm taking you to him right now."

Bobby took his service revolver out of his holster. "Out the back door. Nice and slow. No tricks, okay? I'd hate to have to shoot two unarmed civilians in the back, but I will if I have to."

When they were outside, he motioned toward the boat. "Over there. Around on the other side there's a ladder. Slow. Right?"

He made Jackleen climb up first, then Truman, with Bobby following close behind.

It was an old wood-hulled Chris-Craft, probably from the fifties, Truman guessed. There was a cabin. Bobby opened the door and shoved them inside.

It was dark in the cabin, the only light coming from cracks in the wooden hull. The air smelled of mildew and rot. The cabin's fittings had been torn out, leaving just the wooden hull, littered with junk. Curled up on a pile of faded orange life preservers, fast asleep with his knees drawn up to his chest, was Chip.

"What have you done to him?" Truman demanded.

"Cough medicine," Bobby said. "He's okay."

Truman gave Bobby a murderous look. The pleasant face, brown eyes. He couldn't believe his instincts had been so wrong.

"Son," he said. "How'd you get mixed up with a piece of goods like her?"

"Tammi?" Bobby smiled. "I met her on the job. Last year. She got in a little fender bender downtown. I was the officer called to the scene. She's something else, isn't she? Took me aside, made me an offer if I'd fix the accident report to say it was the other guy's fault. I told her I couldn't take her money. That'd be a bribe."

"Lemme guess," Jackie said. "She offered you something sweeter."

Roberts blushed like a schoolboy. "We saw each other a few times. Then this thing at the track came up, we decided to work together. If it had worked out like it was supposed to, nobody would have got hurt. What happened was, some folks got greedy."

"You're not the one who tried to mug me," Jackie said, puzzled. "That other guy was taller."

Roberts laughed. "That was that dumb shit Curtis. Tammi's old boyfriend. Him and his old man were running around, trying to get hold of the disk too. You don't have to worry about those two."

"No," Truman said quietly. "We just need to worry about somebody who'd beat up an old woman, try to run me down with a car, kill a boy, kill us, for money."

"Kill?" Bobby looked mildly surprised. "Hell no. Is that what you thought?"

"You killed Rosie Figueroa, didn't you?"

Bobby's face flushed. "That was Tammi's idea."

"You cut her throat."

"Shut up," Bobby said savagely. "Shut your goddamn mouth."

He shoved Truman and then Jackie to the floor. He took out the rope and used it to bind their ankles tightly together.

"What are you going to do?" Jackie asked quietly.

"Me and Tammi, we're going out to the track, gonna win us the Festival of States race," he said in a conversational tone. "It's up to two hundred thousand dollars, you know? Should be enough to get us to South America. We got the computer program. They love gambling down there. Especially horse racing. We'll be rolling in it."

"What about us?" Truman asked.

Bobby stood up and surveyed his handiwork. "You? You'll be out of here by, say, midnight. They got phones on planes now. We'll call Cheryl and tell her where to find you. See? I'm not as bad as you thought, am I?"

"Bobby?" It was Tammi's voice.

He went out of the cabin to see what she wanted.

"Honey, you go ahead and change out of that uniform," she said. "I want to run by and check on Wade, make sure he's not misbehaving, then I'll pick you up at your place."

"Suits me," Bobby said.

The boat rocked gently as he climbed down. Soon afterward they heard him start the car and back out of the driveway.

Five minutes later they felt someone else climbing aboard. The cabin door opened.

"Hey there," Tammi said brightly. She knelt down and tested the ropes. "He does nice work, don't he?"

"Bitch," Jackie spat.

"That's right," Tammi said. "Rich bitch after tonight."

She looked around the cabin, moving ropes and other debris until she found what she was looking for. A rusting red gasoline can.

Jackleen and Truman watched as she unscrewed the cap and began sprinkling the can's contents on the life preservers. The air in the cabin filled with gas fumes.

"I'll bet Bobby told you we'd call the cops and tell them where to find you, didn't he? He is just way too sweet to be true, don't you think?

"Shit," Tammi said after a moment. "Out of gas. Ain't that always the way?" She set the can down. "I'll be right back. Don't y'all go anywhere."

"We'll burn to death," Jackie said when she was gone. "This thing is all wood. We're going to burn to death in this boat."

"Hush," Truman said. He looked wildly around the cabin, searching for anything that could be used as a weapon.

"Grandpa?" Chip stirred, then sat up groggily. His hands and feet were tied too. "What's that smell? Is that gas?"

"Hey, buddy," Truman said tenderly. "We're here, Chipper. We came to get you."

"I'm scared," the boy said, his eyes filled with tears. "I want to go home."

"We will, son," Truman said. "Can you wiggle your hands a little bit?"

He held them out. The ropes were looser and he could maneuver his hands slightly.

Truman's eye caught something, something shoved way up in the V of the boat's hull.

"Chip," he said urgently. "See that hunk of metal stuck up there? It's an anchor. Are you strong enough to move that anchor?"

"I'm tired," Chip said, yawning. "I want to sleep."

"See if you can move that anchor," Truman said, trying to keep the desperation from his voice. "Try, Chip. Show us how strong you are."

"Okay," Chip said. With his legs extended in front of him, he scooted up to the V of the hull, reached in, and grabbed the anchor. They heard the rattling of the anchor's metal chain, then the scraping of metal on wood.

"It's heavy," Chip said, grimacing.

"You're strong," Truman urged. "See if you can drag it back here."

Slowly, the child dragged the anchor backward, scooting again on his haunches.

"Over there," Truman said, nodding toward the side of the cabin where the ladder was. "Push it over there as far as you can."

Chip kicked the anchor into place with his feet.

"Attaboy," Truman said.

"What are you doing?" Jackie asked. "That child can't pick up that anchor and hit nobody with it."

"He won't have to," Truman said.

They heard the kitchen door close and then Tammi's voice. She was humming as she climbed the ladder.

"Lie over here beside us," Truman told Chip. "Hurry now. Bring the life preservers. Put them around your head."

"What on earth?" Jackie asked.

The boat rocked and leaned slightly from Tammi's weight on the ladder.

"Now!" Truman yelled. "Roll that way!"

Bending elbows and knees, the three of them rolled sideways, toward the other side of the boat. Toward the anchor. The boat rocked wildly and then they were falling,

falling over and over as the boat tipped and crashed over on its side.

The last thing Truman remembered hearing was a woman's terrified scream.

CHAPTER

THIRTY-NINE

WADE HARDESON GLANCED AT HIS REFLECTION in the car's rearview mirror and startled himself. The face of a stranger stared back at him. The stranger was pale and unshaven, with bags under his eyes and a nervous tic that made his right eye flutter uncontrollably.

He got out of the car, locked it with shaking hands. Tammi's demands were too much. She'd ordered him to print out a set of charts for the Festival of States stakes race tonight. "Get it right," she'd screamed, "or I'll kill you myself."

Enough was enough. He couldn't think, couldn't sleep. He'd stop by Nana's long enough to grab his stuff and get out. It was two o'clock, she should be at one of her club meetings. He felt bad about taking the car, but not that bad. Nana was loaded. She could get another car. He had to get away from Tammi and those other two thugs.

He took the elevator up, got out the key she'd given him, slipped inside.

"Wade?" He froze.

His grandmother came out of the bedroom and beamed at him. She wore a pale aqua pantsuit and a string of pearls.

"Oh, good. You're back. I was just about to call a cab to take me to my bridge club. Now you can take me instead. And we'll just run by the bank too, all right?"

Wade smiled weakly. "Just drop you off, right? I've got a business appointment I need to get to."

She looked at his wrinkled clothes and scruffy face and shook her head. What kind of business was her grandson doing looking like a homeless person?

They went through the drive-through window of her bank. "So nice, Saturday banking hours, don't you think?" she said. She scribbled a check and handed it to him to give to the teller.

"Why nine hundred?" he asked, glancing down at the check. "Why not go ahead and get a thousand if you need it?"

She giggled. "If I write a check bigger than that, they notify Jock McGowan, my lawyer, immediately. And you know how tedious Jock can be. Always questions, questions. You'd think it was his money I was spending."

"Yeah," Wade said. "You'd think."

He pulled the car up to the curb at Sarah Austin's house on Snell Isle. It was a huge beige stucco Spanish Colonial number, only a block from his old man's house.

"I'll be ready to come home at four," Nana said, leaning in the window to kiss her grandson's cheek. "Think you can make it back by then?"

"I'll try," Wade said.

He doubled back to the Bayfront Towers. It didn't take long. He knew where Nana kept the cash. There was still a hundred in the drawer, along with the blue velvet cases that held his grandfather's coin collection, a burgundy leather case that held some of Nana's jewelry, and two books of checks. He put all of it in a pillowcase.

He ripped the page with the list of her bank's branches out of the telephone book. His first stop was at the branch downtown. The check was made out to him in a decent imitation of her wavery handwriting. For nine hundred dollars. He glanced down at his watch. It was 3 P.M. He'd have to go all the way to the beach to find the only other branch with Saturday banking and it closed at four.

No time, he decided. He headed for the interstate. Miami, he decided. He had a full book of checks, and Nana's bank had branches all over the state. He patted the laptop on the car seat beside him. Miami had horse racing, dog racing, jai alai. But what it didn't have appealed to him most. No Tammi.

Butch Goolsby shifted on the thin mattress, trying to find some inch of comfort in a comfortless world. He turned over on his side and saw Curtis sitting at the table in the middle of the cell. He had his headphones on and was bobbing his head to some song they were playing on the radio.

They'd been in this cell since last night, since he'd taken the bolt cutters to that gate at the Florida Marine Patrol dock. They'd made it through the gate, nearly to the dock when the alarm went off. They might have gotten away if it hadn't been for the goddamned ski masks.

Curtis had insisted on the masks. "It's a full moon," he'd pointed out. "This way our faces won't show in the dark. And the stink won't be so bad." Butch had allowed himself to be persuaded, and for that he sat now in a cell in the Pinellas County jail.

In the dark like it was, neither one of them had seen the shrimp boat tied up alongside that barge full of rotting fish. Anyway, Butch asked himself, how was he to know the captured shrimp boat held two tons of marijuana, a kind the cops called Colombian gold, seized by the Coast Guard only the day before as it chugged its way to the Mayhall dock?

Butch sighed and turned on his back. It didn't matter much now one way or the other. In a way, he told himself, it was kind of a relief. If he and Curtis kept their mouths shut, nobody would ever know anything about what was on that barge. They'd do, what, six months for breaking and entering? He thought about what Tammi would have to say about their bungled escapade. About Cookie and her last tirade.

Jail, he thought, was infinitely preferable to both.

Jewell Newby was looking over the week's sales activity reports. "Excellent," he said to himself. Sales were ahead of projections. Two of Jeannette Boynton's closest friends had come into the office and picked out penthouse units like their friend Jeannette's. That left only three units unsold. Pure profit.

His office door swung open. He hated being interrupted like this. "I told you no calls," he said, looking up, annoyed.

His expression changed when he saw who it was.

"My dear," he said. "How's your head?"

"Full of numbers," Cookie Jeffcote said. "Shall we talk?"

EPILOGUE

FUNDAMENTALIST FLEECES FLOCK, FLEES FLORIDA
BY TRUMAN KICKLIGHTER, SPECIAL CORRESPONDENT

ST. PETERSBURG—A controversial fundamentalist minister who sought to establish a financial empire by converting a downtown hotel into a high-priced senior citizen condo complex has fled the country, taking with him hundreds of thousands of dollars in "down payments" made by unwitting church members.

Pinellas County State's Attorney Emory W. Crist said Monday that state and federal authorities believe Jewell Newby, 48, pastor of the self-founded Church of Cosmic Unity, may have duped a dozen or more investors out of nearly $800,000 in a scheme to sell them condominium units in the Fountain of Youth Residential Hotel, a run-down retirement hotel located on First Avenue North in downtown St. Petersburg.

"Our office issued warrants for Newby's arrest this morning, but when we arrived at the church offices, they had been cleaned out," Crist said. "We subsequently learned he may have flown to the Cayman Islands late yesterday. The FBI and the IRS have been alerted about his disappearance. Our investigation continues, and we will not rest until we bring this charlatan to justice."

Crist said that Newby, a charismatic figure who started similar ventures in Texas and Arizona, is also wanted for questioning by authorities in those states. He said authorities in New Mexico have reopened an investigation into the 1992 death of an 87-year-old Scottsdale woman who legally adopted Newby and made him her sole heir shortly before her death. Newby inherited nearly a million in cash and real estate upon the woman's death.

Crist said his office was alerted to Newby's activities by a local attorney representing a wealthy St. Petersburg woman who had arranged to sign over the bulk of her share of a large family estate in return for ownership of a penthouse condominium.

Although Newby apparently escaped arrest, Crist said authorities have arrested Newby's alleged accomplice, 39-year-old Corinne E. "Cookie" Jeffcote, of St. Petersburg Beach. The woman, who was Newby's second in command, was apprehended after attempting to flee to Grand Cayman. Jeffcote was detained by airline personnel at Tampa International Airport after boarding a Cayman Airways jet. When a flight attendant accidentally jarred the wig she was wearing, Miss Jeffcote became agitated and physically assaulted flight personnel.

Police responding to reports of an altercation at the airport discovered $30,000 in cash, a gram of cocaine, and documents outlining the real estate scheme in Jeffcote's bag.

She is being held without bond in the Pinellas County jail, charged with mail fraud, racketeering, income tax evasion, possession of a controlled substance, and aggravated assault. Crist said Jeffcote will also be questioned about the disappearance of a Tampa man, Michael J. Streck, 37, a reputed organized-crime figure whose family has not seen him since last week. He said his office received an anonymous phone call tipping police to Jeffcote's involvement with Streck.

It was hot in the card room. A fan whirred languidly overhead, stirring the warm, humid air only slightly. Ollie Zorn finished reading the story in the *St. Petersburg Times* and set his beer bottle on top of the folded newspaper.

Their voices echoed in the nearly empty hotel. The snowbirds had flown back north.

"You mind?" Truman asked, moving the wet beer bottle off the paper. "That's my first byline. I need it for my clip file."

"Special correspondent, huh?" Ollie dealt the cards, slapping them against the tabletop one by one. His shirt was unbuttoned, exposing his round, hairless belly. "What's that mean, special correspondent?"

"It means he's special, that's what," Jackleen retorted, sipping her tea. "Means those fools figured you don't put a prize specimen out to pasture."

"It means I'm a stringer," Truman said, sliding the cards off the table, rearranging them to his liking. "Get paid by the piece. Seventy-five dollars. Plus a byline, plus gas money and tolls, but no meal money."

"Not bad," Ollie admitted.

Jackie picked up a card from the deck, considered, then discarded it. "Ask Mr. K who sicced the cops on Newby and Cookie in the first place?"

"Okay," Ollie said. "I'm asking."

She jumped back in before Truman had a chance to answer. "You know those Boyntons, the rich ones, run all the banks and all that? Mr. K called the Boyntons' lawyers on those church folks, told 'em Miss Jeannette Boynton was fixin' to give away the farm. That's what stopped 'em."

Truman picked up the card Jackie put down. He smiled. Threw a card down from his hand.

"Just some discreet questions, that's all. Good heads-up reporting. Nothing I haven't done a thousand times before."

Ollie's hand hovered over the deck and then the discard pile, his face a study in indecision.

"Take one or the other," Truman said. "We're not getting any younger here."

"You get a notice from the Mandelbaums?" Ollie asked.

"About the rent increase?" Truman snapped. "Hell of a thing, after all they put us through."

"You ask me, new carpet and paint and half-new wiring don't mean they can get away with another fifteen dollars a month," Ollie said. "You're a reporter, TK, why don't you write an exposé? Or hey, I could call the TV station again."

"That's not how it works," Truman said.

"'Course, I guess you can afford it," Ollie said slyly. "Way I hear it, you got a nice little nest egg stashed away, account of you used that computer program that dead girl came up with."

Jackie stared intently at her cards. Truman's face flushed red.

"Had a nest egg," Jackie said quietly. "Had. All gone now. Good thing you got that newspaper job, Mr. K, even if it is only now and again."

"What happened?" Ollie asked.

Truman picked a card off the top of the deck and pursed his lips. "No harm in talking about it now, I guess. As long as it doesn't leave this room. It was a sure thing. Marion, this woman who works out at the track, she helped us win all the money that first time. Went back out there the next week, after everything with Chip quieted down. She gave us a tip. A sure thing. Twenty-to-one odds. It was a big black dog. Name was Lickety-Split. We'd have won too."

"Except Lickety-Split got bumped a mile coming down the home stretch," Jackie said. "Lickety-Splat, that's more like it. We lost every cent. All of it. Had to borrow bus fare home from Marion. Now what do you say about that, Mr. Truman Compulsive Gambler Kicklighter?"

Truman laid his cards on the table. Three aces, three kings, three jacks.

"Gin," he said. "Another hand?"